Samuel N Fisher is a proud Englishman and father, from the northwest of the UK and lives there with his long-suffering girlfriend of 12 years.

He's been a researcher of all things paranormal, fringe and conspiratorial for 30 years now and uses this knowledge in his writing. He has put the majority of this knowledge into the *The Legion Saga*, something he has been working on for 25 of those 30 years.

He is also a YouTube content creator with 2 channels: TMSSP and Sam Fisher, the former focuses on his music videos.

To Rico

Samuel N Fisher

Dedicated to my grandfather, Jack Fisher (RIP); my mum, Emily; my girlfriend, Kat (thanks for putting up with me all these years), and my son, William.

Samuel N Fisher

THE LEGION SAGA: PROLOGUE

AUSTIN MACAULEY PUBLISHERS™

LONDON * CAMBRIDGE * NEW YORK * SHARJAH

A CIP catalogue record for this title is available from the British Library.

ISBN 9781398419322 (Paperback)
ISBN 9781398419339 (ePub e-book)

www.austinmacauley.com

First Published 2022
Austin Macauley Publishers Ltd®
1 Canada Square
Canary Wharf
London
E14 5AA

Thank you to Austin Macauley Publishers for publishing my book.

Prologue

'There's nothing new under the sun' – King Solomon (Ancient, Mythical, Biblical king)

With Friends Like These

Pripyat (20 miles from Chernobyl ground zero), Ukraine, 13 June 1995, 00:47 am.

Colonel Jason Carmichael slammed against the aged and weathered breezeblock wall with the force of a meteor strike. The air in his lungs, forced brutally from his body, was expelled out of his armoured helmet with a loud hiss. He was unable to cry out in pain from the impact. There simply wasn't enough air left in his lungs. His mouth just silently mouthed his agonised screams. Desperately, his fatigued lungs clawed for air as his body descended six feet to the ash-covered ground below. With a loud 'thud!', his body impacted into the soft blanket, his heavy armour creating a large crater in the foot-thick ash blanket, the displaced flakes gently falling onto and leaving a fine layer over his crumbling body. This time he was able to emit a quiet painful groan as he began to awkwardly shuffle himself into a sitting position against the wall.

Searing pain from his multitude of injuries ravaged his body with every movement, but eventually, he was upright and staring blankly at the adjacent wall and the hole he'd created when he came through it. It was quite a hole he'd made and a testament to the weight of the experimental armour he was wearing. Whatever had hit him and sent him had done so with such force that if it wasn't for his armour taking a rather sizable chunk of the impact, it would've easily snapped him in two. Fortunately, it would seem he was going to walk away with, at the very least, numerous broken ribs.

He leant against the wall of the derelict building he was in, staring at the inky blackness beyond the hole. The ash and dust from the ground swirled and fluttered from the heavy wind, hurtling through this newly formed escape and mixed with the recently commencing blizzard outside. The whole thing looked like the innards of a snow globe after a heavy shake as the ash and snow danced and chased each other in huge spirals in front of him.

If it wasn't for his current situation, Colonel Carmichael could've found the view quite pleasant if a little hypnotic. But the screams coming through his headset suddenly tore him out of his private getaway, dashing any hopes he had of brief tranquillity. He struggled, in vain, to make out a single coherent sentence through the panic and terror ringing through his ears. The fact that he was hearing several languages, all of which he didn't speak bar one, wasn't helping either. French, Russian, Chinese, it was like a United Nation's audiobook. His HUD on his helmet's visor flickered glowing green target displays and distances rapidly in front of his eyes.

All information that, up to now, was rather helpful, but now made no sense to him at all. It's falling and climbing numbers zipped past at pace and just jumbled together in his mind. His fatigued brain desperately tried to make any sort of useful judgement from them but to no avail. The targeting reticule, designed to lock in on a target and assist aiming and a, admittedly, rather useful tool earlier in the day, was now darting, fairy-like, around his field of view, thus rendering it useless and very distracting. Especially seeing as, for split seconds at a time, it would flash red, like it'd acquired a target, before reverting to its haphazard flashing green. Any other time he would've considered there to be a threat close by, but due to his circumstances, he disregarded its questionable warnings. Besides, something in his ear, suddenly, yanked his attention from his private light show and demanded his full attention,

"General Schwartzer! General Schwartzer!"

The hushed female voice, although clearly petrified, spoke English, albeit with American, deep south, accent. Not only that, but it was also a voice he recognised from meeting her earlier during the day. Desperately, he struggled to recollect her name as she continued.

"General Schwartzer! Do you read? This is Delta Recon 262!" she whispered loudly. Panic filling every facet of her tone before, briefly, pausing as she waited for a response. Her nervous breaths, the only sound Jason could hear, until she felt safe to continue, "We encountered unidentified hostiles in Sector 8, Delta 9. Two of them! Like nothing I've ever seen before! My squad leader, medic and heavy weapons are all K.I.A. The remainder of my team is scattered God knows where? Their status, undetermined." She began to weep, uncontrollably, "Sir! I'm sorry! I've no idea where I am. My G.P.S and onboard map are shot! I'm just hoping you can triangulate my signal and send support! Heavy fucking support, sir! I can hear Russian soldiers screaming close by. They're being decimated, sir! I shit you not! What the fuck did you d—"

She suddenly fell quiet. The only confirmation she was still alive was the terrifying breaths down her microphone. But this pause gave Jason time to remember her name or most of it at the very least. She was Lieutenant Tyler, something. He was sure of it! Right now, though he was determined, recalling surnames wasn't a huge priority. All that mattered now was keeping tabs on every shallow, sharp, panic-stricken breath she made proving she was still alive. He waited patiently for a response to her cry for help. None came and just as he was about to answer her call on 'commands' behalf her hushed tone filtered through his earpiece once more. "Sir!" her desperation filled his ears, "Sir! There's something very close by! I can't be certain, but I can see shimmers and weird shadows in the distance and those screams are getting closer to my position," her voice was gradually calming now as she began to compose herself and remember her training.

Good girl! Jason thought to himself. *Calm down and regroup. Help is coming! I can promise you that!*

"I'm engaging silent mode and moving to a safe vantage point," she said with far more composure. "If they pass through here, I may get some decent footage of what hit us at least! I'll give you a SITREP in 60 mins, sir! Hopefully, you'll be in a position to respond by then. Lieutenant McQueen signing out!"

That was her name! Jason thought. *Tyler McQueen! Shit, I've gotta speak to her!*

"Tyler!" Jason's Cockney/Irish cross accent boomed loudly with urgency, "Lieutenant McQueen! It's Colonel Jason Carmichael! Activate Protocol: Delta, Niner, Yankee, eight, eight, three from your onboard CPU! I should be able to track your data signal from here! Sit tight and above all, do not engage! I'll be with you A.S.A.P!"

The knowledge of another survivor and one that he knew, albeit rather vaguely at best, rejuvenated him. But this rejuvenation was all too abruptly shattered as all he could hear from his headset was static. He should be able to hear his own voice through his headset as it travelled the airwaves to her, but instead, he heard nothing.

"Lieutenant McQueen! Tyler! Do you read?" he bellowed desperately, "Lieutenant McQueen, this is Colonel Jason Carmichael of her majesties S.A.S, do you read me?" Again, there was nothing.

It was becoming pretty clear that his mic had been damaged in his impact with either the wall or indeed, the source that propelled him through the wall.

"Fuck!" he whispered to himself, "How the fuck am I—" he cut his sentence, instantly, short. A shimmering, sapphire, blue and jade, green blur grabbed his attention for a millisecond before vanishing as abruptly as it has materialised. It was quickly followed by a barely audible, 'swoosh' of fine gravel being kicked up in the rafters above him, no more than twenty, or so, feet away. Again, he caught a brief glimpse of it, his HUD, frantically struggled to keep up with the shimmering blur as it darted from every direction in and out of the darkness. The once infrequent red warning light in his reticule was rapidly becoming the more prominent over the comforting safety of the green.

He slowly and carefully rose to his feet. His legs, still ravaged by tiredness, were barely able to hold his weight. If it wasn't for the exoskeleton in his armour taking the strain, he would quite easily collapse. He knew full well that any second now, he was going to have to a break from whatever it was stalking him. It was either that or quite likely, die. After all, he had no weapons of any sort and his only means of fighting back was hand to hand, literally, and with the state his body was in, he didn't fancy his chances. Even running, at this point, was still theoretical. He severely doubted that he had even that capacity to do that at the moment. *I need a bit of a boost,* he thought, *something that'd give my legs a sudden kick of acceleration.* For a few seconds, he thought hard about what.

Before he remembered that his suit was equipped with several tiny retro boosters that fired high-pressure jets of compressed air, designed to soften a landing from a great height. If he could time it just right. He may be able to take his unknown hunter by surprise and propel himself away from his position out of harm's way at the last second just as it was about to strike. If anything, this would either:

- Cause his attacker to hit the wall, stunning and/or perhaps damaging it, just enough, to give Jason time to escape or,
- At the very least, the resulting blast from the jets would give him a couple of seconds head start.

Unfortunately, Jason had barely a second more to weigh up his options. As following a loud mechanised hiss, his tormentor revealed itself.

Its armour was very similar to his own but seemed far more advanced than his dull, black armour. For a start, it was dominated by a shimmering sapphire blue colour that looked as though it was liquefying into, then separating from, the crystalline jade colour adorning the backs of his arms and legs and around his bulky looking chest plate. The visor of his helmet jutted out at either side of his face resembling jagged horns. His rapid movements, towards him, together with the liquid effect of his colouring made it almost impossible for Jason to focus on him, causing him to be virtually invisible and at the same time, as the dim light caught up with him and ricocheted off the jagged angles of the armoured plates, he almost shimmered hypnotically as he ducked, weaved and twirled ever closer. Over and over Jason told himself to snap out of his assailant's spell. He needed to concentrate.

"Computer," Jason quietly whispered in a clear and precise tone.

"Yes, Colonel," it quietly purred back.

"Computer, arm hammer jets and prep for immediate dust off. Maximum power, maximum velocity."

"Hammer jet's engaged," it purred again, its voice seeming to originate in his head rather than his headset, which he found a little unnerving.

He knew he should've started using the onboard CPU earlier. This was, however, the worst time to ascertain its capabilities, but he no longer had the luxury of time to acquaint himself with it right now. All he could do was deal with whatever it threw at him regardless of how comfortable it felt.

"Would you like to activate the proximity trigger and lock it onto the advancing target?" Its voice felt as though it was rippling through his mind. Before he had the chance to answer, its voice melted and trickled through his mind again. "Pro-trig activated, generating the target grid. Calculating estimated tracking vectors of the target. Booster power holding at 100%"

Immediately, Jason's HUD sprang to life. A dark blue 20x20 grid manifested over his advancing foe that rapidly mapped out an outline of his body followed by green, yellow and red curved and dotted lines cascading out of his body like a multi-coloured fountain as the CPU plotted the likely paths that his aggressor was likely to take.

Jason didn't like what it was doing; he didn't like feeling not fully in control of his actions and to entrust his survival to a machine was absolutely unthinkable. But he wasn't going to be given time to convey what it was he wanted his CPU to do, despite the worrying fact that his CPU was already in the midst of doing what he was thinking of as his attacker was mere inches from striking distance. All he could do was, begrudgingly, relinquish control to this machine and pray it kept him alive and in one piece.

In a split second, across the bottom of his view and in vibrant yellow lettering flashed the words 'Target in range, HAMJET IGN In 3...' But Jason couldn't see him. *The damn CPU had miscalculated*, he thought. He knew he shouldn't have trusted a machine!

"What the fuck?" Jason shouted angrily, "You're gonna fire too early! You fucking bitch! You hear me?"

'2,' flashed up as the bitch CPU ignored him.

"Fuck! Of all the ways to die?"

'1.'

I'd always hoped it'd be a woman that killed me! he thought to himself, *I just hoped I'd be fucking her at the time and she wasn't a fucking computer!*

Suddenly, there he was. Jason was literally nose to nose with his enemy and as the air from its vents emitted a snake-like hiss, Jason looked at the violet lights that were this metal monstrosities eyes and said, "Nice to meet you, at last," he smiled before following with a chuckle. "But I've gotta g—" he didn't get time to finish as flashing in deep red under his target was 'IGN'.

Jason closed his eyes as the loud bang of the jets kicking in, reverberated around the room accompanied by the very noticeable pressure from the g-forces exerted onto his body as he propelled sideways violently into an adjoining doorway 20 or so feet from his original position. All of this was done within nanoseconds of a devastating punch obliterating the wall where he'd been.

He could hear the perplexed grunt from his armoured nemesis as he realised that he'd somehow missed his target and taken out a wall instead. Something that, according to his tone, didn't seem to occur on a regular basis. If, for that matter, it ever did at all.

He gradually turned towards Jason's new position as he rapidly made the appropriate calculations to obtain Jason's new location and let out what sounded like a snigger hidden under the loud hiss as air jettisoned from his helmet's vents. His eyes, briefly but blindingly, flashed a bright glowing violet as he slowly crouched down. Jason instantly recognised that he was about to pounce on him and instinctively kicked the frame of the doorway he was in.

"Computer! Ramjets 100%—" His loudly barked order was stunned into silence from his jets firing again, bizarrely, before he'd had a chance to finish.

The air in his lungs forced out of him as he flew along the floor, sparks billowing from his back in giant tidal waves as his metal plates ground against the stone floor. The doorframe where he'd kicked himself from crumbled, like the walls of a sandcastle, quickly followed by the surrounding wall. The tremor from his kick's impact also causing the weakened wall his foe had just punched to collapse bringing it down along with the ceiling on top of his assailant.

"A more than satisfactory outcome, for the actions of a bunch of mere ones and zeroes, don't you think?" asked the now, rather troublingly, verging on the seductive voice of his computer.

Jason, reluctantly, had to agree. But then something dawned on him. Had the computer just made what could possibly pass for a joke? *Surely not?* he thought, *It's just a bunch of silicone? Just pressurised sand?* he reassured himself. But he knew he was wasting time thinking about this trivial matter. Because, as was his luck, it would appear at the moment, there were sounds of movement from the now virtually demolished room and he knew his pursuer was wiggling himself free from his briefly encapsulating stone and rubble prison.

"Run, dickhead!" he shouted at himself as he quickly summoned the energy to get some kind of head start. "If you can't fuckin' walk! At the very least crawl, you fuckin' wanker! Come on, knobhead! What the fuck are you doin'?" he bellowed at himself. His cripplingly fatigued body under heavy protest began to build itself up into a rapid commando crawl. Every inch of every muscle in his body spasmed in response to the searing pain as he dragged himself along the ground. His battered and broken body unable to reap the full benefits from the assistance his suit was, unbeknownst to him, providing.

Unfortunately, none of this most heroic of efforts mattered. With barely a bleep from his proximity threat detector and, inexplicably to him, two sapphire blue arms burst through the solid stone ground beneath him, taking him completely off guard. Especially, seeing as there was no possibility of there being a basement bellow him. So, how had he found himself under attack from this angle? He didn't get a whole lot of time to ponder on this issue, however, as he was being rapidly thrust skyward as his opponent burst through the ground bellow him and pinned him violently against the ceiling with unsettling ease. Jason cried loudly in pain, his already battered body unable to block out the pain his injuries were causing. He wasn't sure, but his attacker seemed surprised by his painful outburst, he could've sworn he heard a faint 'huh?' under the pronounced hiss.

"Human?" it hissed with an air of pleasant surprise, "You're human? Not a demon?" Despite the electronic twang, Jason was sure there was a human voice behind it.

"Demon?" Jason retorted in disgust. "What fuckin' century you from? The fifteenth?" Jason groaned loudly in pain. The effort to shout proving to be difficult. He took three deep gulps of air wincing beneath his visor as he did, "If anyone's a demon, dickhead, it's fuckin you! Of course, I'm friggin' human!"

"Oh shit!" it said, chuckling. Jason failed to see the joke, a factor seemingly lost on his attacker. "Well, I never have guessed, you know. Where'd you learn to fight like that? More to the point, where'd you get that armour? 'Cos no offence, but you sure as hell look a lot like and fight exactly like a demon!"

"Well, if you put me down, I'll tell you!" Jason replied with a pained whisper. "It's kinda hard to converse with a…What the fuck are you anyway?"

"Who am I? That's a very good question," it replied cryptically. "But it's also one I'm not willing to answer at this time."

Effortlessly, it slid Jason across the ceiling and flung him down the hallway. Jason lands on the ground with a loud thud, inches from a broken window at the end of the hall. He, gingerly, turns onto his side clutching his left side in feigning pain as he grabs a shard of glass on the floor hiding it under his arm.

"I don't think you're in any position to be asking me any questions, do you?" it continued. The jovial tone now replaced by one of disdain and disgust. "After all, you're the one trying to pass himself off as a demon!" It raced towards him, stopping inches from his face before lifting him by the throat. "Now I'll ask you again, who the hell are you, where did you get that armour from and who taught you to fight like that?"

"Who the fuck am I?" Jason spluttered defiantly as he choked from his assailants tightening grip. "Who the fuck am I? I think it's only polite protocol for the attacking party to do the honours first, don't you?"

Jason smiled under his helmet. He had a plan. He just needed to keep it talking just a few moments more. Admittedly, this was a suicidal plan at best, but it was a plan all the same. He just had to wait for the right moment.

"Cocky little fucker, aren't you?" It laughed, seemingly impressed. "Well my friend, forgive my mistrust, but if I am to adhere to your terms, I must first ask you to remove your helmet. Just to confirm your humanity, you understand?"

"Fair enough!" Jason agreed. After all, he could see no problem with this request. "You'll have to put me down first though!"

Carefully, it lowered Jason to the ground and when it'd released its grip, Jason slumped down to his knees, his legs no longer able to hold his weight. He dropped the shard of glass he was holding, its faint tinkle as it shattered on the stone floor reverberated down the hall. Slowly, he flipped the clasps holding his helmet together at the back and pulled it over his face. The moonlight filtering through the fogged and broken glass of the window gleamed off his closely shaven head. His face was beaten and scarred from the battles he'd seen this night. Blood trickled from his nose, mouth and ears. A cut above his left eye prevented him from opening it fully, but as soon as his attacker could see his blue eyes, it let out a sigh of relief.

"Satisfied?" Jason tried hard to mask his anger to no avail.

"I am," it replied. "Now, my human friend, I will answer your questions." It dropped to one knee in front of him.

This was a rare moment of weakness on its part and Jason was going to take full advantage. With all of his remaining strength, he thrust his arm into an uppercut towards its chin. To its surprise, he very nearly succeeded if it hadn't managed to clasp his wrist mere inched from its chin. Then in one movement, it had flung Jason up into the air and blasted a kick into his side, propelling him through the wall to his right. Jason screamed in pain and kept his eyes tightly shut as he waited to make an impact with the ground. But to his amazement, he never did. When he got the courage to open his eyes, he couldn't believe what he was seeing. He was hovering, upside down above the floor.

His attacker clapped as it approached him. Its chuckles seemed genuinely amused without a hint of malice or aggression. It almost reminded him of a cat playing with its prey.

"Very good! You almost had me there." It sounded genuinely impressed too, but that tone quickly changed to one of anger as it boomed, "But playtime is over now, boy! It's time for you to give me what I ask. Bear in mind, I'm losing patience and will not be asking you again!"

It hissed again, as if about to speak, before suddenly looking back over its shoulder as if distracted by something outside. For a few moments, it held this position, the only sound emanating from it was a light swoosh from it vents as it breathed. This was the first time that Jason had noticed it breathing and he found this, oddly, reassuring. After all, if it breathed, then it was human or at the very least, living.

"Wait here!" it whispered as it turned towards the disturbance and dashed towards the wall opposite.

Not all Surprises are Good

The strange being's footsteps never made a sound, despite its apparent sprint. Even as it closed in on the wall, it's pace never waned and Jason expected it to crash through the wall. But to his amazement, it just melted through it like a ghost would. He hung there upside down in silence. Trying to detect any trace of what his attacker had been so spooked by. His wait, regrettably, wouldn't be for very long. From the other side of the wall, he could hear the barely audible growl of something big and he imagined it very toothy, followed by two long and loud sniffs as it sniffed the air. For a brief moment, there was silence, broken only by a piercing shriek that he at first attributed to the wind picking up outside, but when it was greeted and joined by a second, he knew it was something else entirely. Then, yet again, silence.

He waited nervously for any sort of inkling as to what it was and how far away. Then from out of nowhere, boom! Something very large landed just behind the wall, followed by a second, even louder boom! as it was joined by a friend.

He stared terrified at the wall. His eyes never blinking, in case his eyes shutting for that split second hid this new foe's arrival. Suddenly, the wall glowed a deep red before slowly liquefying as it started to melt in front of his eyes. Then nothing. He stared dumbfounded at the inky blackness beyond this newly formed hole. His eyes desperately attempting to pick out any trace of these new attackers. But he couldn't see anything. The silence he found himself in, was deafening and he was starting to feel, for the first time in his adult life, truly helpless. Whatever had scared off his first attacker and was seemingly toying with him now must, he concluded, be something truly horrific and he began to be resigned to the fact he was very likely about to die.

Then barely noticeably, he could see two glowing red pinpricks of light that were followed by two green ones alongside it. He stared almost hypnotised by them as they pulsed silently growing ever larger. Then from nowhere, the huge jet-black head of a beast shot towards him. Its glowing red eyes burned brightly, its gigantic mouth opened wide baring its huge, foot-long and sword-like teeth. Spines, like dreadlocks on its head, bristled like a rattlesnake's tail as it let out an ear-splitting, unnatural roar. Despite all his training and his vast battle experience, nothing could've prepared Jason for this. In seconds, this beast had reduced him to a quivering mass of abject fear. It was like something that he imagined his closet held when he was a child. The kind of thing that even nightmares are afraid of. Understandably, he couldn't contain himself any longer and he let loose a scream of pure terror, his eyes tightly shut as he expected at any moment to be engulfed by that mouth and then feeling the pain of 100 razor-sharp teeth piercing his flesh.

What seemed like an age passed without the expected painful demise and Jason was beginning to wonder if he was already in fact, dead. *Well, at least it was quick!* he thought to himself, *I never felt a thing,* he contemplated opening his eyes. Naturally, he felt rather apprehensive about doing this. *What if the afterlife that up until a few seconds ago, he was certain didn't exist wasn't something he wanted to see? Or worse still, what if, horrifyingly, there was nothing?*

The latter he quickly dismissed as foolish to think, after all, he was still thinking thoughts and to all intents and purposes, that was a pretty good indicator of there being definitely something or a something there and he hadn't just ceased to exist. He was just a tad reluctant to open his eyes to find out what exactly that something was. Before he'd made the decision to open his eyes, he felt himself spinning rapidly upright followed by a dull thud as something clasped him by the shoulder. His eyes sprang open to be greeted by the face of the beast millimetres from his nose. He screamed in horror, his eyes staring at every facet of these terrifying beasts features. Mostly drawn to its glowing deep red eyes. The absence of a pupil within them making their infinite depth looking directly at him seemed as though they were devouring him alone. Its gaping wide mouth, primed and ready to snap shut when it felt the slightest hint of its prey! The saliva drooled out from between its teeth and hung motionless in the air.

"Hang on a sec," perplexed, he said aloud. "What the fuck is goin' on here?"

The beast was suspended in mid pounce as if frozen in time. He struggled, desperately to get his head around this whole situation. His mind blocking out all other sounds and sights that would distract it from the improbable spectacle in front of him. But the fact that anything, let alone this, whatever it was could be in this sort of state was surely an impossibility. His mind was battling with it so hard, he was sure he was nanoseconds away from an embolism brought on by the overload it was causing.

To help deal with this sight and prevent the ever-increasing fragility of his mind resulting in a brain explosion, he concluded, that he must either be:

A: in a coma brought about by the initial attack that sent him through the wall and, therefore, dreaming. Or equally as plausible,

B: he was, in fact, now dead, in hell and the devil was teasing him and waiting until Jason least expected it before letting lose the full horror of his inescapable and painful demise. Both of these results would, he'd later admit, be a damn sight easier to get his head round than what he was about to discover was his actual fate.

In the several seconds, it was taking for his head to fathom, exactly what he was witnessing before him, he'd managed to forget about what had caused him to open his eyes in the first place. The impact against and subsequent clasping of his shoulder. He turned, hesitantly, in the direction the impact had come from at his left-hand side. His eyes drawn and then, inescapably, fixed upon the barely visible outline of a second figure directly behind the beast but suspended around six feet in the air above it and in a position that seemed to make it look like it'd just leapt up to land behind him. Its body looked like a flawlessly transparent crystal and he couldn't help feel a little disappointed that he wasn't able to witness it moving because even in its stillness, it was already hypnotic. But in motion, it would perhaps be even harder for him to avert his gaze.

His head continued to turn and despite his eyes' reluctance to follow suit, the cause of the clasping feeling on his arm became very apparent and jarringly, noisily real.

"Wake up, boy!" it barked at him angrily. "Get your head out of your colon and listen very carefully! With all of your dallying and trances, we are left with mere moments to prepare and act!"

Jason stared blankly in the general vicinity of where this loud booming voice was emanating from. His ill-prepared mind, unable to cope with the figure of his first assailant, not only shouting at him but now pulling and shaking him all whilst the rest of the world seemed static. He could faintly hear it taking what sounded like a deep breath, before muttering something, in a frustrated tone under its breath. Followed, in a tenth of a second, by it yanking him towards it till Jason's nose touched the edge of its visor and its pulsating and glowing violet eyes blasted their light deep into his subconscious mind, repelling his head violently backwards.

"Listen to me, matey!" Its voice, like his suits CPU before it, was coming from inside his head and not through his ears, albeit minus the pleasantly seductive tones of the CPU.

"I'm gonna count down from 3 and on 1, I want you to think to yourself, very clearly, the word follow, okay? Nod if you understand because I'm gonna get you outta here."

Jason attempted to real back from this thing that had him in its grasp. His near totally fatigued body, barely able to speak any words what so ever, let alone any in protest or in questions. All he could manage was a gravely and deeply forced grunt that resembled to some degree and with quite a lot of imagination the words 'fuck!' followed by 'off!'. The source of his arms clamp, snorted in amusement, followed by a more virulent shake.

"3!" it said with authority. "Get ready to think follow on 1, remember?" Jason stared through it, a blank, vacant expression on his face.

"2!" it paused for a moment to gauge Jason's responsiveness. Upon sensing that he'd very likely passed out, it raised its hand and proceeded to slap him across the face slowly at first but building up to a rapid pace within a couple of slaps. It didn't take long for Jason to come to and with a great deal more of an alert demeanour about him too.

"You awake and with me, young sir?" it said laughing. "I'm moments away from reaching 1 and we're gonna be cutting it fine, son! Ready?"

Jason nodded in agreement only to instantly shake his head urgently. "No! No! Wait!" he shouted desperately and with a mountain of conviction. "Not yet! We need to get someone else first, tell your evac team, heelo or whatever it is, we need to make a detour to get another survivor!"

"Evac team?" it said surprised. "Heelo?" it snorted and sniggered as if Jason had just told the kind of joke that is both offensives but guiltily hilarious in equal measure. "There's another survivor, you say? Care to tell me what they're a survivor of?" Jason didn't get time to answer that question, however, "Never mind! There's very little time to get into that now, do you know where they are?"

Again, Jason was given no time to answer as he felt ripples resonate through his brain. "I see!" it said disappointed. "Well, in that case, picture them in your mind and concentrate as hard as you can on them."

"What the hell just happened?" Jason's shocked tone did very little to disguise the violated feeling he had at this moment. "What the hell did you do? And what's thinking about her meant to achieve?" He didn't need to hear the answer to the former, he already knew what it was.

"I read your mind," it said in a matter-of-fact way, "as for what thinking about her will achieve, do it and you'll see!"

Without realising it, Jason was beginning to conjure Lieutenant McQueen's image before it'd finished its sentence. He'd barely finished imagining her, hypnotically curvaceous figure that began at her pert, firm 36DD breasts and continued to sweep inwards to her waist, then outwards around her hips and round, toned, peach-like rear that was encapsulated by that, practically sprayed on it was so thin, armour that hugged her body, before he realised she was getting him hard. This fact was something that wasn't lost on his would-be rescuer.

"Wow!" it said this time out loud. "No wonder you want to rescue her too! She's fit as—"

That sentence was instantly severed from the rest of it that surely followed as Jason and his companion inexplicably vanished into nothing.

Part-Time Underwear Models, Sudden Frights, Daring Escapes and Long Overdue Explanations

Lieutenant Tyler McQueen lay on her belly facing the entrance to her sniper hole that had been blasted out, six stories up in an abandoned apartment block. She's bolted up to this position to hide from whatever had killed the rest of her squad earlier that night and to get a better look at what she and, as a result, whoever was left were up against and if possible, report back her findings to HQ. What she witnessed terrified her. The image of the huge, armoured beast and its near-invisible companion was forever etched into her mind.

From this position, she had a clear view of her surroundings to a surprisingly great distance. That coupled with the scope on the sniper rifle she'd salvaged from a dead, Soviet Spetsnaz and the optical modes of her suit meant she was able to witness the events unfolding with Jason almost five kilometres away including their miraculous disappearance into thin air.

No sooner had their forms vacated the area, than, unbeknownst to Tyler, the passage of time immediately resumed. The huge beast biting loudly at thin air as its trajectory led it to a violent impact with the ground six feet from its starting position and with such force, it buried its head deep into the stone slab floor. It violently tugged and shook its body as its head was held immobile by its stone prison's vice-like grip. The crystalline figure that so transfixed Jason earlier, realising their target had removed itself, desperately attempted to correct itself but a little too late and landed hard against the beast's back before bouncing off it and crashing through the wall out into the ash and snow. The impact wrenching its form out of its invisible shield and into the visible spectrum it had so skilfully previously avoided. Its twisted and grotesque black armour on full view for all the world to see. Tyler lay motionless, completely in awe of what she just witnessed, an eerie silence filling the air.

A silence suddenly smashed by an unfamiliar voice saying behind her.

"Fit as fuck! What I wouldn't do to her?" it said with a lecherous tone. "No wonder you got a hard-on, pal!"

Tyler, taken totally by surprise, span onto her back, her hands fumbling for a sidearm that simply wasn't there. Her panic heightening further when the looming figure of the blue-green beast she'd just seen attack Jason was stepping from the shadows.

"Please!" she whispered through the sobs. Her mind was, by now, equally as fragile as Jason's had become. "Please don't kill me!"

"Huh!" said the figure with an almost hurt tone. "Kill you?"

"Tyler!" Immediately she focused on this second, more familiar voice. "Lieutenant McQueen! Don't worry, he's a friend…I think?" Jason had to admit, he still wasn't sure whether or not this guy really was a friend or not. All he knew was that he was willing to be their ticket out of there and that was good enough for him for now.

"Well, that's fine!" Tyler's voice still trembled as she edged slowly further and further back along the floor. Her attention was locked firmly on this strange, blue-green metal man, standing in front of her. Jason, however, was covered by shadow and though his voice sounded familiar, she still couldn't be sure that this wasn't a trap.

"It's all well and good you sayin', he's a friend an all," she was beginning to sound calmer now. Her soft deep south accent trickled through Jason's ears creating a calm warmth inside him. "But I can't see you Mr and no offence, but you all could be trying to lure me into a trap."

Gingerly, Jason let out a short laugh, his broken ribs too painful to manage anything more than that. He, ordinarily, hated Americans, but this one was growing on him. Her armour prototype, leaving very little to the imagination, bar the colour of her skin beneath it and the dim moonlight accentuating every line of her toned curvaceous body also helped a little with that of course.

He stepped forward just enough to show his face and then stopped. His attention had been captured by events unfolding in the distance behind her. Where they'd just been, a large plume of smoke had risen into the air and something very big was beginning to displace the thickening blizzards path. Jason knew full well what it was. He just hoped his new friend had spotted it too. Unfortunately, Tyler was proving too big a distraction for him it seemed because although his helmet made it difficult to be sure, he looked like he'd not stopped looking at her since they'd arrived.

"Oh wait! I know you!" she shrieked loudly with excitement as she leapt up throwing her legs around Jason's waist before hugging him as she straddled him.

"You're that sexy Irish, S.A.S guy! Thank God, you're a friend, I thought your friend here was another of them. You know? Those things. What were those things anyway?" The blue-green man was just about to answer when Tyler nervously continued before he could, "You definitely aren't one of those too?" she asked firmly, her gaze switching her eyes to stern and steely.

"I can assure you, Lieutenant McQueen, my dear, that I am not one of those things!" the blue-green man replied and she was sure he was smiling beneath that helmet.

Jason, however, had never once taken his eyes off from the unfolding situation in the distance.

"I think we'd better hurry and get goin'," he whispered with a paradoxical, calm urgency. "There seems to be something…"

Before he had time to finish, the next few seconds seemed to slow right down as the cause of his forced silence came in the form of a rapidly spinning 20-foot lamppost that'd been wrenched from the street below and was hurtling in their direction thrown by the same large beast that'd attacked them earlier. The velocity of this object was so great that Jason knew that they were dead. But his new friend calmly crouched, clasping his hand and Tyler's.

"…coming straight for us!" Jason looked around after finishing his sentence. To his amazement, they weren't in Pripyat anymore. Definitely not. This place was hot. Not only that, but it was dawn. Beside them was a roaring campfire with what looked like two African shamans dancing and chanting in front of it and surrounding that were logs arranged like seats.

The blue-green man walked over to the shaman, finally removing his helmet and revealing long, straight platinum blonde hair, which cascaded over his shoulders as he continued to remove the top half of his armour revealing the sheer size of what was now obviously a man and how little his armour altered that size. The shaman looked at him like his arrival here was a regular occurrence but still had an air of awe and wonder about it. They quietly spoke in the shaman's native tongues, apparently sharing some sort of joke and looking like a group of old friends meeting up after a long period apart. Then he returned to Jason and Tyler. As the shaman left, a huge and very welcoming smile filled his face and for the first time, they were able to see the deep, aquamarine coloured eyes of their rescuer.

"Please, friends!" he said to them with a deep but calming voice, which seemed so ever so slightly odd without the accompanying hiss from his helmet's vents that it once had. "Please friends, take a seat! I think it's time I gave you an explanation of who I am! So, when you're sitting comfortably…I shall begin!"

Part 1: So, From the Beginning?

Prophecies of the Father

I was born in a little village 50 miles away from the greatest civilisation the world has ever known, Atlantis. My mother, Elissa, died in childbirth bringing me into the world, sacrificing her own life to save mine. My father, Helron, wept as he watched her die, clutching her hand tight before kissing her head, then her mouth so tenderly, so lovingly as he said goodbye. The look of forced joy on his face as I was passed into his arms. My mother never got to see me, my father never got to share me, to share that love with her and I don't think he ever fully forgave me for that.

My father was normally an unemotional man, unflinching and solid. He was the leader of our clan and at the time of my birth had only been chief for three years. He was the youngest chieftain at only 29 there had been so far and I suppose, he felt he needed to prove that he was strong enough, despite his grief, to be able to lead our people through whatever fate threw at him and us. So, he hid all signs of weakness and to him, mourning his dead wife was just such a sign. He sealed his grief away, never allowing it to come to the surface again.

He was a big man, broad and very muscular. His hair, a bright platinum blonde almost pure white and very long. His eyes, like everyone's in our clan, were a rich aquamarine, which exploded with deep, bright colour at you when he was fired up, burning with intense heat. It made us look, to our enemies, almost inhuman, a very good and very unique psychological advantage for us in combat.

The women who cared for me, whilst my father was away on 'diplomatic' missions, often commented on how similar myself and my father looked. He was a very handsome man, something that wasn't lost on women who met him. After the death of my mother, every eligible woman in the village vied for my father's attention but to no avail. My father would never, in his eyes, be unfaithful to my mother or her memory and he never was. He always remained true to her even though she was gone.

My earliest memory was from when I was around four years old. My father awoke from a dream, screaming, his face was white with fear, his body dripping with sweat. I rushed into his room, fear and panic gripping my every being. The dim light from my candle illuminating the room only mere inches in front of me. His breath was heavy, his lungs clawing for air. He looked over to me, his eyes steely and emotionless.

"Elissa...my love!" he shouted, wanting and desperation filled his voice. "Elissa!" he bellowed again more urgently this time.

I'd never heard my father mention my mother's name before. He was shouting her name over and over, the desperation in his tone was verging on the crippling. He leapt from his bed looking panic-stricken around his room, his body twisting and turning in every direction. It was then that I realised he couldn't see me or perhaps he didn't want to.

"Elissa," he screamed again. "Why? What does it mean? Why our son? Why must I do this...for what reason? I don't understand...Why?" he spun around on the spot and faced me. The expression on his face was terrifying, full of hate and murderous intent as his gaze firmly fixed on my eyes, the anger in them was burning so hot.

"You..." he boomed, grabbing me by the shoulders gripping so tight, his fingers began to draw blood on my weak child's skin. "Why must I have to do this? Tell me...Why?" I yelped in pain as he began to shake me violently, tears streaming down my face, my cries of pain almost deafening.

Suddenly, he stopped, the realisation of what he was doing striking him like a hammer in the eye.

"My God," he said softly, full of pain, full of anguish after the full horror of what he'd just done had finally sunk in. "What have I done to you, boy? How could you know? You're just a child," he sobbed. "You're just a boy, you couldn't have planned this, you couldn't have known?"

"Known what, Father?" I softly asked as he held me tightly to his chest, kissing my forehead as he rocked me back and forth. My sobbing slowly dissipating as I was reassured of my father's regret and remorse for what he'd done.

"It's nothing, lad...There's no way you could've known..."

He carried me slowly back to my bed, clutching me tightly in his arms. I gazed at him, the light from the torches in the hall drizzled over him. A steely look covered his face, a heavy burden rested on his mind, it was impossible for him to hide it. Only once, before he put me to bed, did he look at me. He smiled, his face, as he did, was full of sadness, relief and a diminishing hope all rolled into one would always remain clear in my memory. Because from that point on, everything changed.

My father never again mentioned that night and I never asked, I never could bring myself to do it, to ask him what it was that so visibly shook him. And to be honest, I don't think he would ever have told me…I think, although I'd never truly know for sure, the idea was possibly far too painful for him to re-visit or he felt that maybe I wouldn't understand.

After that night, things became very different; his manner was stricter, harsher, more disciplined. Over the next few years, we spent a lot of time in what he called preparation for what he always seemed adamantly sure was to come and would affect not just my life, but our tribe's very existence. My training, therefore, was very different from all the other warrior sons. The methods alien to all but my father.

The knowledge he was passing to me was nothing like the traditional fighting methods of our tribe, sometimes it was even in direct contradiction to our fundamental teachings and worse still in direct violation of our laws. Because of this fact, I was continuously tutored behind closed doors and only by my father lest the elders got wind of what he was doing and much to their dismay. He was already angering them by insisting on teaching me himself and shutting out the elders, who traditionally schooled our future chiefs since time began. To those elders, he seemed stubborn and overprotective. But that was only because they hadn't a clue as to the real intentions behind this decision. My father made no secret to the whole tribe that I was to be his heir and successor when he passed. But what I was being brought up to do as my first act when that day came was completely unheard of.

A law, thousands of years old, bound my father to equally as old philosophies, fighting methods, attitudes and rules. Out of respect and, indeed, love for our way of life, he vowed to remain true to these laws with regards to himself. I, however, was a different matter entirely. To him, I was a blank canvass, not just to him, but, metaphorically speaking, for the entire tribe too. Because just as our laws prevented my father from changing how they trained and lived, those same laws gave me the power to radically shift our tribe in the direction it was inescapably about to find itself in years to come. To quote my father's take on this event:

'Our tribe, although powerful and to the known world, the empires proven, unbeatable force. The very visible and only reason for Atlantis to remain unchallenged for as long as the empire has reigned.

It too is ill-equipped and, dare I say it, completely defenceless when in the face of power that is not born of this world, but one that is a denizen of the darkest corner of the spirit realm, who is so powerful, he is able to exist in that world and ours.

Not only that, but he is able to eat the souls of man, sucking everything that makes them great and good and releasing them as a most vile and corrupt abomination. Despite our elders understanding my reasons for enacting change, they will use every means at their disposal to ensure our tribe adheres to traditional tribal law.

Thus, sealing our fate along with, perhaps, that of the entire world damning us to be enslaved by the ruling council of hell.

For this reason, above all others, I entrust the knowledge of this impending cataclysm to you and you alone, to only be divulged to the elders after my passing and your coronation. As only by theirs and our own laws can you be unopposed in our plan. Secondly, when you reach adulthood, at 18, you will be the only grandmaster of this style and beginning to develop and create your own style and methods to its teachings. On that day, my son, I will be truly proud!'

Every morning, he would start my teachings with that same speech and for decades, I would be unable to understand nor appreciate the profound nature and immense responsibility that he was bestowing upon me, but also his absolute faith, even at the age of three when my training began that I was capable of fulfilling my father's legacy.

So, as well as the usual lessons in and reading books about single hand to hand and mixed unit battle tactics, reading our family history and the history of our world, I was forging my own weapons, developing a detailed knowledge of the legends and myths of our tribe's previous skirmishes with demons thousands of years ago and magic, spells and incantations that both sides employed now long forgotten. But also some very strange and extremely powerful new ones as well as sorcery or the practice of developing new spells.

All things that any normal warrior never heard of let alone learned neither would they feel they had to learn. All the while he would never tell me what or who this great evil was that he was preparing me for or when he expected it to appear and nor did I dare ask for fear of harsh punishment for doubting my father, my master. He would always just say, as we trained all those long hours, that I had to do this and it would ensure my survival and the survival of our clan in the future.

I was 11 when I was passed my first sword. My father was a brutal combat tutor, never holding back even though I was at such a young age. There were no wooden, practice swords, it was get used to the real thing or suffer the consequences of not reacting in time, which meant losing a vital limb. Needless to say, I had to learn very quickly how to defend myself and to counter-attack.

I guess to an outsider, his methods would seem cruel, but during those times, it was necessary. You see, I was born into a world that to all who truly saw the world with open eyes, knew all too well, was also harsh and cruel. Out here at the frontier, there was no dedicated police force to aid you or fight your battles for you. No set laws to abide by. To settle differences, disputes or what was seen by that individual to be a crime against them, you had the code of combat, violations of these rules seen as an act of disrespect and a great dishonour. If you didn't feel powerful enough to fight your cause, you could always seek the words of our chieftains, which depended on your wallet size or the relationship you had with them but mostly on their mood on that day. Failing that, you could hire a mercenary, my tribe's main area of expertise. Yes, this world was harsh. You lived by the sword and you lived by your honour. The only place that had a recognisable system of law, to you at least, was in the cities and there it was enforced by an iron but fair hand. But that influence stopped at the city border.

My village was anything but a typical settlement. It was an extremely powerful force in the empire. Its influence and power equalling the ruling families. Despite never once wearing the crown or ever feeling it needed to for that matter. We were an all-conquering tribe, unmatched by anyone in the whole land. The empires strength and size, a direct result of our actions and unwavering loyalty to the royal lineage. As a result, our two families were raised together by both the kings of Atlantis and the chieftains of Xenon as brothers and/or sisters, since the great city was still two huts in a field millennia ago.

Every king of Atlantis was a master in the Xenon fighting style and was the only outsider to first be allowed to become a master of the art, but second able to teach it to a single apprentice.

This was how we made our strength, this was our reputation, this was our village and no one was, in our eyes, brave enough to take it from us.

By the time I was 16, my father had taught me enough to defend myself, my honour and my family name. I was a warrior in bone, in blood and in spirit. Mine was the house of Xenon and it was a name to be feared. Our village was very small compared to most, just under 200 people, but over the centuries, the house of Xenon had either conquered or aligned itself with every village, town and city in the known world either peacefully or by force.

We singlehandedly unified the empire and as a tribute we had but one request, we would take a handful of their men consisting only of their best fighters, soldiers and even gladiators, prisoner and free man alike to be trained in our ways. To us, this was the highest honour we could bestow upon a man. They would stay with their own clan until the need arose to use them. They answered only to the chief of the house of Xenon and no one else, their own chiefs having no power over them and no say in their affairs.

The defence of our village was paramount above all else and our name and banner were both feared and respected in equal measure. We were a law unto ourselves, especially the purebloods from our village and no one dared argue with that.

By my 21st birthday, news about the first skirmishes in what would become a war that would change everything in our world began to reach our tribe. I was so eager to go and fight, but my father on countless occasion had persuaded me not to. He knew this was not a war we should get involved in, not at this time anyway. This was not our fight, we were better to stay out of it, stay at the sidelines and not get involved for the sake of our survival. We needed time to prepare. This was a war we'd never experienced; a war so brutal and destructive that it scared even our elders, a very bad sign. But for some reason, I was convinced it was something I should do. I was being pulled towards it, it was calling me to arms and it was getting harder to resist.

At the time of the beginning of the war, a selected few had heard of him, the great destroyer, the slayer of all. To everyone else, he was just a rumour, a myth, a story you tell to children to frighten them when they're bad. But within two months, it became very apparent that he was real in the most terrible way. His hordes, his armies had obliterated most of mankind from the eastern shore to the western isles. These were small settlements, one still not broken away from the stone age. They didn't have our technology and our advanced knowledge. Atlantis had developed so much, much of it deemed too dangerous, to educate to the outer tribes.

The Atlantian council felt that primitive people would never know how to use this technology wisely or even responsibly, fearing that it would create a war on a grand and highly destructive scale. Hoth took advantage of this to full effect, butchering entire fledgeling civilisations to extinction.

He wasn't human, his eyes were like the fires of hell burning with hate and despair. His heart was as cold as an Antarctic winter and his stance was solid and indestructible. He was a demon of the highest order, one of the first and he'd set his eyes on our realm for his lord. He was Hoth, demon lord and demonic god of assassination and father to a horrific race of demonic hybrids, named night reapers because of their 'black as night' armour, who were unwaveringly loyal to him.

He was the first of his kind able to travel between the spirit world of the damned and ours freely, which made him the favourite son of the rulers of hell. He was brutal and cruel to such a degree that he made it an art form. Every town, city, village, home or person was savagely destroyed in the most horrific manners, imaginable and unimaginable. He didn't want slaves; he had no need for them after all. From what we could gather by his actions, he didn't want allies either. Negotiation wasn't an option and never offered. All he wanted was blood and apparently, the eradication of the human race. It was utter genocide. There were whole countries bathed in the blood of its citizens, body parts, laid out in ritual forms and re-animated corpses delivered the warnings of his imminent arrival to his next target, unleashing a frenzied attack on the nearest onlooker to prepare the settlers for what was to come.

He was creating a new world, a hell on earth and in most peoples' eyes, he was unstoppable. My father knew this, he knew what the world was facing and it chilled him to the bone. He couldn't let me go and face this, not yet, there were things that needed to be done first, so much more training needed and he knew he was going to have to be very persuasive in order to get me to stay. Fate though, it has a funny way of teaching us harsh lessons and at the worst imaginable times. A lesson I was about to learn far too soon.

I practised my techniques in our palace courtyard late at night and when I was sure I wouldn't be seen by anyone. As usual, all were fast asleep as I began my routine. This particular night, a huge storm had settled in and it hid any noise I made perfectly, so I chose this time to brush up on a few weapons techniques. The rain lashed my body as I moved and swayed, the harsh conditions not affecting my performance in the slightest. By this time, I was, nearly, my father's equal in skill. I was slimmer and more flexible compared to him. He'd purposefully trained me to favour speed and technique over raw power. A decision that bore some amazingly beneficial results neither of us had expected. My father, however, was still very old school built for power and not much else and, to all intents and purposes, my exact polar opposite. But despite this, he was still unnaturally and exceptionally quick.

I had sensed him watching me for a little while now. Not just because he was my father, but because I could feel this raw power exude from every facet of his being and it was this presence that I could feel behind me. I knew that his gaze was checking for any mistake any mistimed move and I could tell by his approaching footsteps that he couldn't fault any of them. Each step was confident and immensely proud and soon he was standing facing me. A huge smile grew across his face. It was a smile I'd not seen since I was a boy, a smile full of a proud father's love. He placed his hands on my shoulders and looked me up and down slowly, his proud smile growing ever bigger before finally giving me a long hug.

"Remember this day, son," he whispered in my ear, his voice faintly quivering. "You must remember this day for the rest of yours. For today, you have made your father incredibly proud. Because I no longer see my boy before me nor do I merely see a capable young man. No! Before me, I see a worthy chieftain of our tribe and a warrior, truly unmatched by any on the planet," tears weld up in his eyes as he fought them back. "You must promise me, son, that you will forever honour this day with that knowledge. Promise me?"

If I'm honest, I hadn't the faintest idea what had got into him. But his request seemed utterly genuine and I was honour bound to oblige. Little did I know the price that this promise would demand. A price that was to be paid in full straight away.

My father stepped proudly into the centre of the courtyard and with his loudest commanding voice boomed, "Proud and loyal people of Xenon, hear the voice of your chief and meet me here in our main courtyard. I have a matter of great importance to share with you, my loyal friends."

He paced up and down like an expectant father paces the halls of the hospital as he waits to hear news of his child's birth. He didn't speak again until he was absolutely certain everyone was there.

"Thank you, my brothers! I know it is very late and I respectfully apologise, but this matter cannot wait a moment longer!" The onlooking crowd muttered amongst themselves with electric excitement. Every person was eager to see what was in store. It was bound to be something a bit special they thought, after all, they wouldn't have been woken at this hour by their chief, would they. He allowed ample time for the mutterings to all but disappear before he continued.

"By now, most of you will be aware of the threat that's looming over not only us but also the entire world?" There were nods and faint 'yes' from the crowd. "Well for many years now, my son has trained in secret with a new form of fighting style that if we are to survive and defeat this aggressor, you must all adopt." From the crowd's reaction, they didn't seem to be convinced by my father's words, a fact that he was well prepared for in advance. "I know that some of you will still insist that our methods are unbeatable and forever will be, so I will provide proof! Then you will be in no doubts that the old ways that you so cling to will be this tribe's eventual undoing. My son's new skills are the way forward that we all must take. To prove it, it's our tradition to pit the strongest practitioner of our style, which is me against the strongest of theirs, which is Arkanon. So, I hereby challenge him to a fight to the death for control of our tribe and to determine which style is strongest."

Loud gasps and cries of horror and shock came from the crowd as well as myself. This was unheard of. No chief had ever exercised this right in the history of our people. Also, they had a fairly good idea that Helron had been training alone, so he'd truly know the capabilities of this new style already, wouldn't he? You could feel the apprehension from the crowd growing. Because Xenon law dictates that once a challenge is made, it must be seen through with no exceptions. "For years, I have prepared you for war just like this. But now it has arrived," my father said to the crowd.

My father, as I said earlier, was always strong and immoveable. However, somehow, he was different this time, like he already knew what was about to transpire, the hard rain hitting his face, hid his tears as he spoke. His voice was faintly trembling as he tried to hide his sadness. He knew what he had to do; he'd been preparing for this moment for so long. He was finally resigned to the fact. He knew then, at that very moment, it was time. His determination to stop me and by any means showed in his face.

"I can't let you go, son. I can't tell you the reason why, but I have no choice. If you will not listen, I will stop you by force."

Those words, those fateful words. Little did I know that they were to be some of his last words to me, they were to haunt me and subsequently, change the course of my life forever. Because no sooner had he said them, he had unsheathed his sword. He swiped at me from up high causing me to block, As I did, he spun on his heel and his foot hit me clean, solid and fast in the chest knocking me back, blood sputtering from my mouth. He'd took me by surprise, my mind raced as I tried to fathom what he was doing. Why was he attacking me? Was this a test? Should I strike back? Before I could answer those questions, the hilt of his sword hit me square in the jaw spinning me round. I had no chance to recover, he was attacking me again, swiping to the side of me.

I dodged giving myself enough time to unsheathe my sword and block the next attack. I remember thinking why is he doing this. Why is he making me fight him? We danced around each other in a deadly ballet of slashes and kicks, jumping over all obstacles in our way. The clash of our swords echoing around the yard. For hours we fought, none of us getting the upper hand. Swipe after swipe, block after block, parry after parry, counter after counter, all blurred into one. All imprisoning us in a vicious stalemate. It was killing me mentally, emotionally and spiritually. But I would not stop. It was only because I knew he wasn't going to either!

My father was a proud man, a confident leader of our village and an exceptional fighter. He was so powerful, so mind-blowingly skilful. He was a formidable opponent. To all intents and purposes, I was his student and he always taught me to always respect your master, live and breathe his teachings and follow the purest way. In essence, it was wrong for me to fight him in this way to the death, it was just wrong. Why would he want such a thing?

This fight was taking all my instinct and fighting skill to just keep up. It was testing everything that I knew, that I'd learnt over the years and turned into instinct, it was even making me adopt using new tactics to try and outwit him and gain the upper hand. Then suddenly, he altered his fighting style. Inexplicably, it was as if had given up. I didn't totally realise at first, but he was allowing far too many of my attacks to sneak through his defence as if he was asking to lose. Even after my blade struck deep in his heart and in sheer anger and desperation, I ripped it from him, I couldn't comprehend what had just happened. As he fell to the ground, I lunged forward to grasp him.

"Oh my god...Dad! Shit, I'm sorry! No, no, no, no...Father? Hey...Father? ...Why...What did I do?...Why did you make me do this?..." I said weeping into his bleeding chest.

He coughed a torrent of blood, his breathing becoming shallower as he fought tooth and nail just to live long enough to say his piece.

"Your birth and the mere fact that you live is shifting the fate of the world in our favour, my boy. But both of us cannot live..." his voice was getting fainter as the life slowly drained out of him. What was he talking about, he wasn't making sense. "One of us had to fall, someday you will understand...Someday you will realise that my death by your hand is necessary for our future..." He was fighting so hard now, the strain by just talking was having on his body was telling in his voice. "If I did not fight you, we would all be doomed...Be careful of whatever choices you next make, my son, they may well carry a price far higher than you can possibly imagine...Remember that, boy, be care..." his voice grew silent, his breath shallow.

I had killed my father for reasons that were so unclear at the time. What did he mean? The mere fact that I live is throwing the fate of the world in our favour? Why did he have to die? What was going on? Weeping into his bleeding chest, I threw his last words around in my mind. He didn't make sense. This whole event was totally against everything he held dear and honoured. He always taught me honour and sacrifice, not death and decay. That was Hoth's way, not ours. And how were my choices meant to affect everyone? I was one man, not an army! He must have got it wrong surely, maybe he was delirious through the loss of blood. I couldn't understand.

Soon, the whole village was awakened by my screams of anguish as I knelt in the courtyard, cradling my dead father in my arms. Tears of sadness poured down my face as the pure horror at what I'd done engulfed me. No one dared come near me, all were frightened and in shock.

The screams of our women filled the air as they crumpled to the floor with grief. Confusion and disbelief filled their souls in equal measure. They frantically tried to comprehend what was going on in front of them. It wasn't until, wiping the tears from my eyes, I stood to face the crowd before me that I was ready to pay for my crime.

"Look at me..." I shouted, the pain too great to completely hide. "Look at me...Look at what I've done...I have fought my father to the death and I have won...It was his choice to fight me. I had no other option but to retaliate...There was no one to witness this..."

I stopped, I had no idea what to say, what to do. The storm worsened as if the heavens themselves were angered by my deeds. Lightning crashed and flashed, briefly illuminating my shattered form, casting an unearthly image to the already trembling crowd. I lowered my head, for the first time I was alone. My father couldn't advise me what to do? I had to sort this out myself.

"There were no witnesses, no one saw who instigated it. You just have to take my word as the son of your chieftain, Helron, that my father attacked me. Believe me or not, just do with me what you will…"

I dropped to my knees, the weight of a thousand words crushed me beneath them.

I was distraught, in so much pain.

Silence. The cracks and rumbles of thunder and lightning were the only sounds.

That wasn't what I expected.

Why hadn't they killed me yet? Why hadn't they done anything yet? I looked at the crowd in front of me. Their faces were cold and emotionless. None of them could believe what they were hearing nor, indeed, wanted to believe it.

It was like they were frozen by some spell, motionless and emotionless. This wasn't right, they should be baying for my head, quickly judging me and then dealing out my well-deserved harshest of punishments. But instead, there was nothing…Nothing but silence.

"What are you waiting for?" the desperation in my voice was deafening. "Don't just stand there…Kill me…Kill me…" I began to sob again uncontrollably.

"Please just kill me," I whimpered quietly, "I can't live like this…"

Still, silence, what were they doing? *Come on,* I thought, *Do something, say something, anything…*I couldn't handle them not reacting, not making me pay for what I'd just done.

Suddenly, with a flash of lightning, my grief turned to anger. *If they won't do anything,* I thought, *if they won't claim retribution for my father's death, then I'll make them.* I thrust my arms to the heavens and roared, the ever-worsening storm giving me an almost devil-like quality, in the flashes of brief light. Picking up my sword, I jumped to my feet and took up a stance.

"Then if you will do nothing," my voice was sinister now, the conviction of what I intended reverberated around me like a hurricane wind, "then I will…"

With a violent roar, I charged at the crowd brandishing my sword, ready to kill again. They didn't move, I got closer and closer and still, they didn't move. I raised my sword back ready to make the first strike.

"Wait!" a stern voice said. "This is not the actions of a chieftain...Lower your sword!"

I ignored the request. I swiped downwards with so much conviction, I was determined to kill whoever was in front of me regardless of who they were; man, woman or child. They will have reason to kill me and I was going to give it to them. Before it could cut through its target, an armoured hand grabbed the blade mid-swing stopping me dead.

"Sire," said the voice again, the urgency of it more pronounced, "this is not the actions of a chieftain of the house of xenon!" it boomed. "Now lower your sword!"

A moment of hesitation, a flash of my life up until this point. I turned and faced the voice. The ornate armour had an ancient feel about it. A long history that was very familiar to me. It was Benteran, my father's oldest friend and the wisest man in the village.

I stared blankly at his old, rugged face weathered by his many years of life. His kind eyes peered into my soul and like he just flicked a switch, it was the last thing I was to see that night. I could feel my body give way and I collapsed.

Out with the Old...

The coronation, normally a happy occasion, was drenched in sadness. This isn't what I wanted. I wasn't ready for this all I could think was, why? Why now?

Over and over, I replayed the fight in my head, the words my father said to me. What choices? It didn't make sense. I was so preoccupied, I didn't even notice Benteran pronounced me the chief. The whole village bowed before me, it was sickening. I shouldn't be here. It's not supposed to be my burden yet.

I wasn't ready.

I wasn't ready.

"Sire, as a new chieftain, what will be your first act?" Benteran asked.

For a long time, I was silent, my mind a blank canvass. Then from nowhere, I heard it. It was faint, barely audible. But it was there in my head. My father's voice. I calmed myself and concentrated. There it was, I could hear it.

"Yes, Father," I whispered. Benteran looked at me, a smile growing on his face. I looked at the villagers in front of me, the expectant looks on their faces. I took a deep breath.

"My time with my father was spent mostly in training. But whilst you had the teachings of the house of Xenon, my father taught me differently...very early on, he told me he was preparing me for something. Something that would need a different type of warrior..."

Stunned silence, no one could believe what they were hearing. What I was about to do had never been done before, the looks of shocked expectancy loomed like a shadow across their faces.

"From this day, I will dissolve the old ways. And to honour my father, all shall be taught in the new ways, the ways my father taught me all my life."

Jeers and cheers in equal measure filled my ears, some hated the idea, some loved it, others were just too slack-jawed and stunned. But I knew in time all would eventually follow.

Every waking hour of every day for six months we trained. Trained in the harsh regimes and teachings of my father. I taught the fastest learners first and they, in turn, taught the others. Soon, the house of Xenon was unrecognisable. We were that house no longer, because of this we needed a new name, a new banner to fly into battle. But what?

That wouldn't come for some time. For months and months, we attacked and conquered new territory. Gradually, our armour changed to one of jet black. To all outsiders, we were a new target, one that, mistakenly for them, could be conquered. How wrong they were. Soon, all would realise that not only had we changed, but we were better, nastier and above all uncompromising.

Then word came. Hoth's army was on the move towards Atlantis, towards us. We needed to send a scouting party to make sure the information was correct. I picked 20 of my best men and prepared to set off. We adorned ourselves with our sacred charm. The white star of purity to protect us. We readied ourselves and then set off on the march towards an enemy we knew little about.

For five days, we trekked through the wilderness until through the trees we saw them jumping from treetop to treetop. Grotesque black armoured monstrosities, their armour jutting out with spikes in all directions. The whining of their breath bounced off the trees, the glow from their orange eyes illuminated the area in front of them. We laid in wait, waiting for the moment to strike. Which were the mages? We had to eliminate them first. But which ones were they? From the look of things, it wasn't a particularly big group, a scouting party, maybe like us. 15? 20 maybe?

Then we saw it. A mage. It was bigger than the rest, its helmet was high and tall, its glowing blue eyes gave it away. To bias, my most trusted archer readied his bow and with a quiet whistle, the arrow flew through the air, through the trees, straight to its face. With a roar, it clutched its face and fell through the trees, spiralling down, screaming all the way. The others were alerted now. The battle was on.

We jumped from our hiding place and charged at the troopers, swords ready to strike. The first hit down on its shoulder, our newly designed swords cut through its armour like butter. The weapons that so many of our outside garrisons criticised seemed surprisingly effective against these enemies. As he fell to the floor, I swung my sword around as I span to face my next opponent, with little effort, my sword sheared through his neck lopping off his head.

This was what I was preparing for. The realisation engulfed me like a flame. All around my men were hacking through the troopers with ease. But that all was about to change.

From nowhere a mage appeared in the middle of a group of six of us not ten feet away from me with the swiftness of a cat, it dropped to the floor smashing its fist into the ground. There was a blinding flash, a loud boom like the loudest thunder, splinters of trees and the body parts of my now fallen men flew past me as I was knocked off my feet.

There was no time to react, no time to mourn fallen comrades. The foul creature had leapt into the air, a two-foot spike protruding from the back of the hand was aimed right at me. I couldn't move in time. *This is it,* I thought, *it's been a good life, I'll be with you soon, Father.*

I waited for death. Like in slow motion, the mage dropped towards me. The blade was two inches away when thwack! An arrow as if from nowhere, hit the mage in the shoulder pinning him to a tree…thwack. Another hit his other shoulder pinning that to the same tree.

It was Tobias. *Good man,* I thought, *just when I needed…*

I didn't get time to finish that sentence, out of nowhere another mage's hand appeared from the gloom and slammed him in the chest. There was a blinding flash and Tobias flew through the air tens of feet backwards straight into another tree with a loud thud. He hit it that hard, the tree cracked in half falling on three other night reaper troopers killing them instantly. Without thinking, I launched myself at the mage, driving my sword deep into its neck with a swift flick of the wrist and a very deft turn, I tore the blade from its neck. I suddenly felt a new, very intense rage overcome me and I started to hack and slash my way through the remaining troops. My men seemed to feel it too as body parts and limbs flew through the air as we hacked them all to death.

As the battle ended, I surveyed my surroundings. Blood, bone and sinew glittered on the trees and the ground beneath me. I walked towards Tobias; my heart was heavy at the loss of my friend. I crouched down in front of him, readying myself to say goodbye.

Cough! cough! "What're you lookin' at?" he said wheezing, finding it difficult to breathe.

"I don't know, but it's lookin' back!" I said jokingly. "You OK to stand, old friend?"

"Dunno…I think I may have broken a rib or two…Can you give me a hand?"

I helped him up, his face contorted from the searing pain. We started towards the edge of the forest.

"Sire…You might wanna take a look at this."

"What is it, private?"

"There's one still alive here…" the anxious tone in the trooper's voice said it all. I walked towards him. Ravenous hate gripped me tightly. *Ah, would be an informant,* I thought. The reaper mage wheezed and coughed, it was on its way out, it'd lost too much blood. *There was no valuable information we can glean from him,* I thought. It raised its head, the glowing blue eyes glowing extra brightly.

"White star!" it hissed.

"Who me?" I replied. I assumed it was talking to me.

"Yes, you, white star…Your race is doomed…You will fall to the dark lord's might," it started to cackle. In between wheezes and coughs. I'd had enough. With one move, I took its head and walked slowly away.

"Hey, Tobias," I said.

"Yes, sir?"

"What did that thing call us?"

"White stars, sir."

"I thought so…I kinda like it…"

The Fields of Blood

Two years after I had taken over my village's army, I had turned them into an incredible fighting force, riveling even Hoth's greatest warriors, the night reaper high guard. They were a formidable enemy, nine feet tall and nine feet wider, half vampire, half werewolf without any of their weaknesses, no silver, no stake through the heart, not even sunlight, just decapitation.

They made that difficult with their thick armour covering most of their body. The only exposed spot was their lower neck and their thick, matted hairy chest plates. These were monsters in every sense of the word. Savage, brutal, strong and extremely dangerous, only the foolhardy would take them on their axes, 20 feet in length and weighing more than a tonne, made short work of would-be attackers, that or their, foot-long, razor-sharp claws and teeth. They would tear a man's flesh in seconds. For two years, they kept Hoth's army winning, for two years, they struck fear into any army just by the mention of them and for two years, they cut a swathe through every army that stood before them. But that all changed when they met us.

We were all young, none of us was over the age of 24. To look at us, we looked like we lacked experience, but for six months, we had been repelling Hoth's armies and now he wanted to know why. Our village was the last one before Atlantis, the great city of legend. It was the jewel in humanities crown, the accumulation of all of man's knowledge and worth. We had not to let it fall.

We stood in a meadow surrounded by hillsides nearby to our village. It was green and lush, somewhere our children played, our citizens rested and our warriors trained. This was not where we wanted the battle to take place, it was too close to our village, especially with what we were about to face, but they didn't give us time. No warning, nothing. Thank God, King Feron had seen fit to send help, 2000 Atlantian reserves. They weren't a regular army, but they were better than nothing.

Up until now, we had only fought lower-level troopers and mages. But even they were a task. Nothing in Hoth's army was easy. But on this day, he brought the big guns, so to speak. The high guard waited on the hill 200 yards away, we could hear their growls, smell their foul stench on their breath even from this distance. Hoth stood in front of them, proud and unwavering, his eyes burning red flame licking his eyebrows. A small battalion of troops gathered behind them jeering and chanting in a foreign horrible tongue. It gradually became louder and louder, the will to fight drained from our hearts. The men from Atlantis became restless as panic set in their gleaming golden armour hiding the terror in their souls. My men, though, stood true, unwavering at the horrors that lay before them, so they had not fought high guard. So, what? they thought, they're just bigger versions of his regular troopers. We may have to change tactics a little, they thought, but not much.

I had named my troops the white stars and they had them painted on their chests. In my village, it was a symbol of peace, purity and honour but also a talisman of protection. It had done me proud in past battles. I never seemed to lose many men, so at the time I thought it would be fitting to use it again. Their jet-black armour and their bright white stars made them look like a formidable army to anyone else, but for some reason, the reapers weren't fazed.

We let out a roaring battle cry to counter the reaper's terrifying growls in the hope it would ease the Atlantian men's hearts. Hoth just stood there and with a raise of his hand silenced his men. His eyes burned brighter and within a blink of an eye, he was right in front of me, nose to nose. I'd never seen anything move so fast. I didn't even see him coming, but there he was, his breath washing against my face, the heat from his eyes burning mine and the click of his huge serrated teeth filling my ears.

He was truly terrifying, a true demon in every sense of the word. My heart jumped into my throat as I stared at his demonic form, his intricate golden armour reflected the hot sun into my eyes and I'm sure just for a moment, I could see the pattern move and inspect me trying to weigh me up as a valid opponent or intimidate me. I could hear the hiss of snakes and the cries of a thousand dead souls emanate from it before he spoke.

"Do you know who I am?" he bellowed, his voice was loud but had a strangely relaxing purr underneath, almost calming and sensitive. "Do you know why I am here at this place?" Those eyes burned brighter and brighter hypnotising me. Inside them, terrifying images of dead enemies' souls led a tortured dance through flames, their screams filled my head. They were deafening. *Why wouldn't they stop?* I thought, *Why won't they stop screaming?* Where was it coming from? Was it really coming from him? Or is it just a trick, an illusion to strike fear into my heart? Whatever it was though, it was definitely working.

I was hesitant, a bad thing to do, a very bad thing to do, it shows fear and even though I was, for want of a better word, shitting myself, the last thing you want to do is show fear to a demon, especially to a demon like this.

He sniffed the air long and hard before giving me a sly grin. "I guess you do!" he chuckled as he vanished again only to appear on the hill where he started.

For a long while, there was silence on both sides apart from the faint whimper from the Atlantian army. They had good reason to be scared; before now, we or rather I was the unwavering, courageous champion of champions for the entire Atlantian civilisation, but even the milkmaids 15 miles away could probably smell the shit filling my pants. I was so scared. My mind was mush, I couldn't think straight. *If they attacked now,* I thought, *we would be slaughtered and in my state and also because I was at the front, I would be the first to die.* I was frozen with fear. But then something strange happened. For some inexplicable reason, he turned around and started to leave. We were gobsmacked as he leisurely sauntered off down the back of the hill. The sense of relief coming from the Atlantians was immense, they thought they'd got away with their lives.

They couldn't be more wrong. As their columns began to disperse in relief, it started not with a bang, but a word, a word that I wouldn't hear, used in that way again, for millennia to come, but it was so quiet like a whisper on the wind like it was only intended for me to hear. "Desolate," that was all it was, "Desolate." Within seconds, the ground rumbled as jets of streaming red flame flew from the ground. The Atlantian men were taken totally by surprise, flying into the air, the high heat melting their armour to their skin as they were boiled alive in their so-called protective shells like a lobster in a saucepan. Armour became fused with skin and bone.

I was struck dumb with terror, totally paralysed by the sheer, cunning and stealth involved in this attack. I just couldn't fathom how he did it. Then I saw them as the flames grew into the shape of pentagrams on the ground, their forms revealed themselves. Their bodies black as night, their helmets shaped into grotesque human skulls, their eyes glowing deep green.

This was the first time I'd seen them, the order of the demon tongue. Up until now, I'd just heard stories, tales of them. High mages so powerful that it only took four to wipe out 2000 strong armoured men and Hoth had hundreds of these at his command.

Our plight seemed hopeless, I was still rooted to the spot. Soon though, the sight of the men under my command dying, they're bodies being twisted, torn and violated until they were barely recognisable as human, drove me into taking action. I knew that most of the Atlantians were lost, they were fighting, but they were dropping like flies. They weren't going to last much longer.

I had only one option left and one hell of a gamble. I had to charge with what little men I had left straight at Hoth's remaining army. And hope above all that he'd only brought four of those high mages because I had a high guard to contend with and they weren't gonna be easy.

So, myself and the 30 of my most skilful, most experienced and loyal troops that I had brought with me, proud men and although young, they were the best fighters, be it either hand to hand, with a sword, axe or spear that ever graced the earth, we were the best of the best and today, on this battlefield, we were going to prove it. We turned and charged towards the hill and Hoth.

The screams of agony, fear and death coming from the falling Atlantians rang through our ears as we soldiered on. The closer and closer we got, our hearts pounded further into our throats as we ran. Closer still we got closer and closer, the sight of the reapers on the hill filling us with dread. I don't know why but, at that moment I began to chant to myself over and over, "I will show no fear," the conviction in my voice resonated around my body, "I will show no fear and we will cut them down with all the strength in our hearts!" To this day I do not know where those words came from, but those words somehow gave me power.

Faster I ran and faster I chanted. One of my men next to me heard my chant and saw my resolve, felt the energy from me and began to chant as well. As we reached the crest of the hill, all 30 men were chanting at the top of our voices, "I will show no fear, I will show no fear and we will cut them down with all the strength in our hearts!"

As soon as we came over the crest of the hill, the attack began, not with stealth and cunning like before, but with a 20-foot spinning blade of death hurtling towards us. I managed to duck just in time as the high guard's axe span past my head, missing it by inches and hitting the two poor souls behind me. They didn't see it coming, just as I had very nearly not done, luck was definitely on my side. Their bodies slumped to the ground as their heads bounced leisurely down the hill towards Hoth's army. The high guard that threw it let out a what sounded like triumphant cry as it began to steam towards us. Hoth stood firm glaring in my direction, the flames in his eyes raising above his head. It was that moment that I knew I'd really pissed him off.

He wasn't expecting this and that angered him, it was a weakness that even he couldn't hide. My father taught me, in battle, above anything else, to keep calm and composed, do not let your emotions take over or you will almost certainly make a mistake. I had made mine earlier, not expecting there to be anything as powerful as the high mages. Now it looked as though Hoth was about to make his. He'd underestimated our sheer courage and without doubt, our incredible madness and willingness to try the impossible.

The high guards were getting closer, I could feel their breath and smell their foul odour as they lunged for us. Quickly, I ducked swiping my sword high and hard, hitting one at the weak point between its neck and chest, severing its head. With a loud cry, it fell to the ground, its head rolling back down the hill a few yards in front.

Hoth roared, it was a roar I'd never heard before from man nor beast. It wouldn't be the last time I would hear it and from what I could gather, he was now extremely pissed. Up until today, no one had dared fight with a high guard, let alone killed one before. This was something he'd not expected and he didn't like it. He gestured and wave after wave of high guard and troopers rallied themselves towards us. My men looked on as the mass of sharp, pointy, evil death raged on quickly gathering pace. Soon they were upon us, my men after seeing how I despatched the high guard learned from my manoeuvre and did the same. Most were lucky, some were not. I was down to 20 men and I was losing them fast. The Atlantians were all but obliterated, but the remaining few charged to our aid whilst trying to repel the continuing high mage attacks.

Anyone on the outside looking in would guarantee that we were going to lose, but not us. We were down to 15 of my men and 14 inexperienced Atlantian foot soldiers injured by the mages but still putting up a fight. Our blades dripped with reaper blood, they were thirsty for more and we weren't about to refuse them a drink.

Hour after hour we battled, none of us giving up, reaper or human alike. Night reaper troopers fell by the dozens before the next wave of high guard attacked. Hoth looked on, I could see the anger in him grow and grow. This was unprecedented, no one could battle his army this long let alone survive or, God forbid, may even win. He was furious. His eyes burning white-hot. His hand grasping his sword tighter and tighter as his rage built inside him. For another two hours, he let the battle raged with every troop, mage or high guard that I cut down, I made sure I was looking right at him. I wanted him to know that if I got close enough, then the look in my eyes would be the last thing he would see. I was making my way through his troops, making my way to him or I was going to die trying.

Of course, I just had to find a way of killing him. Hoth wasn't anything like these troops, even the high guard and high mages combined weren't even in his league, he was one of the first. No, Hoth definitely wouldn't go down easy, I'd to try something special for him.

The battle raged on and on and on. Soon it began to dawn on me, the waves coming against us were slowing and dwindling. We were winning, the elation in my heart grew more and more yet again, I cut down the best that he could throw at us. My men could feel it too. We began to chant louder and louder as a high guard after high guard fell beneath our feet. Suddenly, he was there yet again right on my face, snarling angrily, a deafeningly loud, terrifying roar slowly ate its way out of his mouth and the marauding hordes retreated all the while, Hoth never shifted his gaze from my eyes. The flames licked over his head like ballerinas pirouetting high in the air. I knew then that I'd really made him mad.

Suddenly, the roar stopped, his gaze peered towards the heavens as he gleefully began to chuckle. This above all else scared me more. Here we were, victorious in front of him, my pitiful army of what was now 23 had taken on and defeated an army of 500 strong night reapers 100 of which were high guard and here he was laughing, I couldn't understand it. It baffled me, he looked at me and smiled. A faint glimmer caught the corner of my eye, shadowy silhouettes, human in form, then another and another and another. The sudden realisation of what was happening came to me. As did the full horror of what was about to come, high mages. This was it, I was a goner for sure.

He grinned gleefully, "I could kill you all right now…Whelp!" he said, an air of triumph in his tone.

I stayed there, peering into the flames that were his eyes, unable to move, the fear was that strong. "But I won't!"

Now, this I didn't expect, why not? Why was he letting me live? The contorted forms of the high mages shimmered all around me, their eyes brightening through the knowledge that they were about to kill.

"Why not?" I said, the fear quivering my voice as I looked at the odds against me. He just looked at me and smiled, "Today, my young friend, you have shown me a worthy battle. In a sense, you've won. Even though I could kill you where you stand or I could just have my mages kill you. I admire a worthy adversary, it makes things more interesting, makes me look forward to our next battle and to the time we meet again." His tone of voice was so calm but strangely full of a sort of admiration for me.

"Someday, Arkanon, I will watch you die. But for the time being, I think it'll make things…a little…How should I put it? Ah yes, a little more interesting if I let you live. Well, at least for now. You make war here…entertaining. It would be a shame to kill you just yet." A smug smile grew across his face, his sharp teeth gleaming in the sunlight, a chuckle like a child getting up to mischief for the very first time wisped with the sound of the wind. He was finished. I had seen my enemy and he terrified me to the very essence of my being. He bowed his head and vanished before my eyes. The mages slowly turned their backs and followed vanishing into nothing.

As I stood there on the battlefield, I gazed at my surroundings. The stench of death was everywhere. Piles and piles of night reaper troopers and high guard lay before me, their blue-green blood soaking the mud under my feet. Behind me, the bodies of nearly 2000 Atlantian soldiers laid twisted, broken, fused with metal and staining the charred grass with blood beneath them. This had been a momentous battle, we may have lost countless lives to win it, but we did win. And for the first time, we felt hope. If we could win this battle after so many failures, maybe, just maybe we could win the war.

Part 2: Ah! So, You're the 'Organ Grinder'?

Always Remember to Read the Fine Print

Secret gestapo bunker, Berlin, 14 April 1942, 09:27 pm.

Colonel Hans Schmidt sat uncomfortably in a large leather chair situated at the end of a vast tunnel-like hallway. He was a reasonably handsome man in his late 30s with a fairly well-cared physique. He was your stereotypical looking, pure Arian in the German sense, all straw blonde hair, blue eyes and chiselled features.

He nervously shifted position in his seat every few minutes, his fingers drumming against his knees rapidly and noisily. His gaze was fixed on a grandfather clock 20 feet or so across from him against the far wall, counting every second of every minute in his mind. He'd been following this pattern for the past hour, only breaking the repetition occasionally to readjust his uniform before sitting back down. He'd been kept waiting for age and in normal circumstances, he would've complained and demanded to be seen immediately by now. But this appointment was a different matter entirely, so he would begrudgingly have to wait.

He'd been told to arrive for the appointment at 20:30 hrs and was under strict instructions 'not to be late!' The very nature of how he'd received these orders was also the cause for concern and Hans was still unsure if he'd fell foul of a cruel and quite dangerous, practical joke. As he sat back down for the umpteenth time, he began to mull over the circumstances that brought him to this point,

When he arrived home at 19:00 hrs, he'd found a brand-new SS uniform placed neatly on his bed. It was obvious someone had been in his apartment as it wasn't there this morning and he certainly hadn't previously owned one. But the mystery gift giver had left no trace of their intrusion other than this uniform and a white envelope that was placed in the centre of the plush, black jacket and beautifully penned calligraphy had the words, 'Colonel Hans Schmidt: In accordance with your promotion'.

He'd got into the shower before opening the envelope and immediately wished he'd opened it beforehand. Not only was there the information about his meeting, but it informed him that a car would be arriving at 20:00 hrs to collect him and to follow the driver's instructions to the letter, which meant he'd only ten mins to get changed. He hastily threw on his pristine black and silver uniform rather than wasting time reading the remainder of the note and just managed to put on his boots when there was a screech of tires, a clunk of the car door followed by a loud and commanding knock! knock! knock! on the entrance to his building. He dashed downstairs to meet the driver and open the door, rapidly composed himself, saluting the sergeant who was his driver, who promptly saluted back,

"Forgive me, Herr Colonel!" he said. "But I have been ordered to make sure that you wear this upon entering the car and to not remove it until I inform you that we've arrived at our destination," he continued, passing a black cloth bag to Hans with a smile. "I'm sure you understand the reasons why this must be the case?"

Hans smiled and nodded politely in agreement, despite not having the faintest idea why the bag over his head was necessary. Or for that matter, where he was going and whom he was meant to be seeing. He'd not left himself enough time to read that part of the letter.

"We also acquired all the relevant data and files from your office that you could need for your meeting, Herr Colonel!" The sergeant paused for an acknowledgement for his forward-thinking. But all Hans could think was how invasive it seemed. The sergeant, sensing that Hans was anything other than appreciative, continued, "I would hate for you to go into such an important meeting unprepared, sir! And seeing as we're on such a limited schedule and such short notice, I ascertained that you'd have little or no time for a detour to your office. It is 16.3 km in the opposite direction after all!"

The sergeant smiled again waiting for any sign of praise and Hans had to admit he had a point, despite his privacy being violated in this way. But this was the Third Reich after all, so he should expect nothing less and it did kind of did him a favour.

"Very good, sergeant! Good work!"

The young sergeant smiled as he opened the rear door of the car and waited for Hans to enter. Hesitating, Hans looked at the young soldier in front of him. *What if this is all a ruse to take him to his death or an allied trick to kidnap him?*

he thought. *Did this guy look like a German soldier? The Brits were rumoured to be kidnapping scientists, especially Jews, to use in their own labs and workshops! What if they were coming after him? What if they were here now?*

Suddenly, he snapped himself out of his panic and guffawed, unintentionally, out loud causing the young sergeant to notice his outburst. Hans shook his head allowing the guffaw to evolve into a snigger. So, as he entered the car, he patted his young driver on the back, giving him a disarming look, to convince him that his sniggering wasn't at his expense and sat down on the back seat. Then placing the bag on his head, he allowed his mind to, once again, bed into utter paranoia.

It wasn't until he'd arrived at his destination and was allowed to remove the bag covering his face that he became aware of where he was. Because this was the secret bunker of the secret police, the Gestapo and the feared SS, this was the office of Heinrich Himmler himself, so Hans now had good reason to be nervous, even more so after he flicked through the files that'd been picked out for him.

You see, up until this night, Colonel Hans Schmidt had been the head of the Reich's scientific and engineering division. Or rather, more specifically, head of the new technology, acquisition and reverse engineering department and his department had been sucking money from the Reich's coffers at a rate comparable to the weekly wages of an A-list Hollywood actor would demand. Not that the money wasn't being used for anything other than the essential equipment and personnel required. But it was a great deal of money, that he hoped he could justify taking.

Into the Lion's Den We Venture Forth

From the far end of the hall came the, at first quite faint but getting increasingly louder, distinct clip! clop! of high heeled shoes headed towards Hans' direction. He looked up, quietly surprised by what greeted his eyes as he did. A very tall, very leggy, curvaceous blonde stepped seductively towards him.

Her long hair tied back and fastened with a pencil. Her fringe pushed loosely to one side away from her bright blue eyes. Her thick-rimmed glasses balanced delicately on the edge of her nose. She had a lightly golden complexion, though she seemed to look a little pink and flustered in her cheeks. Tiny beads of sweat clung diligently to her forehead as she carried a wobbling tower of files. She wore a flimsy white shirt buttoned up just enough to contain her plunging neckline and ample bosom but always seeming to be ready to fail at a moment's notice.

The only thing stopping that from happening was the stack of files she was carrying tightly against that chest. Her army issue, the tight grey skirt had been pushed up narrowly managing to cover her underwear but still managing to let slip that she was wearing fishnet stockings and suspenders. Hans couldn't help but be mesmerised by her. She was the most gorgeous woman he'd ever seen. He continued to watch her struggle for a few moments more before realising what he was doing and hurriedly jumping to his feet, "May I assist you, fräulein?" he asked as he made his way quickly towards her, bending forward just in time to catch hold of the files and steady them before they fell to the floor.

Instinctively she leant forward at the same time to catch them, trapping his hand between the files and her chest. Slowly, giggling with embarrassment, she stood up releasing her grip on the files and allowing Hans to take hold of them.

"Danka!" she said softly, "I've travelled up to three flights of stairs and past, at least 50 or 60 men and you are the very first to offer me any assistance!" Her soft voice had a tinge of anger behind it that, to Hans, made her sound sexier. "All they did was whistle and letch! Disgusting brutes! It's so nice to finally be in the presence of a gentleman," she smiled at Hans. Her plump ruby lips were so inviting. He would've kissed her right there and then if he knew he'd get away with it.

But, he thought, *I probably won't!*

"I presume you're Herr Himmler's eight-thirty appointment? Colonel Schmidt?" she enquired. Hans just nodded nervously. "Aww!" she said, noticing his trepidation. "Don't be nervous! He's been looking forward to your meeting all day. He has high hopes for you, you know?"

Her voice felt like silk in his ears and he very nearly didn't take in what she'd just said as his soul seemed to comfort itself within it. She turned around and bent over directly in front of him and he wasn't sure if she was doing it on purpose, for his benefit, but he was glad she did. She pushed the button on the intercom and waited for a response. It didn't take long.

"Ya, Helena," the soft-spoken voice of Heinrich Himmler trickled through the air. "What is it that you want, my dear girl?"

She looked over her shoulder at Hans smiling, partly due to what she was about to do and also because she'd just caught him checking out her rather curvaceous rear. Rapidly, he started to look in any direction but her rear or her eyes looking back at him.

"You like what you see, Herr Colonel?" she said with a seductive tone. "Because naughty boys like you need to be punished! Let's see what Herr Himmler thinks of all this," her tone was playful as she teasingly winked at Hans.

"Is that so, my dear? Well, if that's the case, what I think of all this," Helena screamed in shock as Himmler's voice cut through the air and directed at Helena as he playfully scolded her, "if you're going to tease the good Colonel, you should remember to take your hand off the intercom button first. Hmmm! What shall we do with you then, eh?"

Helena slumped onto the desk to hide her embarrassment as Himmler's laugh came through the speaker along with a second voice Hans didn't recognise. After a moment or two, she realised she's still bent over and could feel Hans' eyes taking in every detail of her curves. She took a deep breath and slowly turned round to face him. "I'm sorry, Helena, is it?" Hans interjected before Helena could say a word. She instead just nodded in agreement. "Well, Helena, my dear, forgive my rudeness and my lingering gaze, but you really shouldn't bend over like that, if you don't want me to look?"

She had to admit he was right. She did do it to get his attention. She just wasn't expecting Himmler to hear any of it. Neither of them was expecting what Himmler did next.

"Are you married, Colonel Schmidt? Have a girlfriend perhaps?" the smoothness of Himmler's voice coming through the speaker in such a disembodied way felt almost ethereal. Himmler was a hero to Hans, an idol of his. It almost felt to him that he wasn't just talking to Heinrich Himmler, no, he felt that he was communicating with a god.

"No, Sir, Herr Himmler! Not married and no girlfriend. I am completely married to my work and research, sir!" Hans said nervously. "Why do you ask?"

"Yes, why do you ask?" Helena chirped in, curious as to where Heinrich was going with this.

"No!...No! That won't do at all, Herr Colonel!" Himmler said disapprovingly. "A good man, especially one that will change the world, needs the balance of a good woman behind him." There was a brief pause, then it seemed as though Himmler was asking someone else their opinion and it was hard to make out, but it sounded like Himmler did get a response. Not only that, but the accent of this companion sounded, dare he say it, Jewish. A fact Hans immediately dismissed as preposterous.

"Himmler is fraternising with Jews indeed!" Hans snorted under his breath.

It was still, however, audible enough for Helena to hear and let out a hysterical cackle in response. She was still cackling when Himmler spoke over the intercom again.

"It's settled then!" Himmler began commandingly. "Due to the insulting nature of your prank, Helena, you are hereby ordered to spend the next week at my Carcassonne chateaux as the guest of Herr Schmidt!"

"I insulted him?" Helena shouted angrily at the speaker on the desk. "How the hell have I insulted him, Heinrich?"

"By attempting to make a high-ranking officer of the Gestapo look foolish, can there be any greater insult?" This angry and volatile Himmler was a stark contrast to the quite accommodating and friendly one he'd been experiencing thus far. "Now, my dear Helena! You will obey this direct order and spend the week with Herr Schmidt or I will have you charged with desertion and shot! Am I making myself perfectly clear?"

Helena stood ridged in shock as did Hans next to her. *Surely, he didn't mean it?'* he thought to himself. He looked over at the still shocked Helena and quietly apologised.

"I am, as yet, missing an answer from you, Helena," Himmler angrily barked again. "Are you clear what your orders are?"

"Yes, Heinrich!" Helena replied with disdain.

"What did you say? Should I have you brought up on charges for insubordination? You will address me correctly, girl! Need I remind you that you are only a mere civilian with no military rank and only my secretary as a favour to your sister, my wife. I'm sure I could orchestrate a believable cover for your demise, wouldn't you agree?" Helena burst into tears as Himmler's voice rasped and hissed, unnaturally, with each murderous word. Her fear all too real and in no way fake, which Hans was desperately wishing that it was.

Hans knew then, through Helena's reaction, that this was no idle threat but clear and calculated response to a, perceived by Himmler, unacceptable diminishment of control that would be executed with masterful efficiency. Something that seemed to all intents and purposes to be an unconfirmed certainty that was well-practised also.

"Well!" Himmler barked again, "I'm waiting, girl!"

"Yes! I understand perfectly, Sir Herr General Himmler!" As quietly as she could, Helena ran for the door sobbing and Hans couldn't help feeling sorry for her. He was just starting to think that the stories he'd heard about Himmler were a wild exaggeration to demonise him and make him seem like a monster when the reverse was true. Sadly, the last couple of minutes had done nothing to discredit the stories he'd heard.

"Good! Now then, Colonel Schmidt," Himmler said in a surprisingly calm tone.

A troubling trait indeed, Hans thought. Anyone who, without batting an eyelid, can go from intense and cruel rage to calm as a dead zen master was something to be wary of more so when it seemed as though they held you on such a high pedestal without even meeting you first.

"I apologise for the long wait," he continued. "But unfortunately, this meeting was completely unavoidable and the sheer length of time it is taking is a testament to the issues involved and their importance. I'm sure you can understand?" Hans was just about to answer when he heard a murmuring before Himmler butted in.

"Actually, Colonel Schmidt, would you care to join us? It has just occurred to me that it would be of immense benefit to all involved if you met my companion. After all, you will both have a lot of dealings with each other from now on!"

Hans couldn't believe his luck! But along with that came the realisation of how massive a deal this whole meeting was. He was, after all, about to be privy to something that is strictly reserved for the ruling elite in the Reich. Not an engineer and physics professor.

"I would be honoured, Sir, Herr Himmler," he responded, fighting back tears of proud joy.

"Please, Hans! Enough with the formalities, call me Heinrich. That reminds me you have hereby been promoted to general, more specifically, there is no other rank above yours, but there is one that is equal. Mine! Congratulations, General Hans Schmidt. The door to my office should be unlocked now, please take a seat."

At Last, We Meet Mr Organ Grinder and I Presume This Is Your Monkey?

Although Hans already had preconceptions on how opulent Heinrich Himmler's office would be, nothing could prepare him for the real McCoy. As he opened the large mahogany doors, he was greeted by a room whose size was only narrowly beaten by a small country such as Luxembourg. Its only light source as he entered was from a gigantic, roaring, wood fire in a specially built fireplace and chimney dead centre in the room. The firelight was aided around the room by brilliant white, polished marble about halfway up the walls, the only break in the darkest black marble he'd ever seen. At the very end of the room, Himmler sat behind an ornate mahogany desk in a large, throne-like leather chair and across him sat a figure he couldn't make out from the shadow covering him. Himmler slowly rose to his feet, extending his hand as he made his way out to greet him.

"It is truly a pleasure to finally meet you in person, General," a subtle smile wisped across his face, his eyes obscured by the glass in his round glasses reflecting the fire. Its flames danced feverously in the glass and Hans couldn't help but think that he could easily be here to sign away his soul to the devil himself. Little did he know how close to reality that stray thought would eventually become.

"I've heard some amazing work has been coming from your labs and with some unbelievable artefacts. But then from the amount of money that has been pumped into it, I should hope so, eh?" Himmler roared with laughter. It was the kind of fake laughter a bully would use to gauge whom to manipulate next based on whether or not they laughed too. Hans remained silent, he'd failed to get the joke after all. Their mystery guest, however, seemed as though he did.

"Please, come sit down," Himmler said with excitement that was oddly genuine sounding as he put his arm around Hans' shoulder guiding him towards the desk. "I presume you've brought along some literature covering your latest findings?" Hans just nodded. "Excellent! Are these the files?" He reached down to the group of files in Hans' hand and slowly took them from him. "Now please, tell us what we can look forward to?"

Hans shuffled nervously to his seat as Himmler returned to his. For the first time, he was able to get a good look at the other gentleman in the room. Even in this dim light, he could tell he was old, very old. Exactly how old though was open to debate, Hans reckoned upon late 80s due to the depth and frequency of his wrinkled, leathery skin, which hung loosely over extremely gaunt features. For a few moments, he had to convince himself that Himmler hadn't stolen a body from the morgue as he looked dead. Reassuringly, or not as the case may be, the gentleman moved slightly.

"Ack! Where are my manners?" Himmler said disapprovingly. "Forgive my rudeness, gentlemen, I seem to have neglected introductions in all my excitement. Hans, allow me to introduce to you John D. Rockefeller, founder and president of the central bank of America. John, this is Brigadier General Hans Schmidt, director of the newly founded SS special projects department."

The two men nodded politely to each other in acknowledgement, Hans' was rounded off with a faint sneer. If there was one thing that Hans felt sure he could be certain of, it was his own and Himmler's shared hatred of Jews. But now he found himself in the presence of the great Heinrich Himmler and he was sharing a brandy with one! Worse still, he was an American. He just hoped that there was a good reason to even entertain this vile excuse for a human. He just hoped that the Führer wasn't aware of this because that would just kill all the faith he had in his beloved Reich.

"Would you like a brandy, Hans?" Himmler asked.

Hans shook his head defiantly. *It was one thing to remain in the same room as this garbage*, he thought. But he drew the line at sharing a drink with him. A look of pure disgust and hatred flooded his face whenever he needed to look at Rockefeller's, a fact not altogether lost on Rockefeller either. Himmler wasn't ignorant of that fact either, a sly smile of approval sneaking out when his guest wasn't looking.

"This is the man I was telling you about, John," Himmler stated proudly. "He has acquired something recently that could keep us in power for millennia."

Rockefeller's eyes widened in disbelief. This was a bold statement and one that, he knew, Himmler wasn't prone to making unless he had good reason.

"Would you be so kind as to give Mr Rockefeller a brief idea about what it is you've found, Hans?"

Hans took a deep breath. He didn't have to say anything, but it was very clear that Hans wasn't happy about the idea of explaining anything to this man present. He didn't trust him.

"I'd love to hear it, after all, it's my money that's funding this project," Rockefeller said smugly. Hans gave him one more disapproving look, but at the same time felt some relief. Himmler's reasons for associating with this man-made perfect sense. It was the most basic of reasons too, money. So, looking directly at Himmler, he began to explain.

"Around 18 months ago, a small exploratory force in North Africa stumbled across what's best described as a tomb. Within that tomb were what were first thought to be two empty suits of armour. These suits are made from a material that we cannot place on the periodic table and have no idea how to synthesise. Not only that, but the technology within the suit is way beyond anything we can fathom at this current time."

"Interesting," Rockefeller said with a bred and disbelieving tone but was rendered speechless on first glance at the pictures Himmler was passing him. Hans, sensing that he'd got his full attention now, continued.

"That wasn't the best part," he said excitedly, moving his chair closer to Rockefeller's so he could point things in the photos out as he explained. "Within the smaller set of armour, we found a completely new element that we've named Xerum 528. It is a yet unspecified substance as we cannot determine whether it is a rock, metal or anything for that matter due to its high levels of intense radiation that it floods into its surrounding area." Hans paused for a moment to allow this information to sink in before continuing. "This stuff is amazing, it continuously glows with a vibrant purple light and we feel, quite possibly, could be the most powerful energetic force that exists on the planet."

"A bold statement," Rockefeller remarked, "one that's provable, I presume." Hans laughed at him dismissively and continued.

"If you skip past the next two photos you'll find the only one we could get of it," He waited patiently for Rockefeller to reach the aforementioned picture and smiled at his reaction.

"Is it stood on a piece of glass or suspended from something?" John Rockefeller wasn't entirely sure what he was looking at. All he could make out was a glowing mass in the centre of some sort of reinforced box.

"No! It's not on anything," Hans said, hoping he didn't ask about anything he couldn't rightly explain, which was a rather large blank area about Xerum if he was honest. "It's actually floating in that box, held up by nothing but thin air." Rockefeller looked stunned but still rather sceptical. "That box incidentally is 12-inch thick lead. The radiation is still unimaginably strong even from within that since the man who took that photo was dead seven hours later."

"My god!" Rockefeller gasped. He started to flick through the rest of the photographs before stopping, dumbfounded, at one photo in particular. "Where was this picture taken?"

"At our facility in Bremen." Hans clicked onto the nature of Rockefeller's question immediately as did Himmler. "Why? Have you seen it before? You have, haven't you? You've seen this thing before?"

Hans' excitement had piqued Himmler's interest into what they were talking about and he rose from his seat to see what the subject was. To his delight, it was something he'd never seen before and he too was eager to learn more. "What on earth is that?" Himmler enquired. "I've not been informed about anything, even close to resembling that! Is that a person stood next to it?" Both Rockefeller and Hans nodded silently. "But that must be what? 10, 15 metres tall?"

"13 and a half to be exact," Hans said without thinking. Himmler smiled. "We had originally thought it to be long dead. But as soon as we attempted to remove its armour, it awoke killing eight scientists and 36 armed paratroopers before surrendering." Hans had to think for a moment. "Actually, if I'm honest, it seemed to allow us to capture it! We've actually come to learn a great deal about what it is and where it came from. According to that, it's something called a—"

"A high guard," Rockefeller butted in.

"That is correct, Mr Rockefeller." Hans was amazed he'd known this at all, only a selected few, trusted member of his team knew about it, could one of them be a spy, he thought.

"My father used to tell me stories about them when I was a boy! They were described as looking just like that."

"It talks to you and you to it," Himmler exclaimed, his excitement for the prospect of communing with such a beast growing ever higher. "When can I meet it for myself?"

Rockefeller breathed in deeply, his gaze transfixed to the picture. "I would also wish to commune with beast also if that's possible, Herr Schmidt."

Rockefeller rose to his feet before gently placing the picture onto Himmler's desk. "Forgive me, gentlemen, for my sudden departure, but I have a long journey home ahead of me."

"I'll see you to the door. Hans, my boy, could you wait here a moment, I would like to discuss a few things with you." Himmler escorted him to the door, the pair chatting like lifelong old friends before dashing back to his desk. "I'm sure you have plenty of questions, Herr Schmidt, so feel free to ask them."

Hans shifted uncomfortably in his seat for a moment or two before deciding to come right out with what he had to say. "Forgive me, Herr Himmler."

"Call me Heinrich, please!"

"Sorry! Heinrich! I have to ask this." He thought carefully for a moment about the best way to word his question. "But what the hell is going on? Fraternising with that disgusting Jew, even worse an American coward as well? What on earth has possessed you to involve yourself with him? Does Hitler know? And will we be also presenting my findings to him? He'd surely have a keen interest in this?"

"All relevant questions, my friend," Himmler seemed surprisingly calm. "I'll answer your last question as it will in some way answer all of your questions. Hitler will know nothing of this meeting between us or between me and Rockefeller and that goes especially for your research more than anything. Hitler doesn't need to know anything because Hitler isn't the one with all the power, he is just a...Well, what can only be described as a puppet. A puppet with an uncanny ability to enthral the masses, but he has to use my words to do it! He is a necessary frontman for the Reich that I and I alone have created. Hitler has no more power over the people than a dog defecating on the street. Nor is he able to make, or indeed influence, for that matter policy. He is just a voice and face for me."

Hans tried to get his head around what Himmler had just told him. But all it did was produce even more questions than Himmler had given him answers for. One of which was why the hastily awarded promotion and why was he so looking forward to meeting him.

"Ah that's a good question," said Himmler. "Eighteen years ago, I was involved in a seance. The psychic we'd hired to hold the seance for us channelled a demon that was far too powerful for her, the poor girl. Just before it, quite spectacularly, it tore her to pieces from the inside, it made three predictions." Himmler lifted his glasses and wiped a tear from his eye before continuing. "The first was that the owners of the house we were in would be dead before the end of that week, a sacrificial payment for the subsequent predictions. The house belonged to my brother and his family. And, sure enough, that Saturday night, he disembowelled his wife and sat her in an armchair and made her watch him bludgeon my two young nieces in front of her as she died before disembowelling himself followed by dousing himself in petrol and setting himself on fire. As an event to prove the validity of the demon's power and the accuracy of its predictions, it was quite effective."

Hans was stunned. He genuinely didn't want to know the circumstances surrounding the two further predictions, but he had a feeling that Himmler wanted to tell him them.

"Its next prediction was," Himmler continued, a small, unsettling smile creeping across his face, "the rise of the Third Reich and its domination of the world. But its next was the one that intrigued me most."

"It foretold the acquisition of artefacts of immense age and unequalled power." Himmler turned his back to Hans facing the fire and breathed in deeply. It was the kind of breath that is taken when that final, long-awaited piece of the puzzle has revealed itself to you. Himmler's shoulders suddenly thrust back as he raised his head high as if enthralled by a masterpiece concerto that was playing on his mind.

"Hans…Hans…Hans!" a slight chuckle escaped his lips like the one which would come from a giddy schoolboy before he snapped it silent sucking through his teeth as he turned to face Hans. The dancing shadows and dim light cast from the fire across his face clashed jarringly against the almost blinding reflection moving opposite in his round spectacles. This only grew ever brighter as he slowly lowered his head, a maniacal smile dominated his face. This was the first instance that Hans had ever experienced anything that he could honestly say was close to pure evil. But Hans could tell that this was all Himmler! He wasn't under some kind of possession nor some sort of mind control; this was the true nature of Heinrich Himmler. This was his true face, yet he felt no fear from him. Oddly, he felt indifferent, unphased and faintly disinterested and bizarrely, Himmler loved this!

"The demon foretold your coming to me by name." Himmler paused a moment to allow this knowledge to sink in. "Why do you think I would actively have such a personal interest in your career?"

He walked towards Hans, arms outstretched until he was close enough to crouch in front of him and clasp his hands on either side of Hans' face. "You and I are about to become the rulers of the world. Beginning with your research and subsequent development of your technologies."

Hans tried to hide his apprehension, managing to summon up an exciting looking expression that seemed to have failed. Yet Himmler responded with a somewhat reassuring chuckle and said with a knowing wink, "No pressure!"

Part 3: So, Don't You Think We Should Know How We Got Here?

Uneasy Alliances

Pripyat (Chernobyl), Ukraine, 12 June 1995, 04:32 am

The sun rose slowly over Pripyat, the golden-red glow drenched the pale white buildings of a deserted town. Tower blocks crumbling after years of neglect, trees and vegetation relentlessly through streets and buildings. This place hadn't been touched by human hands since the Chernobyl reactor disaster ten years earlier. Birds and wild deer now owned this place, nature had made its home and was determined to keep it.

Suddenly, the bird song and silence were dramatically disturbed as the roar of a truck engine reverberated around Pripyat square. The truck, over 50 feet long and heavily armoured, was a deep black, its exhausts spewed black acrid smoke poisoning the air as it ground to a deliberate halt.

Inside General Ivan Romanov sat slightly hunched over, his attention fully ensnared by the screen in front of him. Around him, soldiers flitted back and forth like worker bees, busily chatting to each other in several different tongues. Men in very expensive black suits sat menacingly in the shadows. Romanov was a huge man, six feet and seven inches, around 45 years old and built like a bodybuilder, his long grey fringe covered an eye damaged in years gone by. He was highly decorated and respected, not just by his own country, but foreign armies also. He was a battle-hardened man, had seen untold amounts of live combat, some secret missions, most not so secret. In stark contrast, the man who stood beside him was his polar opposite.

General Martin Schwartzer was a fat man by military standards and surprisingly short for a soldier. His military uniform failed to hide his huge stomach and he generally walked with a waddle, gaining him the affectionate name of 'duck ass' by his subordinates. The one saving grace was at least he still had all his hair, which at the age of 53 was greying quite badly. He was a general in the U.S Marine Corps like his father, Leyton Schwartzer, also a general in the marine corp.

Leyton was a highly decorated and highly respected soldier, who fought Dunkirk during operation market garden in WW2. He was also head of the U.S. government's science and technology division based at Groom Lake, a position that Martin inherited from his father and now held. It seemed his father was a little too forthcoming with the information he was giving to his son, guaranteeing him the position to safeguard his silence. To a lot of Martin's peers, he had gained his rank largely due to his father's merits and in a large part, from working his way into officers' functions and kissing ass profusely. The worst part was they were right.

Throughout the cold war, he was employed to oversee the design and manufacture of ways to spy on and in some cases, how to covertly kill Russian targets. This made him deeply mistrustful of the Russians. His combat experience was also shaky at best, somehow managing to get out of getting involved in any combat throughout his military career This in most part, was due to his father's huge amount of favours that were owed to him and had decided to collect.

To Romanov, Schwartzer's lack of combat experience showed. He generally thought the man a coward and was unsure why he was the Americans' choice to be here. You could tell these two men despised each other, the atmosphere in the room was thick. They had been thrown together by their respective governments for what was perceived as a common goal.

They were here to test a new armour newly designed as a joint project by Britain, America, Russia, China and France, the only permanent members of the security council. This was an unprecedented achievement between countries normally at loggerheads with each other and even though it seemed as though their countries were getting along, it was impossible for these two remnants of the cold war to really get along. There was still a lot of ill-feeling held by these two men towards each other's countries. Both of them thought that the other shouldn't be here, that they weren't to be trusted. With that in mind, they kept a very watchful eye over the other. Neither man really wanted to talk to the other yet both men knew that at some point they had to.

It took a young, British private to break their tension. "General Sir Schwartzer, we have arrived at our destination," the private said saluting.

"Thank you, private," Schwartzer said in his most authoritative voice. "Inform the test subjects that we will be ready to begin in…" he turned towards Ivan waiting for confirmation of how long it would take his men to be in place.

Ivan sneered at him, he abhorred the idea that he had to communicate with this man, but he was fully aware that he was going to have to at some point. "My men will be in place in approximately two hours," he said with disdain.

General Schwartzer gazed at Ivan, a vacant expression on his face, the cogs in his brain whirring as he tried to comprehend what Ivan was saying. His accent was very thick, extremely Russian, the feeling that not only did Ivan despised, but was also largely uncomfortable with the idea of having to communicate in English echoed in his voice. It troubled him greatly that the American army would send someone who couldn't understand let alone speak Russian as their counterpart on such an important mission. It seemed clear to him that the Americans were treating this like a joke, a matter of no real importance and this infuriated him.

The private sensing the friction building that went largely unnoticed by General Schwartzer and against all regimental good manners quickly took over the conversation. "Two hours, sir. I will inform the test subjects to be ready at 06:32 hrs, sir."

Schwartzer glared at the young private, how dare he address this Russian instead of him. The private was British, an American ally, technically, he should only answer to him. More to the point, how had this private understood Ivan, he had barely got three words out of what was said.

"Very well, private," a smile faintly washed over Ivan's face as he said it, he knew the private had just embarrassed General Schwartzer and this amused him. "Inform the test subjects to proceed to rally point delta at 06:32 hrs and await further instructions."

Schwartzer struggled to take in what was just said, Ivan's thick Russian accent proving too difficult of an obstacle for him to understand. Ivan smirked at Schwartzer's difficulties. His confusion was written all over his face. The private, trying unsuccessfully, to hide his grin, saluted then very quickly turned on his heels and marched towards his desk.

On the outskirts of the town, a second truck, brandishing the red star of Russia, grounded to a deliberate halt. This was quickly followed by another, then another and another. Out of the back of them jumped Russian soldiers, all in radiation suits and seemingly armed to the teeth. From the front of their trucks jumped their commanding officers, two to each truck. Each of them gave each truckload their orders and in teams of ten, they began to spread throughout the town.

General Romanov watched them on the TV screen in front of him expectantly. He didn't like the idea of this exercise, didn't like it at all. For one: His men were armed with blank firers and laser tagging equipment. And second: He had a bad feeling about this and whenever he had a bad feeling, his gut was normally right. His vast amount of combat experience had taught him to trust his gut instincts. It'd saved his life and the lives of others countless times.

This feeling made him extremely nervous and he couldn't shake the feeling that something was wrong, very wrong. There was just something not right at all. He looked around the makeshift room that was in a truck's trailer and felt that something was most definitely off. He glared at General Schwartzer trying to work out what he was thinking.

Schwartzer seemed nervous, even by his standards. His hand was almost in his mouth, he was biting his nails that much. His foot too was tapping incessantly. *This was meant to be a general in the U.S. marine corps, he shouldn't be as nervous as this*, Ivan thought. Even though he was nervous himself, he hid it from his men if only for their sake as it showed weakness and bred descent. Schwartzer, though, was visibly nervous, almost too nervous. Either this was normal practice for the U.S. army to have such shaky and weak leadership, in which case that would explain why they did so badly in combat, or he was hiding something.

Then something caught his attention; one of the few black suits that were with them started to tap Schwartzer on the shoulder. He turned, the nervousness on his face heightened as the black-suited figure started to whisper in his ear. Ivan watched intently, trying, in vain, to maybe lip-read whatever he could to find out what was being said. Schwartzer noticed him and shiftily put his arm over the suited man's shoulder, turning their backs towards him. The suit, Ivan knew was C.I.A and he didn't trust them at the best of times. He didn't trust any secret service organisation, including his own K.G.B but even this seemed very peculiar and very out of place.

When the two men had finished their clandestine little chat, Ivan took it upon himself to try and ascertain what they were saying and by the only way he knew how. He grabbed Schwartzer by the throat and dragged him to the wall in full view of the highly stunned crew inside the truck. With a loud slam, Ivan had him pinned to the wall. Schwartzer was trying desperately in vain to get his hand off his throat. This Russian was as strong as a bear and about the same size. He had nowhere near his strength and by the look of things, neither did the six, quite large themselves, marines trying to pull him off. The room fell deathly silent as all eyes were on the struggle unfolding in front of them.

"First, I have a bad feeling," Ivan boomed. The determination in his voice sent shivers up Schwartzer's spine. This man was scary, very, very scary, he thought. It would only take just a little more pressure and he might crush his throat. Ivan continued.

"Then you talk in secret to C.I.A man over there, you hide it from me, I see you hide it from me," Ivan was desperate. He knew something was wrong. He also realised that perhaps this wasn't the best course of action to have taken. But if he wanted to glean any truth from this man and seeing as he'd already started down this path, then he may as well see it through. Schwartzer was choking and at the same time was quite surprised to discover that if under extreme stress, it was possible to understand even broken English and quite clearly. He could definitely get what he was getting at now for the first time since meeting him.

"I...," Schwartzer said in a choked, whispered tone between each hard-fought-for breath, "I...wasn't...tryin'...to...hide...anything."

"Liar!" boomed Ivan louder still. Marines were still dangling from his massive frame as they tried desperately to prize him off. "You are hiding something...Why be so secretive with C.I.A? We are a joint operation, that means all information to be shared with all parties. You not sticking to the agreement made by our governments." His accent was growing thicker by the second the angrier he got.

"He was wishing me luck," Schwartzer said fighting for breath and now with more urgency as he felt himself getting closer to passing out. "He was wishing me luck with the mission and asking about my family."

This was blatantly a lie, Ivan thought.

"You lie! Tell truth, little fat man! Tell truth." He whispered menacingly, tightening his grip.

Four additional marines had now joined in the effort to free General Schwartzer from Ivan's iron-like grip. This seemed to be just the boost they needed and after a few more seconds and lucky for Schwartzer, they managed to release him and just before he passed out.

Schwartzer grabbed his throat, trying to ease the pain, he stared at Ivan's insane look on his face staring back at him. He knew that Ivan was right. He knew that what he'd told him was a lie. But he couldn't tell him that. He couldn't tell anyone, not yet. He regained his composure and stood up straight and tall. Well, as tall as a short man can in any case. He then walked over to a desperately restrained Ivan.

"There is nothing untoward about my conversation with the man you saw me with," Schwartzer said with a quiet, almost smug confidence. "He is a close family friend. The reason why he was standing so close to me and I might add," his finger pointing in the air, like a defence lawyer delivering his final argument, "the reason why, to you, it may have looked so secretive was because it's very loud in here and being the not so spring chicken that I used to be, I found it difficult to hear what he was saying."

That should do it, Schwartzer thought, *it should stop the rest of the crew's suspicions at least anyway.* He gestured for the men to let Ivan go.

Ivan calmed himself. He couldn't believe what he was hearing. Did this fat prick of a general actually think that that excuse worked? He chuckled under his breath as Schwartzer walked over to the C.I.A man. He glared at them both, they were smiling and laughing and he knew it was at his expense. The room suddenly burst back into a hive of activity and loud chatter.

"You, C.I.A man two," he pointed at the second black suited figure who was chatting to a female Russian soldier. The man pointed to himself, a little perplexed. "Yes, you…C.I.A number two…You."

"No, sir, not C.I.A, K.G.B, sir, what can I do for you?" the man replied in Russian. Relief enveloped Ivan, he'd found a Russian K.G.B agent, he was totally convinced he was C.I.A before then, but then he always thought all secret service agents looked the same regardless of which country they were from and this proved his point. Better still, at last, he could stop talking English, which he never felt entirely comfortable doing and could start talking Russian.

"Come here, I need information," he replied in Russian. The K.G.B agent quickly followed the order. From across the room General Schwartzer caught a glimpse of Ivan talking to the K.G.B agent. Call it what you will, delusions of grandeur maybe, but Schwartzer had a sudden boost in confidence.

Hang on, he thought to himself, *he's just damn near tried to kill me for doing that exact same thing, talking in secret! That cheeky commie bastard! I've a good mind to go over there and dish out the same punishment he gave me.*

That idea didn't last long as he realised it would probably result in him being injured, possibly quite severely and then thought better of it. But then he realised that Ivan was walking very, very, purposefully towards him again.

"You…fat man," Ivan barked, the time for pleasantries and politeness was over. It was time to show this, as far as Ivan was concerned, stupid American and sorry excuse for a general exactly how much ill-feeling Russia really had towards his country. Yet again, all eyes were on the two generals.

"If you no lie about conversation and you know C.I.A man so well, then what is man's name?" He knew he'd got him here. If Schwartzer didn't know his name after saying he was a family friend, he'd have proven that he was lying and it was a pretty safe bet that he thought he didn't. But Ivan did. His new K.G.B friend had told him what it was. Ivan smiled confidently, folding his arms as he waited in anticipation.

"Who, this man?" said Schwartzer, sheepishly pointing at the C.I.A man. Ivan nodded his head, the smug smile on his face growing bigger. "This man sat here, in this chair, this one," the nervousness in Schwartzer's voice tickling the air.

"Yes him, fat man, him there."

"Can I ask why you want me to tell you his name?" Schwartzer was obviously stalling.

"Stop stalling," Ivan was getting annoyed again. He knew he'd got him, so why didn't he just admit he didn't know his name and then they can get out on to what he was really talking about. Because of his attention being totally focused on Schwartzer, Ivan didn't notice the CIA man skilfully whispering behind the American general's back. Schwartzer smiled.

"OK then, General Romanov, if you insist," he said with newfound confidence. "You want me to give you his name." Ivan nodded slowly, his temper rising once more. "This, General Romanov, is my good friend, Archie…," a loud cough exploded from the vicinity of the C.I.A man and suspiciously sounded like someone's name. Ivan shook his head; he couldn't believe what he was seeing.

"Andy Jackson…Special agent. Andy Jackson…There, are you happy now General?" said Schwartzer, trying to add a bit of assertiveness to his voice.

Ivan couldn't hide his disgust. His frustration was increasingly brewing up inside. He couldn't let him get away with such a juvenile display. This so-called man was making him look like an idiot and in front of all these people, American and Russian alike. He was insulting his very reputation and that he couldn't have. "What about age?" he said determined to catch the general out. "Surely you know!"

Schwartzer stood chuckling and shaking his head, infuriating Ivan even more. "I think, General, I have answered all the questions I need to on this matter, I do not think it is in this joint…" he purposefully overemphasised the word joint as he paused to make sure everyone in the room was listening and heard it. "It is not in this joint exercise's best interests to be quarrelling," Schwartzer's tone turned from quiet confidence to one that is normally reserved for new recruits that need to be reprimanded. "Quarrelling over such trivial matters i.e. how old someone is? Or what the names are of people?…What do you want next? huh…His inner leg measurement or what time he fucks his wife at night? Do you wanna take him out on a date by any chance?" a faint sniggering floated around the room as the soldiers, under their joint command, tried to contain their laughter.

Ivan knew he wouldn't get what he wanted this way. The fat bastard was making him look stupid, even if it was through extremely childish means. Reluctantly, he resigned to losing this argument but only for the sake of avoiding a diplomatic incident. He glared intensely at Schwartzer as he returned to his post. He knew something was going on. He knew that the Americans were up to something. He just didn't know what.

Schwartzer stared around the room, everyone was looking at him. Angrily he snapped, "Get back to work," the room erupted into noise once more. He walked back to Agent Jackson and sat beside him making sure that Ivan couldn't see him, then leaned over to the C.I.A agent and whispered, "Are the specimens ready and conscious?…And are they controllable and ready for testing?"

The agent looked around. He stared hesitantly at the room in front of him. The answer that he was about to give, unbeknownst to the General was to have unthought of repercussions for everyone. Not just here, but the entire world.

Agent Jackson was an intelligent man and he knew what the General was asking was? He'd seen these specimens in action in the lab and even though he knew himself that the answer he was about to give wasn't entirely accurate. Orders were orders and he'd been told what to say in this situation. "I believe the specimens are here and are, indeed, conscious," the agent hesitated, hoping that the general would notice his pause and question why.

General Schwartzer, however, wasn't an intelligent man, so he didn't detect the agent's pause. Agent Jackson knew that the next thing he was going to say wasn't in the slightest bit true, but shaking his head, he continued. "They are also fully under our control and combat-ready." *At least the last bit was true,* he thought, *they were at the very least combat-ready.*

General Schwartzer smiled. He knew this was going to show the world who he was, this was going to make him famous. It was going to make his name. Little did he know that it would make his name but it wouldn't be for the reasons he was hoping for.

Agent Jackson stood up and turned towards the very gleeful general and outstretched his hand. "It was a pleasure working with you, General. But now I must be going, I have…other business to be attending to."

Schwartzer rose to his feet. "What?" he said, a little confused.

"I must be going, General Schwartzer, I have pressing business to attend to elsewhere."

"Ah, yes, of course…Well, my boy, thank you, thank you very much."

"There is an American transport chopper arriving, General Romanov," a young female rookie said nervously. "Should I give it clearance to land?"

Ivan stood motionless and silent. He knew this wasn't right either. He looked over at Agent Jackson, trying to figure out what was wrong. Why was he going and no one else? What were these capitalist American pig-dogs up to? He decided it might be an idea to ask? *Because you never know,* he thought, *he might surprisingly actually tell me the truth?* He smirked at the idea.

"Excuse me, Agent Jackson," he said with polite authority as he sauntered over to him.

"Yes, General Romanov, would you like to pin me against the wall also?" he joked.

"I was wondering where was going?…You are only man leaving. And we have yet to begin exercise. You also get private chopper like film star…Would you satisfy my curiosity…please?" Ivan smiled. He'd pulled out all the stops to make his voice sound as polite and ad none threatening as he could. *This,* he thought, *had better work.*

"I'm to fly to rally point Delta to meet the replacement group commander for bravo team," Jackson looked around as he spoke trying to avoid eye contact with Ivan, "as you know Captain Lefevre was involved in a car accident."

"Ah, yes," Ivan tried as hard as he could to act consolable but to no avail. "Yes, very unfortunate business."

"Well, I've worked with his replacement, Colonel Jason Carmichael of the S.A.S, several times before. It was thought that it would be better if I was to brief him when he lands. Be a sort of a friendly face in amongst people, whom he may perceive as not having his best interests in mind. He still hasn't been briefed on his reasons for coming here and will more than likely need to know. But before he meets you all. I'm sure you understand?" He stared at Ivan to gauge his reaction. Ivan's face was blank. He knew he was lying but he couldn't work out why. Nor, yet again, could he prove it.

"Well, agent Jackson, give Colonel Carmichael my regards and have a very safe trip." He extended his hand. Jackson clasped it for a handshake and Ivan gripped it tight.

"Good luck, comrade," he said a sneer across his face.

Jackson let go of his hand and walked out the door. The now bright morning sunlight and dust were thrown up by the rotor blades of the chopper outside trickled through the open door. Then with that, he was gone.

Ivan stood silently fuming. Another hour, just another hour and then, whatever his gut was predicting was going to hit. Whatever it was or what form it would take, he didn't know. But his gut was never wrong and he was damn sure that General Schwartzer knew and he wasn't telling anyone.

Baby Steps

The helicopter's rotors roared violently as it landed at the makeshift camp on the outskirts of Pripyat. Out of it climbed the heavyset and muscular frame of Colonel Jason Carmichael. He scanned his surroundings and sighed. Though he'd fought in many campaigns and missions, from the Falkland's to the siege at the Iranian embassy in the U.K. and more recently Kuwait and secretly behind enemy lines in Iraq during the gulf war. He had been a hardened and seasoned veteran of the U.K. special forces, the SAS, for many years now. Little did he know that this mission would be the one to test him the most. Partly because of what lay in store but mostly because at this present time, he had no idea what he was doing there.

The man who greeted him was a small, wiry French special force's corporal. His thick French accent gravelled out as he spoke. "Colonel Carmichael, it's a pleasure to meet you…" Jason looked at him blankly, clearly unimpressed with the individual in front of him. He hated the French and thought they were snobby and arrogant.

"Spare me the pleasantries, Corporal," he snapped. His northwest accent still not untampered by his stint living in the south. "And just tell me what the fuck I'm doing here!"

"Yes, sir, right away, sir…," the corporal clearly taken aback by Jason's aggression, fumbled his words aggravating Jason further and he wasn't afraid to show it. His steely gaze pierced through the hapless Frenchman. This man is just a desk jockey, a clerk, he thought. They have sent a fucking clerk to greet him.

"Forgive me, sir…erm…You are to report to tent 1a…for the outfitting of your test suit and you are to report to General Macmillan for your briefing, sir."

"My what?" he couldn't believe what he was hearing. But even he had to admit it was intriguing. "My test suit?"

He tried to mull over in his head, what kind of tests they were doing here? It couldn't be weapons tests on him, he thought, they conduct hazmat and biohazard tests on grunts. No! It must be something else. Immediately his thoughts turned to new toys, but not the kiddy kind. Oh no! This was the secret government and untested, fun kind of weaponry. He didn't give the corporal chance to explain as he barged past him, heading for one of the many tents dotted around.

As he entered tent 1a, men in white coats were busily running around carrying bits of what looked like black metal garments. Gauntlets, leg grieves, chest plates, all were being connected to computers running some kind of diagnostic tests that Jason couldn't and more to the point didn't want to understand. He quickly walked to the nearest, most important looking individual he could find.

"Excuse me?" he said in a rather unaccustomed to, polite tone. "Colonel Jason Carmichael reporting for outfitting." The man in the white coat stared at him blankly. He tried again but slower-acting out what he was saying.

"My name is Colonel Carmichael…I am here for outfitting," his hand gestures resembled a badly played game of charades.

The man smiled and then, to Jason's surprise, uttered something in Russian. Jason couldn't understand.

First, I get greeted by a French guy, now I'm talking to a Russian. What the fuck is going on! he thought to himself.

"You…Russkie…R…U…S…S…K…I…E?" he said to the man.

He nodded his head, a wide grin filling his face.

"You speak English…E…N…G…L…I…S…H?"

The man took a moment to take in what he thought Jason might've said. Then shyly ducking his head, he shook it from side to side.

"Fuck that's all I need," Jason uttered under his breath. He scanned around the room looking for anyone who even remotely looked like they might speak some English. Around him were all manner of nationalities. Some very obviously Chinese, as were some of the Russians he spotted obviously Russian.

An assortment of different languages intermingled with each other almost drowning each other out until they were just one noise. He was finding it hard to pinpoint anything that sounded anything like something he could understand. He was just about to walk to the next nearest and an important-looking person he could see which just happened to be a rather attractive brunette, who also looked very suspiciously far too young to be involved in anything like this when a voice from behind him caught his attention.

"Excuse me, hunny!" The accent was unmistakably American, possibly Carolina, he thought and even better, young and female.

When he turned towards the direction of the voice, what greeted him made him slack-jawed and struck dumb but not by terror. This woman was gorgeous, absolutely drop-dead gorgeous. She was around five feet and ten inches tall, had shiny, shoulder-length blonde hair and she was dressed only in her underwear, which was suitably camouflaged. This camouflage showed off the silky-smooth bronze tan of her complexion. The longer he looked at her, the more he found he surrendered to her as he mentally photographed every inch of her. Her eyes were a rich sapphire blue. Her legs, long and shapely and seemed to go on forever. Her breasts pert and firm that looked just on the verge of a DD cup size. She was the most gorgeous woman he'd ever seen and judging by the direction their eyes were pointing so did every red-blooded geek male in the tent. It wasn't until she politely coughed that Jason realised he'd been staring at her for quite a substantially, inappropriate amount of time.

"You lost in your own lil' world there, hunny?" she chirped. Jason just shrugged, still dumbstruck. She cheekily chuckled. Obviously finding his inability to muster a coherent response quite funny, "I get that a lot, babe, don't worry about it. So, are you the replacement platoon leader?"

"Wha…What?" he quickly composed himself as best he could. "Yes…Erm…Er?"

"Lieutenant … Tyler McQueen. But my friends call me Stevie," in some ways, she was sickeningly chipper and typically American.

Jason hated Americans almost as much as he hated Russians.

But even though she's a Yank…she's fuckin' hot! he thought to himself, *and you can't have everything.*

"Shame about that French guy you're taking over from. A car accident was it? Unlucky!" she pretended, rather badly, to act remotely bothered about Jason's predecessor. But it was obvious, she couldn't give a shit.

"Yeah…Very unfortunate," he coughed, readying his next words. "So…Um…Stevie, eh?" It took a moment for the plainly obvious reason for the nickname to come to him. "Ah, I get it…yeah! Stevie McQueen…I like it…Like the actor?" There was an awkward pause followed by an equally as awkward, simultaneously forced giggle to break the stone-cold silence. Someone had to speak, Jason decided it would be him. "I'm Colonel Jason Carmichael. British

S.A.S," he said it with such pride but with the full intention of showing off. Tyler whistled as if she was impressed.

"Wow!...Really?...A real-life British S.A.S soldier, huh?...Cool." On the surface, it looked like he really had impressed her. She was genuinely flirting with him now, making a conscious effort to touch him and flaunt her sexy body as much as possible. But underlying that, she had a tone in her voice that gave him the feeling she was humouring him.

"Oops...Silly me," she said, her hand quickly covering her mouth. "Gosh, where are my manners?...I didn't salute," she smiled at him.

He knew this smile. It was the same butter wouldn't melt smile that every beautiful woman uses. The kind that says I'm innocent. I didn't just fuck your best friend. Please forgive me. And which up until now had never worked on him. Not until now.

Damn, she's good, he thought. Unfortunately, it was one of those stray thoughts that exit via your mouth without you realising it. He hoped she hadn't heard it. She laughed and shook her head.

Shit, she had.

"So, I guess you're here to get fitted up then, huh?"

Jason just nodded.

"You'll probably find these guys pretty useless, they don't speak any English," she pointed as she spoke.

Jason's attention was firmly fixed on her and she knew. She kept slying a glance at his eyes as she pretended to point things out. She knew he wasn't really listening, that he was just watching her and she liked it. She knew that she could, maybe, have some fun with him and besides he wasn't that bad looking. She might even let him see more of her at some point.

"They have real problems with communication here, too many languages and shit...But there's one real, nice girl. A Russian chick. Think she's called Ivana, somethin' or other? She should help you out?"

Their conversation was cut short when a voice came over her radio telling her to report to her station to suit up. Jason stared at her baffled, where the hell was her radio? Where had she put it? He couldn't see it anywhere. She reached into her bra and pulled out a very small walkie talky and grinned before responding that she was on her way.

"Cool place to put it, huh?" she said with that now trademark sexy giggle.

Jason laughed and nodded in agreement.

"I've got a better one though," she said winking before pulling open the front of her panties and to Jason's surprise, dropped the radio down them. His eyes followed it all the way making sure to take in that slight glimpse of her previously hidden snatch for however brief it was. But before his eyes could reach it, it was skilfully and timed to perfection covered. She was such a tease, he thought, or was she genuinely interested? His mind wasn't going to be easily made up on this one.

"Well, Mr Colonel…I'm on Alpha, so I guess I'll see you again when this is all over." she turned and slowly walked away with the style and grace of a catwalk model. But with the sexy wiggle in her bum and hips like a lap dancer.

Jason managed a quiet see her later before she bounced back round to face him, her breasts jiggling up and down as she did, magnetically attracting his eyes. "Oh dear, there I go again…I forgot to call you sir…And I forgot to salute again," her smile still so sneakily innocent to beyond the verge of sexy.

How could he resist her? He knew he had to or she would tease him until she was getting away with murder. But what if she was genuine? He couldn't be sure? Couldn't be sure at all? That was until…

"I guess you're gonna have to think of some way of punishing me for my very bad behaviour, Mr Colonel Sir," she purred saluting. "I'll report straight to you after the exercise for my orders, sir!" She turned on her heals quickly and started to march forward, sneaking a lingering look back at him before exiting the tent.

Jason grinned to himself. *Definitely a fuckin' tease,* he thought, *this is going to be fun.* He looked around the tent once more. Which one was Ivana? It could be any of the many women in here? Well, admittedly there were only 4, but it was still a task to figure out who out of those she was? It was so noisy in here too. He couldn't think straight. Without thinking and in his loudest order giving voice he boomed, "Right!…Silence please!" A sudden hush stifled the sound as nobody dared move. It looked as though he'd finally found something universal that everyone understood. "Thank you…I am looking for someone called Ivana. Can Ivana please step forward?"

Nothing. No one moved. This wasn't going well. Maybe Tyler had set him up? *Cheeky little bitch!* he thought. *Very clever.* The sexy brunette he'd noticed earlier removed a pair of headphones as she looked around her, curious about why everyone had stopped.

"OK!…I will ask one more time…Is there an Ivana here?"

The brunette stood up straight glaring right at him over the top of her glasses. She had that secretary look about her. The kind that if you had your own company, you'd want to see to your every need. Her brown eyes were large and like Tyler, they had a mesmerising quality to them, even if they were spitting daggers at him right now. They were the first thing about her to reel you in.

"Who wants to know?" she said in a thick but still quite sexy, husky, Eastern European accent.

He looked her over again. Part of him thought he'd died and gone to heaven. Here he was after being shipped off to the middle of nowhere and with no idea why he was there. Yet it looked like he'd been dropped in the middle of what may as well be the playboy warzone. This woman was just as gorgeous as Tyler. She had long, dark brown hair tied into a loose bun at the back with a pen. She had a slim yet very athletic curvaceous body. With dark caramel coloured skin, her tan was that deep. But she looked far too young to be a civilian scientist involved with black projects. She only looked about 24 or 25 at the most. Far too young to be whom he needed to find. But at least she spoke English. So, if anything, she might be able to point him in the right direction.

She casually walked towards him with a disgusted look on her face.

Even when she's angry, she looks sexy, he thought. Yet again, his brain let slip through the mouth and she heard every word. Even worse, she didn't look happy.

"Well, if you've quite finished undressing me with your eyes and have burned my image into your tiny mind enough, do you mind telling me who the hell you are? And what are you doing frightening my scientists?" She was not happy at all.

Jason decided to try and ease the tension responding by making a joke out of how he enjoyed mentally undressing her. This proved to be a very bad idea.

"How dare you! Do I look like some sex object to you?" she angrily shouted. What followed was a tirade of abuse aimed solely at him, which if he was honest, he wasn't paying attention to.

"Look, woman!" he said calmly, stopping her in mid-sentence and stunning her for just long enough that he could follow up with a question. "All I want to do is find this Ivana woman and then I can get out of here."

"Well, you've found her," she was clearly very pissed off but tried to remain relatively calm. "My name is Captain Ivana Romanov. I am the lead scientist and head of research at this test site. You must be Colonel Carmichael?"

Jason nodded in agreement. A sense of relief came over him. He was getting somewhere at last.

"Well, Colonel, I assume that you have had no briefing informing you why you are here," she said in an authoritative voice. He didn't need to tell her, she already knew. She began to guide him towards the back of the tent,

"Didn't think so…Well…we…as in the security council have been working in secret together to develop a new type of battle armour. It offers 1000x the protection of Kevlar but has only half the weight…This will be the first field combat test that we've attempted…We're very excited," clearly, excitement filled her face. "If all goes well, we'll be able to start mass production in the next two years."

"A new type of battle armour, eh?" Jason was suspicious. "Tell me, Captain, why would five countries that aren't the best bosom buddies club together to develop a battle armour that they could quite easily develop in secret and use against you?…What are you not telling me?"

She avoided eye contact. Clearly, she was hiding something? Or more likely, she was under orders not to say anything.

"OK. So, you either don't want to or you are unable to give me any more information on what the hell is goin' on here." He didn't trust this situation he was in one bit.

All these years, he'd been led to believe by his superiors that the Russians and the Chinese were the enemies. His opinion of the French, as being a minor annoyance, was merely his personal view. But now, he's meant to forget all that and sit shoulder to shoulder with them and why? Because it turns out that in reality, we were all friends, we just pretended to be enemies. He wasn't readily going to accept that and Ivana felt it.

As they reached the back of the tent, Jason couldn't help but notice the test armour. It was a strange sight, almost alien looking. In fact, for a split second, he really thought it might've been alien in origin. But quickly dismissed that. *UFOs, yeah right*, he thought. The first thing he noticed on closer inspection as he approached was that it was thin. And not just a little thin but barely a few millimetres thin. It looked too flimsy to stop even a BB gun, let alone be the 1000x strength of Kevlar that was being suggested. It was jet black and had a strange reflective quality to it that didn't quite reflect the light but seemed to absorb quite a lot of it instead.

"Impressive, isn't it?" Ivana said, a smug grin stretching across her face.

She was clearly very proud of this prototype. "You are lucky, Colonel…You have the latest build. We have managed to incorporate suede stealth like quality to this model. It's one of a kind, so be very careful with it." She smiled at Jason and ushered him forward, "Go ahead, try it on."

He stepped hesitantly forward and with the aid of a few helpful scientists started to put it on. Every piece that was carefully attached to him tightened and moulded to his body, startling him a little. He didn't expect that and didn't seem the only one to have that reaction either. From over two tents away, he could hear Tyler's giggles as she shrieked, "It tickles!" and through an open door at the back of his tent and one in her tent, he could see Tyler wriggling as the suit moulded to her contours. God that was a nice sight. She could essentially be naked if it wasn't for that suit. But then he realised so could he? This managed to bring a smile to his face and eased his tension a little.

"Remarkable stuff, eh Colonel?" Ivana had that smug smile again. "We are not entirely sure why or even how it does this? It seems to be a side effect of the chemical process involved to give it a sort of memory. It's quite bizarre but very useful…One size fits all, so to speak," she chuckled, a geeky chuckle that only someone in her field might have.

"It's definitely weird shit," he said, though he was starting to get used to it now. It felt extremely flexible along with extremely durable. It also felt strong yet light too.

"You think that's good? Just wait till you see what you can do with it?" Ivana's words grabbed his attention by the balls.

"What do you mean?…You mean it's gonna do something to me?…What?…What does it do?" He couldn't hide his concern that something he knew nothing about that now seemed to have attached its self to his body may also have some degree of control over him. It wasn't a nice thought. Even worse, they were starting to stick little electrode like things to his head.

"Relax…Colonel…It merely enhances certain physical characteristics of the wearer," Ivana tried to use her most reassuring of tones. All she got for her trouble was a raised eyebrow.

"Certain physical characteristics, eh?" it was obvious what he was getting at even before he started to look southward. "Really?…I like this suit already."

He didn't get a chance to hear a response as the technicians started to put on his helmet. This felt just like a balaclava but without the eye holes and like the rest of the suit, this too moulded to his face. Quite quickly, he thought he'd discovered a little set back at this point. Well, if he was truthful, quite a major setback. He couldn't see. There were no eye holes, which he saw as quite a major flaw. He was just about to point it out when his ears were filled with a slight whirr, almost like a computer booting up. Then suddenly and miraculously, he could see and perfectly clear.

"What the fuck just happened?" he exclaimed with surprise. This was a very bizarre experience. One moment, it's dark, then a whirr and then in the blink of an eye, he could see. He was also starting to realise that he could see a lot better than he normally ever could.

"What's going on, doctor? This is so fucking weird."

"Relax, Colonel," came Ivana's familiar voice, but somehow it seemed sharper, clearer even. "The suit is enhancing your vision and your hearing…At the moment, we still have you hooked into the computers, so don't try and get up yet. We just have to test a few things first."

He was beginning to admit that this mission, despite its shortcomings, was actually becoming pretty cool.

Ivana bent over in front of him to access the computer. "Right. Those electrodes attached to your head monitor your thoughts. So, don't worry, it's not for mind control or to spy on what you're thinking."

"That's a good job…You'd probably slap me if you knew what I was thinking right now," he said trying to slyly look at her ass.

She chuckled and quickly turned round to show Jason the computer screen showing what he was viewing through the helmet. She looked at him with a disapproving yet playful look before shaking her head, tutting and wagging her finger.

"OK…So, it monitors my thoughts but doesn't monitor my thoughts." *Get her on the science bits again,* he thought. She won't notice him eyeing her up.

"So, what the fuck does it do?" She stood thoughtful for a moment, before answering.

"OK…So, say like you have a target 200 metres away, but you want to be able to recon the area before you engage…OK?" Jason nodded. "OK, all you have to do is think what vision enhancement you need for that specific task?"

"In English? Or another language? Because I'm fucked if it's not English?" He thought it was best to ask, he'd be screwed otherwise. She nodded giggling.

"So, are all the suits programmed in English, that's a bit—" he didn't get a chance to finish his sentence as a stray thought about zooming in activated it.

With a surprised gasp, he quickly thought of a way to use it. Turning his gaze towards Tyler again, he thought of what he wanted to zoom in on. In a split second, he was zoomed in on Tyler's perfectly formed breasts. Her armour hugged them perfectly as it did the rest of her body as he zoomed very slowly back out. He looked her up and down and Ivana giggled in the background at what she was looking at on the screen.

"Do you maybe wanna try some of the vision enhancements for a moment?" she said sniggering.

Quickly realising that she could see exactly what he was seeing, he turned his attention to her. Thinking of heat vision, the thermal goggles kicked in.

"Wooooh!…My word, you've got a hot body!" He was trying to embarrass her and to some degree, it was working.

Through the thermal imaging, he could make out every contour of her body and it was showing up on the screen. Because he was embarrassing her, then she became suddenly flushed with heat, her embarrassment then became further magnified by the heat sensors.

"Jesus, hunny, you really are hot…hot…hot…hot."

She was not all too impressed, however, and giving him a dirty look turned away from him. She muttered something in Russian to the technicians and then he was cut loose.

"If you go out of here and go straight ahead, then take your second left, you'll be where you need to be for your briefing, Colonel…And…Be Careful."

Did he just hear what he thought he heard? Jason thought, did she just tell him to be careful? He didn't get time to ask.

"I meant be careful with the suit. It's one of a kind that one remember?…Oh before I forget, the stealth functionality has not been tested fully yet…Well, not at all actually…It may have a few bugs, but if you would be so kind as to inform us of any problems on your return, I'd…I mean we'd appreciate it."

He raised his thumb to show he heard her request. "Admit it, Ivana love, you just want an excuse to see me again, eh?" She didn't answer. She just mouthed fuck off. Then laughed.

Jason carefully stood up out of the chair and then took his first steps outside with his new toy.

Don't Shoot the Messenger

Xenon village, 15,000 years ago.

A few months after the battle outside his village, Arkanon was awoken in the middle of the night. An Atlantian messenger had arrived and had very noisily requested to see Arkanon with an urgent message. He wearily gathered himself out of bed, wrapped himself in a loose-fitting robe and slowly made his way to the courtyard yawning loudly and scratching an itch on his bum. He knew this must be important. Why else would a messenger come at this hour? Disgruntled, he threw open the large doors to the courtyard and was greeted by an extremely nervous looking man.

He was dressed normally, no armour or regalia of any kind. To say he looked basic, almost peasant-like was an understatement. He was rough and weary-looking from his long journey and the only way that Arkanon could tell that he was military was by the short crop of his brown hair and the regimented look in his stance. Even so, he seemed very young and a bit inexperienced.

This better be important! Arkanon thought to himself as he slowly walked down the stairs. He struggled to prevent a stern look from flashing in his eyes, which at first seemed to freeze the young man to the spot. But once realising where he was, the young man dropped to his knees and bowed his head.

"My Lord, forgive my arrival at this late hour. But I have a message of the utmost urgency from my master, King Feron of Atlantis," the messenger said hastily. His head still pointing to the floor. "I request a private audience with the chief of the House of Xenon as my orders are to deliver this message to him and to him alone."

Arkanon could tell that his gaze made the young man even more nervous as he confidently walked towards him and gestured for him to stand. His unintentional steely looking gaze seemed to penetrate right through the young soldier making his heart beat faster. Arkanon could tell the young man had never felt so scared.

"What's your name, boy?" he said as the young man slowly rose to his feet with his head still nervously pointing to the floor.

"Rexas! Son of Metaxas, sire," the man said quietly and with a nervous tone.

"And how old are you, Rexas, my boy?"

"19, my lord."

"How long have you served, lad? And stop looking at the floor, look at me, soldier."

Gingerly, Rexas raised his head. Clearly, he was in awe of Arkanon and he could tell. When Rexas' eyes met Arkanon's, all at once Rexas' mind went blank and he felt even more uneasy. He'd heard stories about Arkanon and of the House of Xenon from his father and his grandfather. But to just be in their presence was feeling a little overwhelming. *What had he just been asked?* Rexas thought, worry beginning to set in his face.

"Pardon, sir?" Rexas said with a puzzled tone. Why was he being asked all these questions? he thought. All he wanted to do was get this over and done with. Just deliver his message and get the hell out of here. At least Arkanon seemed friendly enough though!'

Arkanon could tell what he was thinking and just grinned. Rexas' nervousness amused him and so did his worried and confused look.

"Don't worry, lad," Arkanon's voice fluttered with a calm, fatherly quality. "Take a few deep breaths in through your nose and breath out through your mouth. There's no need to be so nervous, boy, this isn't an interrogation. It's just a conversation between friends." Rexas did as he was told.

"That's it! Just relax." He paused for a moment to give Rexas time to calm down before repeating his question. "So, how long have you been in service?"

"Including today, about four months and 18 days, my lord," Rexas felt more relaxed now but still grinned apprehensively.

Arkanon was astonished but fought hard not to show it. *Why was someone so young, sent on such a dangerous mission?* he thought to himself as he slowly circled the boy looking him over as he did. *Why wasn't someone with more experience sent?* he pondered, unsure of what decision had led to this young man's appearance. *Sending someone so young, this far out...alone! With no protection! The route to Xenon even during peaceful times was still a dangerous journey. Even more so now with Hoth and the Reapers out there. What was going on in Atlantis? What were they thinking? Still he had made it all the same,* Arkanon thought, *and unscathed too, by the looks of things.* He had to admit it, this young man had impressed him. Not everyone can make this journey without any incident. This kid was either:

A) Very skilful in the art of blending in and staying out of sight.
B) Very ballsy and able to talk his way out of a situation or ballsy and able to fight his way out. Or at the end of the day,
C) Just plain lucky.

Either way, he'd impressed Arkanon greatly.

Gently he placed his hand on Rexas' shoulder and began to guide him towards the large wooden doors of the main hallway. "Follow me, lad. We'll get to somewhere more private," Arkanon said with a cheekily knowledgeable grin. "And for god's sake! Call me Arkanon...My lord feels too formal. After all, we are friends now, aren't we?"

He laughed heartily to ease the growing tension. Rexas just nodded, he was still a little unsure whether his question was serious or not, but he did as he was told anyway and followed close behind.

They chatted casually as they walked through the dimly torch-lit corridors. Rexas was amazed by how welcoming and friendly Arkanon was. This was the chief of the legendary House of Xenon. But he was chatting to him like an old friend. The stories he'd heard made him think they were hard and brutish people. And although they were very heroic, they were also meant to be treated with caution. Yet, they didn't seem like that at all. It was amazing. Definitely, something he could tell his grandchildren.

He expected Arkanon to have said 'What the fuck do u want?' as soon as he saw him. Instead, Arkanon was asking him questions about his life back home in Atlantis, his family and his platoon.

He listened intently as Arkanon told him, in great detail, of the battles they'd had with Hoth and about how and why they'd changed the name of his tribe to the white stars. Arkanon even seemed impressed as Rexas gave his views on Atlantian politics, despite his knowledge of them being quite elementary. He wished they could've had more time to talk, but all too soon, they reached their destination, 'the great hall'.

Rexas was stunned by this room. It was huge even by Atlantian standards. It was circular in shape with large marble columns surrounding the outside that stretched high into the air, stopping at a huge domed ceiling adorned with depictions of past victories carved into it that were surrounding a huge circular hole in the middle allowing milky moonlight to gently float down. On each of the pillars, a torch, dimly illuminated the room in front of them. The flickering flames made the shadows from the carvings dance to life but leaving the walls behind them in total darkness.

The floor was a jet-black polished marble, which reflected the ceiling above and the pillars around, making the whole room seem like you were inside a giant ball. In the middle of the room stood a great polished granite table that had cushioned stone benches on either side and a great golden throne at the head. This table virtually filled the rest of the room. Rexas was gobsmacked.

"Quite a sight, isn't it?" Arkanon said smugly. "I'm impressed every time I come in here." Rexas had to agree. "You want to see it during the day. The light from the morning sun fills this room…It's pretty impressive to look at. You can't see half as much at night."

Arkanon loved showing this room off and Rexas could tell. "Mind you! I bet you've seen even better in Atlantis, eh?" Rexas just grinned sheepishly. If he was honest, he'd never seen anything like this anywhere; he'd never been anywhere this grand in Atlantis, so he had nothing to compare it to. The only thing he could imagine might be this grand was maybe the throne room in Atlantis, but seeing as he'd never seen it, he couldn't be sure.

"Come! Sit with me," Arkanon said, nearly dragging him over to the table, "and deliver your message."

He sat on the bench beside Arkanon and looked around nervously before sitting forward. A look of concern filled his face as he gazed at Arkanon's expectant face.

"Forgive me, sir!" Rexas began quietly. Arkanon looked at him sternly before Rexas realised his mistake. "Sorry! Forgive me, Arkanon!" Arkanon grinned, his eyes looking intense as he waited for Rexas to carry on. "My master ordered me to come to see you. To request your help."

Arkanon's face changed to one of great concern. He could tell this was going to be bad news. When someone as powerful as King Feron requests your help, then you know things are very bad indeed. He dreaded what was coming next.

He hoped it was just an order to help with a training exercise or something like that, but knew deep down that that was wishful thinking.

"A few days after the attack on your village," Rexas continued, "we got the first word of an attack on one of our outer settlements." Arkanon's heart sank, he knew what was coming next.

"A small contingent of reaper troopers had arrived in the night and taken everyone…There was no sign that they'd killed them. They were just gone! Fifty people vanished without a trace…men, women, children…everyone, just gone!" Rexas' voice began to grow heavier as he continued.

"A week later, in the district at the outermost wall where I lived, we found out where these people had gone," Rexas' eyes welled up, but he fought back the tears as he talked.

Arkanon placed a sympathetic hand on his shoulder and beckoned for him to continue. "I don't know the precise details and I was on exercise at the time. I just heard from the few survivors that were there. And saw the aftermath for myself when we were sent to investigate," tears began falling down his face and Arkanon could tell that this was going to be brutal. "I'm sorry, Arkanon sir! Forgive my tears."

"Don't worry about it, son. Take your time," Arkanon said with a consoling tone. He waited patiently for Rexas to gather himself. "Tell me, son, what happened there?" Rexas gave him a look that Arkanon knew all too well. The kind of look that tells you something truly horrific happened. The kind of thing that'd traumatise any man, farmer and soldier alike. "What was it, son? What happened?" he said with a little more urgency.

"From what we could gather," Rexas said quietly, his voice quivering as he still fought back the tears. "From what we could gather, the attack began at dawn. The first of them were seen on the horizon. There was only a few of them, maybe five or six, advancing slowly on foot. But they were masked by the sunlight, so from a distance, no one could tell what they were."

"Reapers?" Arkanon said, troubled. *This was bold, even by their standards,* he thought to himself. *Just strolling up like that…What were they up to? Was it even reapers?* He had to make sure, "Were they reapers, son?"

"No!" Rexas said, fear and confusion filled his eyes. "Worse!"

Arkanon was stunned. He sat back in his throne, his eyes darting in all directions as he tried to comprehend what could be worse than a reaper attack.

"Worse?" he said. "Forgive me, son! But what can be worse than reapers?" He couldn't hide the disbelief in his voice and he thought it may have been too harsh, but to him, something worse than reapers was unheard of. Rexas looked at him, that same look of abject terror was in his eyes.

"Yes, sire! Worse! I know it's hard to believe, but…but, they sent our own people against us…But they weren't our own people," desperately he looked for some sort of sign on Arkanon's face that he understood. But he couldn't find one, Arkanon just looked stunned and confused.

"Your own people? But not your own people? It doesn't make sense, boy!" Arkanon said with calm desperation making Rexas jump back in his seat. He didn't mean to scare or even upset the boy, but it just wasn't making any sense. "Were they your people or not? What the hell were they? People, not people? Out with it, boy!" he shouted, his voice reverberating around the room.

"I'm sorry, Arkanon! I know it doesn't make a lot of sense…It still doesn't make a whole lotta sense to me either even now…Even after everything I've been told, everything I've seen." Rexas fought in his mind, desperately trying to think of a way to explain. In the end, he just came out with it, "They used to be our people. When they got closer, it became all too clear what had been done to them. They weren't alive anymore. They weren't exactly dead either. And what had been done to them…" he had to stop. He had to pause for a moment as the images flashed in his mind taking away his words.

Arkanon waited patiently for him to continue, a look of stunned horror on his face. This was unheard of! He had no idea that reapers had that much power that they could raise the dead. He also had to admit it was a horrible thing to envisage their own people advancing slowly towards them. Then finding out, when they got close enough that they were dead and then from behind them comes the real attack. It was an ingenious plan. What better way to instil fear into your enemies than to send their own dead people against them. It would be hard for any one of the same clan to attack them straight away and would serve as an inescapable distraction, remarkable!

Arkanon let slip a sly chuckle, he was impressed. Rexas looked at him shocked. He knew what Arkanon was thinking and couldn't believe his reaction. He wasn't meant to be impressed; he was meant to be horrified yet he wasn't. Then again, he hadn't heard the rest of it. He glared at Arkanon, waiting for his eyes to meet his, his fists clenching on the table as anger began to boil up inside. *How dare he!* he thought to himself, *How dare he be impressed by this heinous act…Why wasn't he, at the very least, a little upset, by what he was being told.* Slowly, Arkanon's eyes met his and Arkanon could see the distaste in his eyes. All at once, Arkanon knew he'd done wrong, he knew his reaction wasn't what the boy wanted to see and quickly his face changed to one of sympathy and regret.

"Sire, I must insist!" Rexas said with a modicum of defiance. "What transpired there was far worse than what, I presume, you are imagining."

His insistence shook Arkanon a little. Firstly, because he was amazed by how he could possibly know what he was thinking, even most of his most trusted generals didn't have a clue what he was thinking half the time. Secondly, when someone uses the phrase 'far worse than what you are imagining' in a sentence, it never bodes well. And lastly, this boy had balls and as far as he knew, from what he'd seen of him previously, he didn't seem like he had any. But Arkanon knew he was in the wrong, what he didn't count on was that this kid was gonna tell him. This was something that only his closest allies dared to attempt, most of the time, to no avail. Yet, this boy had only been in his company for a half-hour at the very least and here he was, a lowly private in the Atlantian army, one that had barely been in service for five minutes, for that matter, reprimanding him! A chieftain of an entire tribe! Arkanon looked at him like a child does when he's getting a severe telling off and silently requested for him to continue.

"My family! My whole family died in that attack, Arkanon. How could you, the chief of the fabled House of Xenon be so disrespectful? And no matter how good a tactical manoeuvre, you may think Hoth used, you are practically spitting on the graves of my family and the others that died there!" Rexas knew he was probably insulting him right now. Arkanon just sat still stunned by this young man's outburst but very quickly decided that due to his emotional state, he would probably be better letting it slide this time. *Boy!* he thought, *He really did know what I was thinking! That's impressive! And he's ballsy too!*

Rexas, though, knew full well what his status was and what the implications might be, but at that moment, he didn't care and he didn't care if Arkanon knew it or not. Even so, he knew he'd have to lessen the insult somehow, he would have to apologise. "I'm sorry if I'm being insubordinate, but you can punish me later if you wish. It's just that you have to understand what happened there!"

Arkanon stared at him as if weighing him up. He knew the boy was right. Yet, he was still impressed by his insight. How did Rexas know what he was thinking? He stared at him from across the table, an impressed look crossed with anger shot like daggers from his eyes, as he tried to figure him out. He was starting to realise why Feron had sent him. *He must've known that I'd like him. Wiley old bastard!* he thought to himself. *Well, the kids apologised! I guess I better had to too.*

"I'm sorry, son! Forgive my disrespect! I was not intending to nor was I trying to condone what Hoth has done…You'll have to forgive my manner, it's just that although Hoth is an evil bastard, to be sure…I can't help but be impressed by his actions on the battlefield. Maybe when you've spent as much time on the battle as we have, you'd begin to understand why I reacted this way…And I'll also admit that at times, my judgment with regards to expressing my admiration and the right time to express it leaves a lot to be desired." He smiled at Rexas, hoping that he'd accept his apology. And then started to wonder why he felt he should apologise. "Shit! We all have our faults, kid!"

Even though it wasn't much of an apology, it was an apology all the same and Rexas thought he'd better accept it, besides, he wasn't sure what Arkanon would do if he didn't.

"Why don't you carry on telling me what happened? And I promise I'll try and keep the inappropriate comments to a minimum," Arkanon smiled. It was sort of an expectant smile crossed with a hint of murderous intent like if Rexas didn't agree, he was going to kill him. Rexas just nodded quickly and leant forward to continue.

"When the first attack came, as I said already, there was just a few. They were approaching from the rising sun. We think to mask their appearance." Rexas thought about the next part carefully before carrying on, "One of the guards on duty described them as limping towards town like they were injured from battle. They thought they were maybe escapees from the settlement that was attacked. That was until they got within about 50 feet or so. Then they realised something was wrong," he stared at Arkanon's face, looking for any sort of a hint that he was going to get a reaction like before. It didn't take long as Arkanon quickly butted in.

"So, they limped towards them? They're pretty slow-moving then. How'd the hell did they do whatever it was they did?" He was starting to think the Atlantian army had gone soft. Slow-moving enemies and there were only five or six? He smirked again. Rexas noticed and glanced at him angrily.

"Sir! Arkanon, sir!…You didn't let me finish," this was irritating him now. Why wouldn't he let him finish? "As I was saying, as they got within 50 or 60 feet, they realised something was wrong. A couple of them only had half a face, one had no eyes and no guts…You get the idea?" Arkanon just nodded. "Then they attacked. The people who survived described how they charged, screaming, blood-curdling screams. Of how what looked like five or six quickly turned into ten, then 20, then 30. In my district, there were only 100 guards normally stationed there. But that day most of us were on exercise, so there was only a handful, around ten or so, left behind and they were quickly overrun. Only two managed to get out and the 70 or so villagers, including my mother, brother and sisters, were left to defend themselves or run if they could. Only six made it out alive," tears welled up in Rexas' eyes again. "They didn't stand a chance, any of them, arrows did nothing…even aimed at the head. And swords! Cut off their legs and they keep coming, crawling and biting, cut off their heads and they just ran around like headless chickens, flailing their arms around and tearing at anything they touched." He paused again as if trying to find the words to describe what he was visualising in his head but struggling fruitlessly.

"Rexas! You don't have to carry on," Arkanon said in a reassuring tone. "Why don't you tell me why Feron has sent you here instead?" Rexas gathered his thoughts back together and stared at Arkanon with a look that told him there was worse to come.

"It's OK!" Rexas said with a chilling calmness as if he was somehow managing to disassociate himself from what was going through his head. "The reason why I'm here is tied into what happened at my district. Everything that has gone wrong happened almost immediately after that attack." Arkanon reached over and squeezed his shoulder again. Strangely, this time, Rexas felt some comfort from it and found the strength to continue. "The next district is only two miles away, so the survivors were found very quickly and word spread. The walking dead were gone, well, the ones that were left as were the intact bodies of the dead from my district. All that was left were the torn remains of the dismembered and…" he paused again for a moment, looking at Arkanon as if he was trying to fathom if he'd believe him.

"Go on, son! No matter how fantastical it may seem, what you're going to say, have faith we'll believe you," Arkanon meant what he said. In the past few months, he'd seen amazing things that, quite frankly, should only be in your imagination, not a living, well, livingish! Breathing reality. And Rexas could feel that from him.

"The most badly damaged bodies still moved, still tried to attack. Heads hissed as they gasped for air and still tried to bite. Arms still grabbed and scratched wildly…it was terrible to behold. It was only a matter of hours before the next attack. This time just reapers and on the other side of town, it was deep within the second inner wall, deep inside the city. There was just three of them and they did unimaginable things. That settlement had at least 300 people and at least 150 highly skilled, highly experienced guards and they decimated them all." Arkanon nodded knowingly, there was only one type of reaper that had that much power, he'd seen them before.

"High mages, only they could do that! They are so powerful. We've yet to defeat just one of those. They can appear at will from anywhere and can destroy a whole legion in a matter of seconds with a single attack." Arkanon smiled as if he had a kind of respect for them. "One day we will kill one though and then…How many attacks followed?"

"Thirteen in all…All in a matter of hours and then they just stopped, we've heard nothing for three months now. I haven't heard anything else since I left last week to get here." Arkanon nodded and stroked his chin in deep thought. "What is it, Arkanon? What are you thinking?" Arkanon stared into space for a moment, his mind wandering as he mulled over what he'd just been told. What was Hoth doing? Why attack thirteen times and then suddenly stop?

"How many casualties have you had and how many settlements still remain?" he asked hurriedly, sitting forward as he spoke. "How many able and experienced soldiers are there left?"

"Erm!…Er!…" Rexas struggled to think as Arkanon glared at him with icy coldness, like he was demanding a quick response. "All in all, there were 28 outer settlements and districts. Fifteen of those remain. Out of those 15, only one has an experienced squad of around 20 men, the rest either have none at all or all new recruits and there was about 20,000 but now there's only 3,000 of those. The rest have deserted. None have seen any battles." Arkanon's heart sank as Rexas continued, "As for casualties, out of a population of around 400000, about 150,000 are either killed or missing. There is a bright side though!" Arkanon's ears pricked up. "The main city inside the inner wall is undamaged and has yet to be attacked. There are roughly around 10,000 of the king's high guard in there, protecting 50,000 people…But, as you'll understand, they have to remain within the city walls to protect the king and the elite."

Arkanon nodded in approval. He could understand why those men were being held back. What he couldn't understand was why Hoth had ceased the attacks on the city when all was looking like a very quick and very decisive victory? What was he up to? He needed to think on this more, he had a bad feeling about this, a very bad feeling and he knew whenever he had a bad feeling, something terrible always followed.

"So, I guess your next question is how soon can you get your men here? And how many men can you spare to help?" Arkanon said. Before Rexas could answer, he answered for him, "I personally will arrive within the week, if it is a smooth journey. And I will bring 300 of my best men. That should be enough to stop most reaper attacks, including Hoth's high guard. As for now, Rexas, my boy, you shall stay the night and we shall leave at midmorning. I would like you to travel as my escort, my boy. I like you and I think you could become a valued addition to our ranks…That's of course if you would like to. I promise I will train you myself…so what do you say?" Rexas didn't think about it too long.

"Are you kidding? Of course, I would…I'd be honoured, Arkanon sir," he said with boundless enthusiasm.

Arkanon rose to his feet extended his hand towards Rexas and smiled. After shaking his hand, he began to lead him out of the great hall and back down the corridor to the courtyard before summoning a handmaiden to escort Rexas to his room.

"Oh, I just have one more question to ask, Rexas. Why did Feron send you and not one of his other more experienced men?" somehow Arkanon knew what his answer was going to be, but he just wanted to hear it from his mouth.

"I…er…," Rexas was hesitant, but he realised it was best just to tell him, "I volunteered, sir!"

"I thought as much."

The Princess and the Palace Guard

King Feron's castle, Atlantis, 15,000 years ago.

It was many years before Hoth would attack Atlantis again. This didn't mean he wasn't active elsewhere though. Tales of his horrors gradually trickled through to us sometimes by survivors, sometimes by witnesses who saw villages and towns burn from afar. The white stars and Arkanon were under orders to stay in Atlantis as a sort of replacement for the city guard so they could be close by and ready to defend it in their time of need.

The king of Atlantis, Feron, was very old, at around 102. He was toothless and it seemed he was going senile and getting rather forgetful at times. For a long while, he was convinced that Arkanon was his daughter, which he found a little insulting. Arkanon could never understand why that was. For one, he was a man and secondly, his daughter was black. Whereas Arkanon was white with blonde hair. What perplexed him further was the fact that Feron was also white, as was his wife. So, how did they have a black daughter?

There were many times when we would joke about it, commenting on the fact that his wife was very young, around 36 and extremely beautiful. So, it was a safe bet that she probably strayed away. Or she was a secret love child of the king's, perhaps by some servant girl, he ended up giving some extra royal duties too. It wasn't until one hot and very bright day during late summer and also a particularly quiet period concerning attacks that a visitor arrived at Feron's castle. Arkanon was summoned to the castle at once.

The great hall was huge, at least a mile in diameter. Its circular hall towered upwards as far as the eye could see. Great columns around 20 feet towered up to the distant roof. At the top, a feint hole could be seen, letting light through that was shining down on the throne below with a vast shaft of light illuminating the king. You could tell that if you were to go up there, the hole would be huge, but from down here, it was like a pinprick.

Beside him stood his advisors, two on either side. The two on his left were dressed in bright blue and green cloaks. Their white beards stretched down to the floor in long flowing curls. The two on his right troubled Arkanon greatly. They wore dark red and black hooded cloaks. Their faces obscured from view. Their presence chilled him to the bone. He had no idea why they were there and that really did bother him. They were sort of out of place. He slowly approached Feron. You had to as he startled very easily and he didn't like that at all. When he was within talking distance, Arkanon announced his presence.

"Who?" Feron said perplexed. "Arkanonof Shenon?…Never heard of you…What do you want?"

Arkanon began to explain that Feron had summoned him and he had been the commander of his palace guard now for quite some time.

"Bollocksh," he said disgruntled, his lack of teeth slurring his words. "What do I need palashe guard for? I could defend thish shity myshelf, from any threat, any army, any danger and all the while blindfolded!" he said confidently standing to square up to Arkanon before his legs promptly gave way and he fell flat on his face.

"Ish it night time already? Todaysh gone bloomin' quick…Well time for bed…"

His advisors looked to Arkanon for help. Gingerly, so as not to hurt the poor old soul, Arkanon helped him to his feet,

"Cashandra!" Feron said gleefully. "Itsh nishe to shee you…You know you've alwaysh been my favourite daughter!"

"Erm sire, as I said earlier, I'm not your daughter," Arkanon said as calmly and as tactfully as he could.

"I know that, you bloody baffoon, I washn't talkin' to you." Feron shook his head and began to steady himself on the arm of his throne. "I wash talking to her!" he raised his hand slowly and with all of the strength pointed his cane behind Arkanon.

"Thank you, Father, it's nice to see you too…How's Melaina?" The distance in her soft and sultry voice as she mentioned the Atlantian Queen's name reverberated around the great hall.

Everyone but Feron noticed it. The advisors breathed a sigh of relief. Arkanon slowly turned towards her, "She is doing well I hope?" Cassandra's voice rippled through Arkanon's body sending tingles up his spine.

Before him stood what, at first glance, wouldn't be expected to be Feron's daughter. Her skin was a light chocolate brown that looked so soft even silk would be jealous. Her hair was as black as the darkest night and stretched all the way down to her small back, just missing her pert, perfectly formed and round rear. Her legs were long, so very long they seemed to go on forever and with thighs so shapely, they were like the gods sculpted them themselves. She was at least six feet tall, with breasts shaped like big, ripe watermelons.

She was an African goddess, curvaceous in all the right places, with eyes you could get lost in for decades. From that moment, Arkanon was in love.

"Casshandra, meet Arkanon…Heesh…Er…Heesh…Erm," Feron looked helplessly at his advisors, seeking guidance. "Heesh…Eerrrr…," the words for some reason wouldn't come, so Arkanon intervened.

"I'm commander of the royal guard and sworn protector of the city of Atlantis," he was sure that was going to impress her.

"Oh really," she said, politely, extending her hand.

"His high exalted worshipfulness would like you to escort the blessed and purest of the pure princess wherever she wishes to travel…You are to be her bodyguard…so to speak," one of his bright coloured advisors said in a rather snooty tone.

Arkanon nervously took her hand before bending down to kiss it. Her skin was so soft, without realising it, he forgot to let go and stood there staring at her hand, mesmerised by the softness. He'd never seen a woman so beautiful.

She looked at him expectantly waiting for him to set her free from his clutches, but he was spellbound. Eventually, Feron intervened.

"Let go of my daughter, you blithering imbesheile!" he said angrily beating Arkanon with alarming ferocity for such a frail old man, around the head with his cane.

"Sheesh going to need that hand, you know?" Cassandra turned her head towards her father. Her eyes never leaving Arkanon.

"Father?" she said in her best daddy's girl voice.

"What ish it, my dear girl?" Feron said, spellbound by his daughter's voice. "What can your alwaysh devoted father do for hish darling daughter?"

There was something magical about her voice. You just knew that with that voice and her striking beauty, she could even bend the gods to her will.

"Can I please borrow him for other duties a while? Whilst I'm here? I promise I won't take up too much of his time."

Arkanon was shell shocked. The princess of Atlantis wanted to borrow him? He was trying to work out what for, but quite frankly, he didn't care. She was amazing.

"Borrow who, dear? What dutiesh? Whom are you taking? Me? Him?" said Feron, clearly a little confused, pointing at one of his advisors.

The advisor smiled, his eyes gleeful like he'd just gone to heaven. He looked at her expectantly.

"Your commander of the palace guard, daddy, silly!"

The advisor shrugged in a 'you win some, you lose some' sort of way. Feron shook his head sternly at him, glaring at him with daggers flying from his eyes. The advisor sheepishly hid behind the throne out of Feron's gaze, who'd quickly realised what Cassandra had just said and he snapped at her, "Eh…but I haven't got one, have I?" the confusion on Feron's face grew,

"Well, who's this then?" Cassandra snapped back. "OK…Can I borrow this rather handsome…" she said calmer and smiling at Arkanon, "gentleman here…For a little while? We have a lot to discuss?"

Feron nodded silently. Arkanon couldn't believe what he was hearing. He was being dragged away for some sort of purpose, which he was secretly hoping involved a bed and himself and her in it and her father was agreeing or so he thought. However, what he'd assumed was Feron nodding in agreement was actually him dosing off.

Cassandra instinctively knew what Feron was doing. "Daddy!" she shouted, hitting him gently on the chest but just hard enough to knock him backwards, sitting him back on his throne. "Eh! What? What'sh wrong, dear?"

"Daddy, this man here…Can I…" she started to do a shoving motion to indicate to Arkanon to start moving along. The king was not cottoning on.

"What are you trying to shay?" The frustration grew in Cassandra's tone.

"I'm taking him with me…" she barked. She grabbed Arkanon's hand to drag him away, but the king stopped him just for a second.

"You want to watch tho she Ashumertran women, my boy," he whispered. A slight whistle eking out in his voice just barely masking a rare moment of lucidity.

Cassandra tugged Arkanon's arm to get a move on. He couldn't hear much of what else Feron said but the last thing he caught was, "They have a way with wordsh no one can reshisht…"

From this moment he realised that although Feron seemed like he was losing the plot, he was, in fact, very much aware of the plot and most probably the key player in determining how the plot was to unfold.

As Cassandra and Arkanon left the great hall, they arrived in the palace's public gardens. It was an area where the aristocracy of the city could mingle with royalty. Feron came up with the idea around 70 years ago to keep his first wife happy and occupied whilst he did what every normal king did during that time. Go off and sow his royal oats with the townsfolk and to be honest, anything with a skirt and a pulse. The gardens were beautiful, as well as huge. There were trees imported from the four corners of the globe that were so huge around the base that tunnels were cut through them to let the paths through. And so tall that from the ground, they looked as though they touched the sky. Walkways with terraces, swings and elaborate lifts with pulley systems snaked their way through the treetops connecting each of the trees.

Beneath them lay the pathways around the gardens, winding maze-like through hedgerows, vast, brightly coloured flower gardens with fountains and huge deep, fish-filled pools. All of this was surrounded by a 100 feet tall, bright white wall covered in murals depicting Feron's past battles in his younger days that were awash with colour. It truly was a wonder to behold. Every time he entered them, Arkanon was in complete awe. It really stunned him and now he was here with Cassandra. It just felt even more magical. She glanced at him out of the corner of her eye and smiled as he gazed in wonder at what he was seeing.

"I can see by your face that you really love it here…" she said, that voice of hers taking Arkanon away into a sort of dream world.

"I don't think I've ever seen anything so beautiful," he replied in a lovesick puppy tone of voice. He couldn't help it. All he could see was her. Her skin seemed to glow more with the sunlight giving her a radiance that outshone even the light bouncing off the pools. Arkanon was feeling himself getting increasingly mesmerised by her brilliance.

She looked deep into his eyes and he knew she could tell what effect she had on him. "The gardens are beautiful…Aren't they?" she said softly.

"I didn't mean the gardens…I was talking about you!" As soon as he'd said those words, he felt himself cringing. He couldn't help saying it. He couldn't stop himself from saying them. She looked at him and chuckled.

"You're not really used to talking to women, are you? But thank you for the compliment all the same…"

For the first time in his life, someone could see his main weakness. Arkanon was never very confident around women. He always said the wrong thing and normally would put his foot in it at some point. This usually resulted in them running a mile, or worse into the arms of one of his friends.

When he was 15, his father took him to see the most experienced woman in the village so he could lose his virginity and as his father called it, 'to become a man', Saleyna was called and even though every man in the village, all 76 of them had had her, including the oldest men in the village, the 97-year-old Auroch twins, she was absolutely stunning. Saleyna was 32, blonde, blue-eyed, skin like freshly fallen snow and she shagged like a jackrabbit.

He fell for her too, but alas, it wasn't meant to be. After Arkanon tried, unsuccessfully, for three months to court her, she married Bentreden Auroch after Tier Auroch died during a rather over-energetic tryst also with her. But for some reason, this felt different with Cassandra. He couldn't tell if it was her striking looks or her sultry, hypnotic voice, but he was spellbound, completely.

They walked for hours as they talked about life before Arkanon came to the city, including the time he just mentioned, which left him feeling very embarrassed. Fortunately, she just laughed it off and looked deep into his eyes again.

"Aww! You poor thing," she purred softly, "I'd never do a thing like that to you."

Arkanon's head hit the clouds. What was she doing to him? Why was he feeling like this? But then why did he care? It felt good being with her, so good. They made their way to one of the tree lifts and started up and pretty soon, he had to ask, "Where did you come from?" he said nervously. "…The truth!" Arkanon was hoping she'd understand what he meant. There was a long pause and a look in her eyes he'd never seen before. He could tell that was a question she wasn't used to answering.

She turned to him and smiled. "It's a long story," she said. The tone in her voice trying to hide the nervousness apparent in her stature. "My mother is an Asumertrian queen…She was a princess when Feron met her…He was on a diplomatic mission to create open trade between Atlantis and our kingdom…He ended up taking a few things he…well…which he really shouldn't of…" She began to giggle. Arkanon could tell that this was something that amused her greatly.

"Little did he know that his kingdom and mine would be tied together forever…He hated the idea…I always knew that, but the first time he clapped eyes on me, that all changed…He didn't have any other children and seeing me brought his fatherly instincts to the surface…Now Asumertria and Atlantis are powerful allies and in a way, it's all down to me." A smug smile began to grow across her face. "The only catch of this arrangement is that, as well as his own advisors, he had to have ours as well to balance it out. What's in his best interests, may not be in ours…"

Arkanon could tell that this troubled her a little but the reasons for which would not become clear for some time to come.

Arkanon now knew what those dark-robed advisors were. They were the Asumertrian ones. But that still didn't explain the feeling of foreboding and dread that engulfed him whenever he was near them. Surely, they shouldn't give him that feeling. From that moment, he had to find out what they were up to. Arkanon just had to figure out how to do it.

The Best Laid Plans

Even though he'd got into the great library, he didn't have the faintest clue where to start or for that matter what he was looking for. He didn't even know why he was doing this. He just couldn't shake the feeling that there was something just not right with this whole situation. The Asumertrian advisors were his main cause for concern.

Why was there that feeling of dread whenever he was near them? He knew it wasn't just because they were always in dark robes and always hid their faces from view. Although it was strange, considering the bright colours so befitting of Atlantis, that they should dress as they did. No, it wasn't that. What troubled him more was that the feeling he got when he was near them was so strong, so intensely dark that it was all that he could concentrate on. Worse still, it seemed that he was only the one that seemed to notice it.

Then there was Cassandra. Although he was completely besotted with her, felt so in love, something about that also didn't feel right. It felt unnatural and to the point of, dare he say it, sorcery or even witchcraft. But then again, it could just be his own insecurity causing his doubts about her. Simply, because she was just so stunning and a princess of two of the most powerful kingdoms in the known world. Added to that, she was incredibly wealthy and extremely powerful, so why was she interested in him? It just seemed too good to be true, which usually meant that it was exactly that.

She could bend your will with a single word and have any man she wanted out of all the royal elite. Yet, for some unknown reason, she wanted him? He considered himself nothing more than a soldier. Though, to be fair, he wasn't just any old soldier but was one that was born and raised purely for that purpose and also the leader of his clan. But in his eyes, he wasn't nobility, so he wasn't what a princess should've been looking for.

This was troubling to him. He couldn't get her voice out of his head either. That sweet beautiful voice. Just hearing her speak practically made him melt and he was powerless to resist. She was tightening her grip on his very being and he knew that there was nothing he could do to break her hold. He needed answers to why this was the case and he needed them fast. But where would he start? This was why he was at the great library. He thought that if he could find out everything he could about Asumertria, such as its cultural beliefs, myths and legends, then maybe, just maybe he'd know enough to not be surprised when he either went there, which he knew that someday he would have to. Or, God forbid, he had to predict a possible Asumertrian strategy against them.

He stared at the row upon row of bookcases that stretched out in front of his as far as the eye could see. When he looked upwards there were at least 10 levels of shelves holding millions of scrolls. On seeing this he began to realise how daunting a task he'd set himself?

After many hours searching alone, he conceded defeat and caught the attention of a passing librarian, who pointed him in the right direction. He climbed up several levels and walked through several stacks, before he reached his destination. To his surprise, the Atlantians had a rather large amount of very detailed information about the Asumertrians and after finding a comfortable place to sit and study, he opened the first scroll. Suddenly, everything went black.

Asumertria was a gleaming city. Like Atlantis, it was huge. Columns and statues filled its squares and temples. Marble and gold littered the place, like disused cans on a London street. It truly was a wonder to behold. Arkanon awoke, sat against a wall overlooking the huge main plaza. Passers-by dropping coins in his lap, assuming him to be a beggar. He stared at it in awe. His eyes couldn't comprehend the beauty of what he was seeing. The pavements were marble and not just in the main plaza, but everywhere. This was a rich kingdom and it wasn't afraid to show that fact off. People around him seemed to take less notice of this fact as they rushed back and forth from civil building to café, to another civil building. They never seemed to drink in the sheer scale of the city in front of them.

He was astounded, he really was, but was more astounded by how he was there. What the hell had just happened? How had he got there? For a few moments, he contemplated what the answers to those questions were. Before concluding that he probably wouldn't be able to come up with a plausible reason and would perhaps best use his time here constructively, he went to the Atlantian library to gather intel on this city. So, seeing as he had found himself here, he may as well get the information about the place that he needed.

He got up and walked the marble pavements to the city square. Giant halls with columns made of jade and onyx towered above him. This easily rivalled anything he'd seen in Atlantis. The square was huge just on its own with giant marble fountains that dotted the landscape that themselves were overshadowed by a giant spire dominating its centre. Each of the buildings had a number from 1 to 12 with the shadow from the spire being cast on each in turn like some sort of immense sundial. It was truly amazing. It would have had him totally spellbound if he wasn't so focused on his quest.

He needed to figure out what the connection was to the bad feeling he had when he was around those dark advisors? Something in this city had to give him some clue. Or some shred of evidence that would either prove his worst fears that this was still an enemy kingdom and an extremely powerful one at that. Or as he sincerely hoped, he was wrong and those guys were just fucking weird and he was being paranoid. Whatever it was, he had to know. If not for his sake, then just to prove that Cassandra was genuinely in love with him and, as he feared, wasn't trying to use him as a willing pawn in some devilish plan.

He decided that his first port of call should be one of their temples that had caught his eye. It was strange that he was so drawn to it and he assumed it was because it was so different to any he'd seen before. The black onyx pillars seemed darker than the blackest tar. Its curved outer walls bent inwards to a large spire in the middle. There was no colour at all here, just black empty darkness. This place was, he thought, maybe the best place for him to find some answers.

He entered through a large opening in its front and was shocked by how dark it was in. Torches high in the ceiling dimly lit the huge marble statues inside that stretched high into the inky blackness that was its ceiling. They depicted strange and grotesque creatures that were gods dedicated to the darkest forces of nature and man's corruptible instincts. Gods of torture, betrayal, murder and rape, they were all here. All of man's baser instincts, he wouldn't consider them god's, however. To himself and the Atlantians, these would be demons, not gods. It wasn't any wonder that this side of Asumertrian culture wasn't well known if at all. It disturbed him deeply how a civilisation that seemed so cultured on the outside, so vibrant and intelligent could worship monstrosities like these. The thought chilled him to the bone.

The further he entered inside, the more disgusted and confused he became. It felt like a nightmare and as he reached the last altar, he was met by two, very large, very heavily armed guards across from it that guarded a curtained over the doorway. This looked to him just a smidge suspicious. *Why would a temple need guards, or more specifically, guards like these?* he thought to himself. They stood right in front of the entranceway and completely blocked his view.

"You there!" one boomed at him as Arkanon tried to find some way around them to see what they were guarding. The guard's voice was full of authority and menace. "What business do you have here?"

Arkanon looked at him and politely smiled. The guard glared at him, his gaze seemingly piercing into Arkanon's soul, it was so intense. It felt like he was trying to weaken Arkanon from within somehow. *Was it sorcery or just something natural to the people of this nation?* Arkanon thought. His partner stood there silent. An equally disturbing stare coming from his eyes too. Arkanon stood his ground and thought for a moment.

"Just browsing," he said. This was the only excuse for why he was here that came to mind. "I'm just trying to think of which god I should worship…I'm new to the city, just moved here for diplomatic purposes and wanted to sample your culture." It seemed like a perfectly plausible reason to him, the guard, however, didn't seem all that convinced.

"Ah, I see," he said in a calmer tone. "So, you thought you'd pick one of these? I don't think you'd be very interested in one of these mates," he looked at Arkanon and sniggered. The other guard didn't move. A look of genuine disgust covered his face.

"I'm afraid this area is off-limits to any and all outsiders and seeing as you fit into the category of an outsider 'cos we've never seen you before. I think it best if you just fuck off!"

"Erm…What is this place and why can't I have a look round?" Arkanon said curiously.

The guard looked just at him and sneered. He knew for certain that Arkanon was snooping around and not browsing like he'd said, but he could tell he wasn't going to leave unless he told him something. He let out a long, exasperated sigh. "OK…mate…This temple is off-limits to everyone but visiting royals and their escorts, members of the royal senate and the Asumertrian royal elite…You seem like none of those, so if you don't—"

Arkanon didn't let him finish his sentence. "I'm a visiting dignitary, I'm an ambassador from Atlantis."

This wasn't exactly a lie. He was, after all, from Atlantis. He was also quite a high rank, so that sort of made him an ambassador. The only thing was no one, as far as he was aware knew he was there. So, in effect, he didn't have any official business here.

"So, if I'm an ambassador, I should be allowed access, shouldn't I?" he said.

"Nice try, pal…" the guard smiled and gestured for Arkanon to move along with his hand and the other glared at him threateningly. He knew he wasn't going to like what was coming next as they both drew their swords from their huge backs. They were massive weapons, very sharp and very painful looking things.

"Thank you for your help. You've been very informative," Arkanon said quickly turning on his heels and headed for the door.

He had two options now. The first was to go to the palace and somehow get permission from one of the royal family to get past the guards. But this, he assumed, would be highly unlikely because he'd no official business with any of them and he doubted that they'd see him on a whim. The second was to wait until nightfall and attempt to sneak past the guards when they weren't looking. This was a prospect with a high chance of certain death if he screwed it up. He opted for option two, the sneakier option. So, he decided to wander around town until night will fall.

When night fell, he returned to the dark temple. In the moonlight, it looked even more menacing. The shadows seemed to contort and twist around the pillars, shimmering with a dark light. They looked as though they were and if he wasn't in such desperate need to find out what was going on in there, he'd have turned around and walked away. It really did look like it wanted to eat him. He quietly sneaked through the arched doorway that was the entrance and darted into the shadows behind a nearby demonic looking statue. Slowly and silently, keeping low, he made his way down to the altar.

All the way down he was trying to get a better look at what those guards earlier were trying so hard to hide. As he reached the halfway point, he quickly had to stop as those very same guards walked past in front of him muttering to each other. *Shit!* he thought. *Do these guys never sleep?*

For what seemed like an age, he hid as he waited for them to get well out of his view and then slinked his way further and further down the giant hall, darting between statues as he went.

As he began to get closer, he began to make out what they were hiding. There was another small, red-curtained doorway behind an altar that would've gone totally unnoticed as it was camouflaged within a larger red cloth backdrop. But due to a fortuitous breeze coming from behind it, it revealed itself very faintly.

A bright light shifting in and out of view darted out from behind it before being smothered by its cloth captor. This intrigued him because logically, there had to be a tunnel leading to somewhere else, outside perhaps. Whatever was there, it had to be very important, otherwise, it wouldn't have been so well hidden. He stealthily made his way closer to it. His heart pounding into his throat. *God, this is a rush!* he thought to himself. *I'd forgotten how much fun doing this was!*

When he was stood outside the small curtained doorway, he crouched down and gently parted the curtains peering inside and quickly scouting for any additional guards hidden from view. This tunnel was bigger than the opening and unusual compared to the rest of the temple as it was very well lit. When he was sure it was safe to enter, he ventured inside.

A cold breeze washed his face as he looked down the vast tunnel in front of him. Hesitantly, he made his way towards the end. The same feeling of foreboding and dread that he'd felt from the dark advisors reared its head again. But why? He began to realise that in the grand scheme of things, this was probably a bad idea coming down here. A very, very bad idea. Reluctantly, he continued forward. His curiosity spurring him on until he reached the light at the end.

The light was blinding, but he could just about make out a statue. It was of a man. The closer he got and the more he could make out, the more the sheer horror of what he was beginning to see began to dawn on him. He'd entered a large courtyard out the back of the temple when he realised he'd seen this person before. But not as another statue. He'd seen him in real life and terrifyingly on the battlefield. He'd fought him and nearly died. This bastard had spared him for sport. This horrific statue was of Hoth.

It was unmistakably him. He was the Asumertrian's demon god of assassination and by the looks of things, considering the size and placement of the statue, he was an important figure in Asumertrian culture. Not only that but, logic would dictate, he was very likely one of their strongest allies. Arkanon couldn't believe what he was seeing. They were working with the enemy. More importantly, they were the enemy and yet no one outside of this city apart from him knew the truth. Something else began to dawn on him now too. Cassandra, dear sweet beautiful Cassandra, she was royalty, she'd have to have known about this, after all, like the guards said, 'only the royal elite could freely enter here'.

He was heartbroken. He began to try and find any explanation as to why she couldn't possibly be a part of this. Desperately trying to think of any reason why she wouldn't have known about any of this. Perhaps her being half Atlantian meant they wouldn't allow her to know about this, fearing she might divulge the information to our king thus ruining whatever plans they had.

Or maybe she did know but couldn't tell him out of fear for her own life. All of this was pure speculation though and he soon realised was also completely futile. She was a master manipulator. She was using him for her own kingdom's ends. Perhaps in an attempt to try and dispose of him to weaken the royal guard and the white stars. Or maybe manipulate him into betraying the Atlantian king. His head was spinning with disastrous scenario after a disastrous scenario. The more he thought about it, the more it filled him with dread. They were in trouble, unbelievably serious trouble.

He didn't get long to think about it all, though as a sudden strong wind blasted behind him, startling him and causing him to spin around on the spot to face whatever was behind him.

But there was nothing. He quickly put it down to paranoia, on account of his current situation and location. But then he heard something. Faintly at first, but he heard it. A maniacal laugh he'd not heard since that fateful day outside his village. It gradually grew and was coming from behind him. He spun around again to face his attacker. Yet again, nothing. Shadows on the statue danced around it but then strangely started joining together as the laugh grew ever stronger and louder. Soon the shadows began to take form and rise out of the stone and it was then he realised what form they were taking and just before it had fully revealed itself. Quickly, he turned and ran towards the exit. It was Hoth! He was certain! He couldn't believe he was here. How did he know he was here? He ran faster and faster, reasoning that it was better to tackle those guards than face him. But then suddenly, there was a loud bang as he was hit hard in the back knocking him off his feet forward towards the floor.

"Arkanon," Hoth boomed. That unmistakable hiss in his voice echoed down the hall, "how pleasant to see you here!"

For him, pleasant wasn't a word he'd have used to show how much he wanted to see him right now. Arkanon slowly rolled himself over to face Hoth just as he stood over the top of him. Hoth's eyes burned a bright red, an evil smile stretching across his face. "It's so nice to have guests, especially ones from so far away…To what do I owe this pleasure?" there was that word again.

This for him was anything but a pleasure. With a flick of his hand, the torches were snuffed out and a red glow hit the walls illuminating only a part of his face. Arkanon knew what he was trying to do. Hoth was trying to intimidate him and it was working. He grabbed Arkanon by the throat and lifted him, effortlessly, high into the air, choking him slowly. Hoth's smile was barely visible in the red hue that scattered around his face. He chuckled to himself again.

"You know? You're a smart man, Arkanon. I knew I was right to spare you." The happiness in his voice chilled him to the bone.

"Why? Thank you very much," he spluttered defiantly. "It's nice of you to say so. Now if you don't mind, I'd rather die quickly and if possible with a small amount of pain or better still none at all."

"Why, Arkanon, my good friend?" Hoth said smiling.

The thought of him addressing Arkanon as a friend was a little disconcerting. He didn't want a ten-foot, psychotic, extremely strong and extremely powerful demon as his bosom buddy, although the idea did sound as though it'd have its uses.

"I'm not going to kill you. I may just hurt you a little bit." This idea was a little strange to him, considering he was still unsure why Hoth was letting him live. He didn't get much of a chance to think about it though as Hoth threw him twenty or so feet through the air back down the tunnel and straight into the statue.

He slammed into it hard and then dropped heavily to the floor with an equally loud bang! The wind was knocked out of him and he struggled to get himself up onto his feet. He managed to get to onto his knees just before Hoth was again in his face.

"I thought I asked for very little pain or none at all? This feels like lots of pain," Arkanon wheezed gasping for air.

Hoth smiled at him, taking hold of his chin and then clenched his fist. With the back of his hand, he slammed it across Arkanon's face back and forth, back and then forth striking him across his face with both sides of his hand. Blood began to pour down his face as he struggled to keep conscious. When Hoth suddenly let go.

Arkanon slumped to the ground. His face was numb with pain and he coughed and spluttered as he began to choke on his own blood.

"Not yet, Arkanon! Not yet," Hoth said with a calmness in his voice, "don't pass out yet. I have so much to tell you…By now you'll have realised that this is my city…Although it is ruled by a king, it is still mine…I just allow them to think otherwise…" he paused for a moment to check Arkanon was still awake and listening before he continued, pacing up and down slowly in front of him.

"I orchestrated the arrangement that this kingdom and your own has enjoyed! I essentially…How should I put it?…Hmm," he rubbed his chin as he began to think. "I persuaded Cassandra's mother to seduce Feron for the sole purpose of bearing him a child…a child that would inevitably unite both of their kingdoms…Atlantis needed to open a trade deal with Asumertria or face war. As they battled over trade routes…That would have been very messy."

He grinned like a schoolboy. The thought of that gave him intense pleasure that showed across his face, his forked tongue licking his lips. "Yes, very messy. So, in order to make sure that she wouldn't fail, I gave her a demonic power. I gave her the ability to seduce any man with just a single word."

Arkanon was starting to realise that Cassandra possibly wasn't a bit player in this after all. If anything, she 'was' the plan. She was the lynchpin that held it all together. She did know what was going on. She probably knew from the very beginning what role she was to play in all this.

"Why?" Arkanon coughed, blood splattering on the floor. "Why go to all this trouble? Surely, it'd be easier to just let them kill each other, instead of doing this…You just wait for either side to kill each other and then take over whatever's left. Job done."

"I see your point," Hoth said. Arkanon was quite impressed with himself. He'd actually shown Hoth the error of his ways. Sadly, he was wrong. Hoth continued, "But the thing is, I needed to make sure that Atlantis was the one that fell. I couldn't risk them beating the Asumertrian's…You see they have something I want. Something that is very valuable to me…Something that was denied me at the dawn of time and rightly belongs to me! I needed it back…This then seemed like the better plan."

Hoth's plan was beginning to make sense to Arkanon now and it was horrifying in its simplicity. It was no wonder that no one saw it coming.

"So, to cover your tracks, you start a crusade, vanquishing our allies and occasionally attacking Asumertrian allies to make it look like you're mounting a full-scale war across the world. When all the while you're planning an Asumertrian takeover."

"You're almost right. But it's ingenious, don't you think?"

Arkanon had to admit he was right. Although it pained him to think so. Hoth smiled again. "Time to sleep."

Then with the force of a truck, Hoth hit him square in the face knocking him out. Moments later, in the blackness of unconsciousness, he heard Hoth's voice again, "Wake up, Arkanon," he bellowed, "wake up."

With a jolt, Arkanon awoke and in the great library at Atlantis. He had no idea how he'd got there. A scroll on the city of Asumertria was laid out under his head. Was he really there? Or was it all a dream? He couldn't tell. He saw a passing librarian and signalled for him to come over.

"Excuse me? Have you been here all night?" he asked, still a little groggy.

"Yes, I have," he said. "Did you enjoy your forty winks?"

"Did you see me sleeping?"

"Yes. You haven't moved for about an hour. You took that book on Asumertria and as soon as you opened it you passed out."

A feeling of relief washed over Arkanon that was almost whelming. It was just a dream after all. Thank God!

The librarian looked at him and smiled before his eyes shifted towards the scroll beneath him. "Oh dear, oh dear, oh dear, oh dear."

Arkanon couldn't work out why he was panicking so much. That was until he looked at the scroll. Blood was everywhere all over the length of it.

"How long was I out?" Arkanon screamed at the librarian almost in a blind panic and startling the old librarian.

"An hour! Just an hour…I have to ask. Do you normally punch yourself in your sleep at all?"

Arkanon didn't answer. The realisation that it wasn't necessarily an ordinary dream filled his head. He stood up and a searing pain shot across his back, then his ribs and took hold exactly where he'd hit the statue and floor. Hoth was toying with him that much he knew; but why? Why had Hoth essentially divulge his entire plan? It just didn't make any strategic sense to Arkanon. What was Hoth up to? Why do this? What benefit did Hoth have to gain from this? None of that really truly mattered though at this moment. He had to tell the king. He had to go to the palace!

A Question of Patience

Like an Olympic sprinter, Arkanon ran. He had to tell the king. He had to tell him about his dream. Everything depended on it. Absolutely everything. The fate of the Atlantian people. The fate of his village. The fate of the entire continent. The fate of the world and humanity, in fact, all depended on him, on his premonition, on his dream. Whatever it was, he just knew it was important. He had to tell the king.

Through alleyways and gardens, he ran. Trying to take the shortest route that he could to save time. Every second counted. Every brief moment he wasted brought the world closer to death. After the first mile, his legs began to weaken, but he still carried on, still sprinted, still charged towards the palace with every last ounce of energy in his body. The pain coursing through his muscles was nearly unbearable, but he still soldiered on.

As he reached the great square outside the palace, thousands of people stood in his way. All of them were going about their nightly business, laughing, joking. All of them were largely unaware of Arkanon as he barged past them, knocking them to the floor and much to their annoyance. He had no time for apologies nor time for pleasantries either. He needed to get through.

His focus was unrelenting as the palace gates drew closer and closer. Relief began to envelop him like a warm, comforting duvet the closer he got. Just a few more feet. Just a few more and he'd be at the palace gates. Then he could just borrow one of the palace horses and ride the rest of the way. Just a few more feet! Just a few more…

As he reached the gates, a loud boom suddenly echoed around the square. Arkanon turned towards the noise behind him. The same red flames and pentagrams that he had seen outside his village erupted from the floor sending people flying into the air. Their faces contorted with pain as the searing heat ate away at their flesh and bones. Screams of pain and blind panic suffocated the air. People ran in every direction to take cover as the shadowy images of the Reaper

High Mages flickered into view. Their twisted forms hacked and slashed at the populace sending limbs, heads, blood and sinew high into the air. Surely Hoth couldn't be that cruel. Surely, he couldn't give him all that information only to then attack mere minutes later. But then he was a demon and demons, by their very nature, were cruel.

This was the first time that Arkanon had seen a full-scale reaper invasion. They were everywhere. Thousands of them, trooper, high guard and high mages alike. All of them killing, maiming, burning and levelling everything in their path. They were appearing from all over, suddenly manifesting out of the shadows. It was then that Arkanon realised the power of Hoth's army. What he had seen before, that was just for show. Just a ruse. All to inspire confidence in his army. Hoth had played them. Played them all like a virtuoso pianist and now he was showing his army's true strength.

They were decimating the entire city and Arkanon realised that it wasn't about warning the king anymore. It was too late for that, far too late. Now he knew he had to protect him. He charged through the heavy gates knocking them open like they were old west saloon doors. The guards didn't even notice him as he flew past. Their gaze firmly fixed in horror at the sickening spectacle that laid before them. The adrenaline pumping through his body as he ran was the only thing keeping his buckling legs going.

A feeling of relief began to set in as he reached the throne room. He'd made it. But it was all too quickly taken away from hi, as he was grectcd by the sight of one of the dark advisors hovering in mid-air above the king. Feron lay motionless on the floor. The advisor was almost spectral in appearance. Its dark cloak rippling under some sort of ghostly wind as it sucked the king's essence from his rapidly deteriorating body. Arkanon stood motionless staring at the monstrosity in front of him just as it turned to face him. It's eyes burning bright blue under the blackness of its dark hood pierced into his very soul. With an ear-splitting scream, it opened its cloak making it seem infinitely bigger than it did before. Its arms stretching out made his long billowing sleeves look like vast wings.

Arkanon knew he had to get to the king quickly. But by the looks of things, this beast, this demon wasn't just going to let him take him. It seemed as though it was readying itself for an attack and besides, it looked extremely pissed. He knew he was going to have a fight on his hands here. But how the hell was he gonna fight this thing? It was, to all intents and purposes, a spirit, nothing but a ghost. It lunged forward at great speed. Its screams, like a wailing banshee, cutting the air like a knife as it got closer and closer before it sent one of its wing-like arms hurtling into his chest, knocking him tens of feet into the back wall. Arkanon hit it hard and slumped to the floor. He managed to raise his head just in time to see it float gracefully through a pillar before lifting him by the throat.

Pulling his face right up to its own, it screamed violently at him before tossing him into the air and then raced after him. It began striking him over and over again, crippling blow after crippling blow causing Arkanon's body to crumple and contort with every impact. Each one sending him higher and higher still into the air. Then suddenly and without warning, it grabbed him again before hurling him towards the floor. His battered body crashed into the marble floor with a loud crack and with such force that shards of marble erupted into the air as he hit the ground, blood spurting from his mouth.

He lay there motionless. The spectre hovering silently over him gazed at his shattered body as if it was in two minds about what next to do with him. Gently, it glided down towards him until its nose was virtually touching Arkanon's and slowly opened its mouth.

As if out of nowhere, Arkanon unsheathed his blade and drove it deep into the wraith-like monsters gaping maw. The sound of its splintering skull as the blade pierced through the back of its head was like splintering twigs and with a shattering, tortured scream it shot into the air, spinning as it ascended higher and higher, blue flame jetting from its mouth and the wound in its head. Arkanon's hand still clutched the blade that was now firmly lodged in its skull. A maniacal grin stretched from ear to ear across his battered face.

"Fuck you! You translucent bastard," he bellowed as he pulled his face up to meet his assailants. "Not so fucking tough now are you, eh buddy?"

The advisor climbed higher and higher, its screams growing louder and more panic-stricken.

"Well, you little fucker, it looks like this is the end of the road for you," he said, an air of retribution in his voice.

He swiftly ripped the sword through the top of its head with a violent roar and heavy twist of his body. It trailed skull fragments and black, putrid blood through the air before he started on his rapid descent to the ground below. The still spinning advisor violently fishtailed in the air before it followed behind him. The wound in its head was still spurting blue flames like a raging volcano, twirling round it as it plummeted downwards.

Arkanon gazed at it pirouetting like an aerial ballet dancer. Its body twisting and turning. Its long, flowing robes fluttering as it fell. It was strangely hypnotic. Almost soothing. It was the last thing he saw. With a loud thud and a searing pain, it all went black. He had reached the ground.

After what seemed like an eternity, Arkanon awoke. The body of the advisor lay in a crumpled mass on the ground next to his own and the king's, it's in motionless form lay a few yards away. He gingerly got himself to his feet, the pain from his injuries seared through every part of his body. He'd really done a number on him and Arkanon dropped to his knees as he began to make his way towards the king. "Sire," the pain turning his shouts into a pained groan, "sire, answer me."

The lack of response worried him, Was he alive? Was he dead? From this distance, he couldn't tell. He began to think the worst, but still, he battled on. He had to know. If the king was dead and without a true heir to his throne, Atlantis was lost. But judging by the devastation outside, it would seem that Atlantis was lost anyway.

He began to wonder what was so important about this place that had made Hoth so desperate to destroy it. What was it he feared so badly? All that became irrelevant as soon as he saw the king move.

"Sire!…sire!" still no response. "Sire, if you can hear me, give me a sign." The king gently rolled himself over onto his front and raised his head.

"Arkanon, my good friend, I think I'm on my way out," the king was almost whispering as he spoke. The pain he was in scratching at the back of his voice, never mind the lack of any slurring. Feron appeared to be speaking with unusual clarity and free from senility. Before Arkanon could enquire about this however, Feron continued. "Come to me, old friend, quickly, we don't have much time and there is much I must explain?" Feron coughed, a small fountain of blood erupting from his mouth, causing Arkanon to throw himself onto his stomach as he desperately tried to reach his dying friend. "You likely have questions, but you may have to resign yourself to not getting all the answers.."

Arkanon battled with his legs to stand up before hobbling then hurriedly stumbling towards the king and collapsing in front of him.

"What would you have me do, my lord?" Arkanon said, trying in vain to hide the pain. "What is your wish?"

The king glanced at him and let out a pained chuckle. Arkanon was a sorry looking sight. His face was swollen, blackened and bruised. Blood streamed from lesions all over his head and body. He lay on the floor next to him, his body contorted with pain every time he moved.

"Well, my friend," he said, it was so hard to contain his amusement at Arkanon's question as he let out another chuckle, "you're not gonna do a lot in that state, are you?"

Arkanon looked himself up and down. He hated to admit it, but he had to agree with the king. He was a bit worse for wear. They looked at each other and laughed. A pained sort of laugh.

"So, what do you suggest I do then, my lord and how come your slurring gone?"

"Listen to me," Feron said in a hurried tone, blood sputtering out of his mouth as he spoke, "I needed her to believe I was oblivious to her intentions. She was my little girl and I loved her, but let's face it... She was still of enemy stock, eh? Though I see she enchanted you, good and proper?" Feron coughed loudly, as he attempted to laugh, "She's a looker, got her daddy's genes though, inherited my ravishing looks eh?" Feron sighed as he chuckled quietly and for a brief moment, Arkanon thought he'd gone. Thankfully Feron confirmed his continued life by mouthing the word Boo!, followed by a pained snort.

Arkanon could tell that Feron's injuries were worse than what was apparent from the outside. He was fading fast, so was Arkanon.

"Listen, old friend," Feron spluttered, "there isn't much time…but I have to show you something…something I've kept secret for so many years."

Feron carefully began to pick himself up onto his feet. Arkanon followed suit. Both of them wincing at the pain, coursing through their battered and bruised bodies. Arkanon carefully propped Feron against him holding most of his weight as they travelled down towards the back of the throne.

"What is it you wanted to show me, sire?"

"All shall become clear, my friend," said Feron. His voice was turning into a whisper and Arkanon knew he was fading quickly. "There is a button on the back of the throne, push it."

Arkanon did as he was instructed. He carefully propped Feron against the throne and then he looked carefully all over its back. It was massive and he was trying to find something that was either very small or very big and in a very short space of time.

"Where is it, my lord?"

"Near the bottom, it just looks like a panel that has started to stick out."

He found what he was looking for. He quickly pushed it in. The whole back wall of the throne room started to shake the rest of the room as it moved back and then slowly to the side. It was an amazing sight, the part of the wall that was moving was at least 100 feet high, 50 feet wide and at the very least three feet thick, but it was moving effortlessly. In what seemed like an age, the wall finally stopped moving. Behind it was a huge open room, easily the size of the throne room. How the hell had he not known this was here? The room was bare apart from a huge stone covered in carved hieroglyphics that dominated the room dead in the centre. He didn't know why, but it was somehow mesmerising. There was a low, almost inaudible hum emanating from it. What the hell was it?

"Quite a sight, isn't it?" Feron said with a pained chuckle.

Arkanon turned to him, a look of bewilderment covering his face.

"Don't be afraid, old friend. Go to it. It's calling you, isn't it?" Arkanon nodded in agreement. "Then go to it, go on," Feron beckoned for him to go forward and tentatively he did.

The closer Arkanon got the more massive the rock became. From here, he could see the hieroglyphs moving. How was this possible? he thought to himself. They shouldn't be moving. As he got closer, they started to glow a deep rich blue, getting brighter and brighter the closer he got.

"It's amazing, isn't it?" Feron said in a knowing tone. "I remember the first time it did that to me, it's not something you forget."

"Why's that, sire?"

"You'll see," said Feron, slowly positioning himself behind the throne.

When Arkanon was within only a few feet away, a shaft of blue light struck and then enveloped him.

"That's why, old friend, I have guarded this secret for you for so long and now you're here, I can at last pass it to you, its rightful owner."

Inside the blue light, Arkanon was transfixed by the stone before him. The low hum growing louder and louder when suddenly and without warning, he was suddenly in the middle of a meadow. No buildings. No hills. Just flat open grassland. Where was everything? he thought. More to the point, where the hell was he?

Suddenly, the sound of combat filled the air. It was deafening. Clanging shields and clashing swords strangely ricocheted and echoed off invisible walls. Cries of pain and victory lay hidden behind the sounds of the swords. Yet, he couldn't see anything in front of him. But the noises sounded so close like they were right in front of him. But there was nothing there. Nothing. Just a green field.

Suddenly, the ground shook, throwing Arkanon to the floor. When the shaking stopped, he quickly sat upright. *What the hell?* he thought as he looked around. The sounds of battle were getting louder and louder. Underneath, he could hear a faint rumble, a low, almost inaudible hum. Arkanon was confused. Where the hell was the battle? It sounded so close. Almost like he could touch it in front of him.

Yet!

There was nothing. Just this green field and blue sky as far as the eye could see. He attempted getting himself back onto his feet again and just like before, the ground shook, knocking him back down.

OK! he thought to himself. *Obviously, I'm supposed to sit here then.*

He looked around a little more, trying to place where the sounds were coming from. They all seemed to come from, well, everywhere. From all around him. But it was impossible to pinpoint exactly where from. He sat motionless before looking up to the clear sapphire blue sky and in the politest voice he could muster shouted, "What the hell do you want me to see?"

The sounds of battle grew louder as he shouted drowning out his voice. It was almost as though someone or something was doing it on purpose to shut him up. It was almost like he was being taunted, not tested.

He wasn't happy. Whoever or whatever was doing this was taking the piss out of him and he didn't like it. As far as he was concerned, he wasn't going to stand for it. Arkanon cleared his throat with a loud cough and in his loudest voice, looking towards the sky shouted again, "I'm sorry, whoever you are, but I haven't got time to sit here, I need to get back to the king…to Feron." He was sure that mentioning Feron would hopefully speed things up a bit. After all, he was guarding this secret from the rest of the world. This stone or whatever it was would surely recognise Feron's name. Then hopefully, after hearing his name, it might allow him to leave and rescue the stones former protector. It seemed to Arkanon that this was the idea that had the highest chance of success. Unfortunately, as was becoming his habit lately, once again he was wrong. He would have to find a different approach.

"I need to get back before my city is destroyed. Before maybe everything is destroyed. You see…There's this demon, Hoth…His name is Hoth…and he's killing everyone." It was useless to try and hide the desperation he felt. He knew he didn't have much time. He knew that soon Hoth could quite easily have laid waste to the city by now. If he could just get this over with he might be able to get back in time and maybe still help.

"Please?…I…I can't let him do that…The longer I'm here, the less chance I have of saving my city. From saving my people…From saving…Well…you." He was sure that the last part would sway whatever or whomever it was to either speed things up or set him free. He waited expectantly.

For what seemed like an age was, in reality, more likely around five minutes, he'd still not heard anything. Every time he tried to pick himself back up off the ground, he was quickly knocked back to the floor by another earthquake. Whatever or whoever he was waiting for, by all accounts, wanted him to be sitting down for this, he concluded.

"Please…Please just let me go, I need to help my people," Arkanon was becoming frantic.

He was trapped on some sort of grass plain. With no way of leaving. No way of knowing where he was with no way of finding out the fate of the city or his friends and his tribe. All he had for company were the battle cries and blood-curdling screams of men that weren't anywhere to be seen. He decided to try pleading just one more time.

"Please, I can't plead with you enough…I need to get out of here…I'm probably by now the last hope for my people…So, please just take me back to them. If you're not going to show me anything or do anything, then please just let me go to where I'm actually needed."

Still, there was nothing. This was becoming torturous. The sounds of the ensuing battle still raged around him, yet he was still here bound to this plain. He couldn't move and he certainly couldn't leave. Yet, he could still hear the terror, still hear the painful cries of his countrymen, the cries of anguish from the people that he had sworn to protect.

He crossed his legs and began to lower his head into his hands. The sudden, brutal realisation that he very likely wasn't going to get out of this in time began to make Arkanon, for the first time in a long time, feel totally powerless. He truly was at the whim of the gods and they weren't interested in playing fair.

For hours he sat in the same spot, the same position, rocking backwards and forwards to comfort himself. All the while trying to block out the sounds of war that filled his eardrums. They were just loud enough to drown out his own thoughts but just quiet enough so that it didn't deafen him. This seemed to him like cruelty in the highest form. He was very quickly getting to the point where he was starting to break.

He knew that it wouldn't be long now. Soon he was going to cross that very slim threshold between sanity and insanity and that he would never be able to crawl his mind back ever again. The one saving grace that he had was now he had nothing to lose. It was time to give it one last hard push. With his eyes closed tight, he threw himself as fast as he could up onto his feet with a loud, menacing roar. He roared until every last bit of air left his lungs before taking in another deep breath.

"This has gone on long enough," he boomed, a manic and verging on the psychotic, anger filled his voice, "whilst I sit here, unable to move. Unable to leave. Unable to do anything, my people are dying." He listened out for the sounds of battle. Strangely they had stopped. "In fact, by now, they are probably already dead." He knew the sudden silence was a bad sign and it was telling in his voice. He'd failed. He dropped his head and with his eyes still tightly shut began to shake it slowly. The guilt he felt for not being there to help hang heavy on his body.

He began to think of how he could've done things differently to prevent this from happening. Every path he walked in his mind would always lead to the same point. It was his fault; he was solely to blame. He was the one who had to satisfy his curiosity and touch the strange, glowing and humming stone. But it drew him in, he thought. It took over his mind. It seduced him, called him. He was powerless to resist. So, it wasn't his fault!

But then if he hadn't gone into the room before all that happened in the first place, if he hadn't had to be the big hero and save the king, then he would've been able to help defend the city. But oh no! he thought to himself, he had to listen to his ego, he had to be the big hero and save the king from doom. That's where it all went wrong. He should've let the king die. Although it was awful to even think of it, it did seem to be the most likely point where it all went wrong as far as he could see. If he'd let the king die, he wouldn't be in this mess. He'd still be in Atlantis, either dying whilst fighting alongside his brave and loyal brothers and the rest of his kinsmen. Maybe by some miracle, him being there could be the deciding factor that would turn the tide of the battle, winning them the war. But he was never going to know because he saved the king, he'd never know. It was then that he decided it was the king's fault, not his. Without the king, he wouldn't be here. So, it was the king's fault.

He stood still, chuckling to himself, before slowly opening his eyes to? Darkness?

Silence?

Nothing was in front of his eyes. Nothing ran around his ears. Not a single sound. Apart from his heavy breathing. At least, he knew he wasn't deaf, he thought, however, it would appear that he was now blind. He couldn't see anything just blackness.

"So, it's not enough that you prevent me from helping my people?" he said with a bitter, biting tongue, "You now have to take my sight? Have you not punished me enough already? What possible enjoyment can whatever or whomever you are get from punishing me in this way? Do you not think I've had enough now?" He paused waiting for an answer and as usual, it didn't come.

"Hmmm?…Keeping that secret, are you? So, what's next? You gonna kill me in the slowest manner possible? Or even better…leave me here in this field until the day of my death? Did you decide that having to see this field every day wasn't punishing enough for me, so you had to take my eyes too?"

Again, he paused, awaiting an answer that still didn't come. A manic smile slowly began to creep over his face. "Even now, you're still not willing to answer me… You're a coward whatever, whoever…You're a coward."

In a sheer act of defiance, he took a step forward. "Eh?…Hold on?…What the?" Arkanon suddenly realised he could move again as his foot touched the ground. Then he realised that there was no grass beneath his feet. However, what surprised him more was the fact that he felt nothing at all below his feet. He was standing on literally nothing. His foot wasn't feeling anything, yet he was still standing and more surprising still, he was now walking on what, for all intents and purposes, was nothing but air. Yet it was solid. *It had to be a trick?* he thought. Had it taken the sense of touch out of his feet too?

He dropped quickly to his knees with a surprisingly loud thud and frantically began to feel around where he thought the floor should be. But even then, there was still nothing. There was no coldness of stone, the softness of grass nor anything that would indicate to him that he was anywhere. This whole situation was beginning to get very, very strange.

He sat motionless puzzled by the situation that he was finding himself in. He began to think long and hard about where he might be. But at least he had an explanation for why the fighting suddenly stopped. It was because he wasn't anywhere near it anymore. This, he concluded, brought a little ray of hope back to his situation. The battle could still be raging, he could still be in with a chance. Even better, he might not be blind either after all. It could just be very dark. So dark he couldn't see. He slowly rose back to his feet with a renewed confidence that filled his body. He began to take a few more steps forward.

"STOP!" a voice said in a heavy and ordering tone.

Like the battle sounds before it, this voice didn't seem to come from one specific direction. It seemed to come from all around him and from nowhere yet still from somewhere. Tentatively, Arkanon dared to answer back, "Why?…Who are you? Where am I?…Why have you brought me here and what happened to my people?"

"ALL SHALL BECOME CLEAR SOON… BE PATIENT AND THE ANSWERS WILL COME."

Be patient? What the hell did this, whatever it was, think he was already doing for however long it was that he'd been there? He'd been patient enough, now it was time for some answers.

Part 4: So, Now We're All Caught Up...

When Friends Turn Against You

Unknown location in Africa, Arkanon's camp.

For all in intents and purposes to everyone at NORAD, Jason, Tyler and everyone in their team were dead. Nothing more than a sad footnote in a blacked-out and heavily redacted dossier and the sad victims, according to the cover story created, of a helicopter crash during a training exercise in the Rocky Mountains.

So, to say that a request for immediate rescue coming from Jason and Tyler and debrief coming as a bit of a shock was an understatement. Even more surprising was the coordinates that they gave for their pick-up location that was thousands of miles away from where they disappeared and on a completely different continent. Not only that, but there would be three to pick up, the third person being an asset they'd run into.

The young corporal that had answered the call initially thought it was a prank as this was his first day and his unit were well known for hazing new members. He was just about to cut Jason off and ignore the request when Arkanon decided to intervene.

"Private!" Arkanon boomed angrily. His voice causing an unusual hiss to crackle through the airwaves.

"Actually, it's corporal, sir!" the young man said dismissively, "and if you don't mind me asking, this is a restricted channel and only to be accessed by military personnel on black projects and in emergency situations."

"Can you believe this, twat?" Arkanon said in a slightly muffled tone, covering the microphone with his hand. "He wants to know how we got access to this radio channel."

Two other voiced mumbled something in the background that was just about inaudible enough for the young corporal to hear followed by sniggering. The young corporal waited a few seconds as he calmed down his angry demeanour before irately snapping.

"Mike? If this is you and Cash in fucking around, so help me, I'm gonna kill you…"

He was suddenly interrupted by loud mumbling in the background, punctuated by Arkanon asking in a very direct manner, "Who's the General on duty there, lad?"

The corporal was just about to give him the old 'I can't divulge that information as it's top secret' line when Arkanon answered the question for him.

"Is it Powell or Schwartzkopf?" Arkanon asked his mumbling companions. "It can't be Graff, he's dead for sure!" this was followed by further mumbling. "Is Graff dead?" he asked the corporal, who had, at this point, all but stopped listening and without thinking answered yes to his question. He very quickly backtracked on realising his error.

"Er…I mean, I can't answer that question Mr…I didn't catch your name."

Arkanon seemed preoccupied with his conversation with the mumbling voices before he answered dismissively, "Corporal, I can guarantee that your security clearance doesn't grant you the ability to be privy to that information…"

The sounds of what was turning into a heated mumbling argument resumed in the corporal's ear. He was again getting to the point where he was going to end the call when Arkanon suddenly barked back at them.

"Graff's dead! I'm pretty sure of that. What about McCann? Is McCann on duty?"

Arkanon then turned his attention once again to the corporal. "Listen, son…There or not, deliver this message to either Schwartzkopf or Powell."

Deciding to humour him, the corporal agreed. He was certain there was a punchline coming at his expense, but these guys seemed invested in this prank enough to pique his curiosity into what form that punchline would take.

"Go ahead," he said feigning interest.

"Use these exact words: The round table is in session and King Arthur is returning to Camelot," Arkanon said slowly and deliberately. "You got that, son?"

"Yeah, I got that!"

"Good! Now repeat what I said?"

The young corporal was silent. He hadn't been listening so hadn't written anything down. He was just about to admit to this fact when a stern voice stopped him dead in his tracks.

"I'll take it from here, son."

He turned to face the voice and immediately stood to attention and saluted.

"Yes, General Powell, sir! Right away!"

"Thank you, son, you are relieved," Colin Powell turned to face the room. "In fact, you're all relieved for the next hour. That'll be all people."

He waited until everyone had left the room, before taking his seat and placing the headset over his ears, carefully placing the microphone over his mouth.

"We've been monitoring this call old friend and I got here as soon as I could," Powell said in a very professional manner. "It's been a long time and I hear you have a couple of our best and brightest with you."

"Colin!" Arkanon said with a feigned friendliness. "It has been a long time. Is cough drop there too or you on your own there?"

Colin Powell couldn't help letting slip a little snigger. He'd not heard the nickname cough drop for years, in fact, the last time was the last time he spoke to Arkanon. The nickname referred to General Schwartzkopf or his tendency to involuntarily cough due to heavy cigar use and Arkanon seemed to like using girl's names or sweet things to berate people on occasion.

"No, I'm alone, but cough drop is on his way," Powell smiled, he'd forgotten about this aspect of Arkanon. "So, what can we do for you, buddy?"

"Well, I had a trip to Pripyat, I felt like glowing for a week or two and found a curious thing. I think I know what I'm talking about." Arkanon sounded a little annoyed to Powell and for good reason.

"Hmmm!" Powell said, as he feigned ignorance. "Care to enlighten me? I'm not totally sure what you're referring to?"

Arkanon gave a heavy sigh. He knew Powell was lying. He'd warned the U.S. military decades prior to stay away from the reapers and they'd obviously ignored his warnings. He also warned them what would happen to their very tenuous relationship if they didn't stay away. Powell knew this and was desperately attempting to come up with an excuse.

"I know what you're up to, Powell? So, I'm going to give you a single warning, don't lie to me," Arkanon said sternly.

Powell remained silent, but along with the faint sound of automatic doors sliding open, the running footsteps and gasping apologetic voice of General Schwartzkopf in the background, he could also hear something else, something he prayed wasn't what he thought it was.

In an instant, time froze. Arkanon stretched out his hand and an invisible wall rippled reality in front of him as he pushed his hand through that wall.

Immediately, an invisible force yanked him through and instantly he was in Cheyenne mountain, the headquarters of NORAD.

Why is Good Advice Never Taken?

NORAD central command bunker, Cheyenne Mountain, 18 April 1995.

Arkanon stood in front of a frozen in time Colin Powell sitting at a radio desk in the control room of the Cheyenne mountain bunker. The dim light of his computer monitor, the only light source in the room illuminated his face. Behind him was an equally frozen Norman Schwartzkopf in the mid running stride. The rest of the darkened control room was devoid of any other soldiers. This didn't come as a surprise. The existence of Arkanon was only known by a very select few people. Even presidents weren't privy to that information most of the time. The same also went for the knowledge of the reapers too. Powell and Schwartzkopf were two of those select few and were, up until now, considered friends and trusted allies. So, their involvement in the Pripyat incident came as a major disappointment. The strange yet familiar sound in the background was a major concern though and he had to make sure that his fears weren't justified.

He began to slowly walk around the room, carefully taking in his surroundings as he walked. He was looking for anything unusual. Anything out of place, no matter how small that would confirm his worst fears. It didn't take him very long to find what he was looking for.

Even in the shallow darkness of the room, he could make out something behind Norman Schwartzkopf. A darkness that was a deeper kind of darkness floating just above and behind his shoulders. He waited a few seconds and began to close in on Schwartzkopf to allow his vision to adjust to the inky gloom and the unmistakable ethereal and shimmering outline of a reaper wraith began to gradually become visible.

"Oh no!" Arkanon said out loud. "I knew it!"

He quickly spun on his heels and stared at Powell looking for the same kind of shimmer. His wraith was a little more difficult to spot, but it was still there.

"Fuck!" He knew now that whatever he told these two former allies, would have to be a lie. More importantly, his two new friends were likely in a great deal of trouble and needed his protection more now than they did before. He couldn't let them fall into their hands. They'd either been killed or corrupted for sure. He couldn't let that happen.

He closed his eyes and instantly he was back. He could hear Powell on the other end of the line filling in Schwartzkopf with what was happening. Then the clunk and hiss as he plugged in an additional headset to join the conversation.

"Hey there, buddy!" Schwartzkopf sounded condescending, Arkanon hated that. He sounded like he was talking to a confused geriatric rather than a being who was far superior to him in every way. "How can we help you?"

"How about you shut the fuck up and let the adults speak?" Arkanon replied dismissively. Powell couldn't contain his laughter as Arkanon continued, "Seriously...Did he have to be here? I always said he was an asshole and that condescending bullshit he just came out with confirmed it for me!"

"All I said was hey!" Schwartzkopf was defensive.

"Just let it go and let us speak," Powell said in a hushed tone. "You know he's never liked you...Why you here anyway?"

"I got the call...I thought it was your night off."

Arkanon could hear the two men mumbling an argument. He was glad they were because it was giving him time to think. He almost wished he never made this call now. But then he'd probably never have found out how dire the situation had become. He couldn't believe that the U.S. military had got in bed with the reapers, he just didn't know to what extent or indeed how much they knew. This was something he would have to find out, but Tyler and Jason were his top priority as were the two shamans who were his students. They needed a place to lay low and one that wouldn't be known to the U.S. military. He put down the headset, the mumbled arguing from the two generals crackled through it as he approached Jason.

"We need to get you and your friend out of here," he said in a hushed tone. "The U.S. military is compromised as are the allies, I assume. That means the U.K.'s too. I'm not sure to what extent any of the other nations will be either. I need to find somewhere we can lay low—"

"You there?" Powell's voice coming through the headset interrupted him midsentence. Arkanon returned to the headset and put it back on. "We've tracked your location and sending a welcoming committee as we speak!"

Arkanon knew what that meant and it wasn't welcoming in the slightest. He dropped the headset and signalled for everyone to come to him.

"OK! Things aren't good, we need to leave now!" Arkanon sounded genuinely concerned. "I just don't know a safe enough place for us to go to."

"There's my dad's place!" Jason blurted out. "It's off the grid in the middle of nowhere…As far as I know, no one knows he's there."

"Well, that's as good a suggestion as any," Arkanon said with a smile. "Where is it?…Actually, you know what…There's no time, everyone, grab my hand and Jason…Think of your dad!"

He looked around him, the faint sound of a planes jet engine at high altitude could be heard closing in. *At least,* he thought, *it was a plane.* Then it dawned on him that it wasn't a plane. It was a missile.

"Do it quickly though, Jason—"

His words were cut short as the missile struck the ground and the explosion drowned out his words.

The Nine Lives of an Alley Cat

Somewhere in Central Africa, 18 October 1943.

Ronald Taylor had only been in the army a year when Hitler invaded Poland and World War II began. From then on, he quickly rose through the ranks. His natural talent for shooting helped in some part. He was an exceptional sniper, both as a marksman and as, in the words of his captain at the time, an incredibly stealthy bastard. A phrase that only the Glaswegian accent of his captain could truly portray the true essence of.

Another reason for his rapid rise was his fierce and unflinching loyalty to his unit, likewise his king and country, which didn't go unnoticed. Nor did the nine occasions he'd risked his life to save that of a fallen comrade, all ensured his superiors knew who he was.

By all intents and purposes, by now, he should be dead or at least dead for the sixth time now, technically. Especially, when his exploits meant he narrowly missed landmine explosions, sometimes by inches and some of the most astonishing by their mere bizarre nature, feats of pure luck, ever witnessed on the battlefield. A good example of which being his once saved by a half-empty packet of tissues, an occurrence no one neither could nor wished to try to explain.

This trait of his along with his scruffy and weathered looks, an unfortunate of living in a hole for five days at a time, had earned him the nickname of 'alley cat', a nickname that stuck. But also, because his unit at the time really did think he had nine lives.

Those days seemed like aeons ago now, despite only, in reality, being a matter of weeks, since he'd been reassigned and loaned to the OSS along with his newly assigned spotter. Apparently, the U.S. were short of truly experienced and gifted snipers, so he had been, effectively, loaned to the U.S. army for this rather special mission and now waist-deep in a swamp, deep in the jungle of central Africa.

A sniper's first duty was to press a few days ahead of the rest of the squad to the target destination, dig in, usually in a hole, and gather as much intel as possible. Guard routines, notable additional targets, unusual occurrences, all needed to be made note of ahead of the strike team's arrival.

He'd been both honoured and elated to have been chosen to join the fledgeling OSS. He was even more honoured that the American generals had asked for him by name. Likewise, his newly assigned spotter had also been requested, yet Ronald knew little about him. He'd been sad to leave his former unit as the familiarity of the men in his previous unit also came with a great deal of trust in them too and he had no idea who this new guy was. To make matters worse, this guy so far hadn't uttered a single word and they'd been hiking for three days straight. Granted normal operating procedures, especially when behind enemy lines, called for absolute silence so as not to be detected. But even so, the odd word or two wouldn't have gone amiss. He had to admire his professionalism as a result though.

He began to reminisce about his former unit partly to alleviate the lack of communication but mostly to block out the feeling of the waist-high, oozing, almost gelatine-like and deep tar brown swamp water engulfing his lower extremities. This would be the norm for this last leg of their hike, but it would also be the part of their journey that would take the longest. This was partly due to the very nature of the terrain and also to ensure they weren't spotted by any enemy patrols that may chance by.

He remembered how thankful he'd felt to get beneath tree cover and escape the searing heat that they'd faced as they trekked across almost totally wide-open savannah. But he was now beginning to regret his feelings of relief as they replaced that for high heat and humidity. Yet, it wasn't only their surroundings that were making Ronald uncomfortable. Ever since they were given new orders, mid-mission, towards this new location, he'd developed a bad feeling. Something about this whole mission from then on just didn't feel right. He understood that his U.S. counterparts had received intel that a very level Nazi officer had been spotted in the area. One that, in all likelihood, really had no business being there. Nor should he be there with the bare bones protective detail he'd apparently arrived with, especially given his importance. The Americans were desperate to first, get confirmation of the target's identity and then second, make note of his actions in the area.

Their target, according to them, was none other than Brigadier General Hans Schmidt, aka Hans Komler, the head of the SS black projects division and if it did indeed turn out to be him, this would be a significant win to the allies either as a prisoner or cadaver; taking him out would seriously diminish the Nazis ability to hold their technological advantage.

He looked up at the canopy above him as his legs struggled free from the deep swampland, the trees looked like pillars holding up a leafy green sky. A faint mist hung all around them sticking to their combat gear and gradually ate away at their camouflage paint on their faces.

During the night and early morning hours, their conditions felt almost tolerable, but by late morning and mid-day through to the early evening, the swamp water felt more like being in a bain-marie as it slowly cooked their flesh through their clothes.

It was nightfall when they finally reached their destination, a rare break in the tree cover at a cliff edge. Both men were utterly exhausted and dug in for the night, ready for their task in the morning.

Robes, Torches and Other Suspicious Merchandise

When Ronald awoke, his spotter was already awake, looking through his binoculars. He commando crawled slowly and silently up beside his spotter and gestured for the binoculars. The other man dutifully obliged with a smile and passed them over. Below them was a wide ravine with an equally as wide, slow-flowing river running through the middle, ending in a rough pebble beach on the opposite side. He slowly trained his eyes up the cliff on the other side. But instead of a cliff face, what lay before him was, at the bottom, what looked like a huge entrance, either side of which stood two enormous statues, brandishing equally as large axes that almost looked as though they were standing guard. Their upturned axe heads buried into the ground and their hands rested atop their hilts. From his vantage point, he'd guessed they must both be at least 15 to 20 feet tall and what kind of being they depicted he couldn't tell, but he was certain they weren't human.

As his eyes continued upwards, he noticed balconies and walkways snaking in and out of doorways carved into the rock. Each had a smaller, somewhat less detailed statue guarding them. The top of the cliff was covered in grassland and a stark contrast to their side. He couldn't help let out a gasp of surprise.

"I know," his spotter whispered in a thick, southern Irish accent, "that was exactly my reaction too!"

"So, a Mick then?" Ronald said with an equal amount of surprise.

"Ah! A racist then?" the man replied. "The name is Seamus…Seamus Carmichael."

He held his hand out to shake Ronald's and was relieved when it was accepted.

"Ronald…Ronald Taylor," Taylor replied with a smile, his eyes remaining firmly fixed on the scene in front of him.

"What the fuck have we stumbled across here?" Seamus asked, a thin veil of concern hung in his inquiring tone.

"Good question?" Ronald passed the binoculars back to Seamus, who continued to recon the area.

Seamus turned over onto his back and closed his eyes. "Maybe they'd gone off course somewhere, as this couldn't be the target area, surely?"

He was just about to check his map when Seamus gestured, he saw movement on the cliff top and was horrified to discover it was the strike team, they were early.

He reached to Seamus' large pack, opening it up to reveal a radio and was just about to demand an explanation from HQ when Seamus gestured, he'd spotted movement on the beach.

Ronald scrambled for his rifle and looked down his scope, first at the strike team readying their equipment as they prepared to abseil down, then to the beach. Near to the water's edge were two robed figures that almost resembled monks. But something was just extremely off about the pair of them. It was the way they moved almost gliding around the beach and there seemed to be an odd, very deep green glow emanating from within their hoods. He knew he'd have to make a decision and fast, monk or no monk, they could alert whatever was residing within the cliff monastery. Worse still, the strike team were unaware of their presence on the beach. In that instance, he decided it would be best to take them out.

"I'm taking the shot," he said with certainty to Seamus. "Calculate range, son, we've gotta act fast."

Seamus looked through his rangefinder and rapidly calculated the distance to the two monks on the beach.

"The one on your left is closest, 600 yards, no wind."

Ronald trained his sights on the monk's head and as he was gently squeezing the trigger, the monk suddenly turned its head towards him almost as if it knew he was there and just in time for the strike team to begin their descent down the cliff. The monk's eyes flashed bright green just as Ronald's shot rang out and the bullet hurtled towards his target. Immediately, Ronald began to line his sights up with the second monk, not noticing the first monk vanishing the split second before the bullet hit and sending its robes spiralling through the air,

"Miss!" Seamus shouted in confusion. "You missed!"

"What the fuck!" Ronald exclaimed, equally as confused "That shot hit! How the fuck did it miss?"

"I don't know? He just..." Seamus paused for a second, he knew he was going to sound crazy, but it was what he saw. "He just vanished!"

"What do you mean he just vanished?"

"I mean that one minute he was there...the next he was gone! You know...Vanished!"

"You must've been mistaken, he can't have vanished."

Ronald took his eyes off his other target to check Seamus hadn't missed its body falling somewhere. Yet, when he looked...nothing. Frantically, he searched the immediate vicinity for any signs of a body. But there wasn't one. By this point, the other monk had thrown off its robes and vanished just in time for Seamus to catch it doing so in his sights. He was dumbstruck!

How is that possible? he thought to himself just as a frantic Seamus was slapping then punching his arm to get his attention.

"What?" Seamus bellowed, taking his eyes from his sights.

But Seamus didn't get a chance to answer him, as the sounds of an ear-splitting and unnatural roar accompanied by the sounds of splitting and then falling rock, reverberated around the ravine.

This caused the first members of the strike team that had now reached the bottom of the cliff to freeze to the spot. Seamus immediately trained his sights on the location of the doorway in the cliff just in time to see the second of the huge statues sheds it's rocky skin and revealing an enormous reaper high guard beneath.

Its massive jaws widened as it let out a huge roar of its own. Its quill-like spines in its head quivered and shook giving off a rattlesnake like sound as it slowly sank onto all fours, placing its axe on its back and charged towards the strike team.

Both Ronald and Seamus were too dumbstruck by what they were seeing unfolding in front of them that they completely forgot that there were two of these monsters. It wasn't until the other was waist-deep in the river and heading in their direction that they remembered only to look at it just in time to witness it spin once, then twice, it's axe held flat and edge at its side, then on the third spin, it let go of it sending it spinning and hurtling straight at them. Its loud whooshing sound getting increasingly louder the closer it got and the two men, just realising what was happening, had just enough time to cover their heads and pray as the axe splintered the trees around them with a deafening crack.

Both of them looked up as the men at the bottom of the ravine were being easily ripped to pieces by the other high guard. Their body parts and blood being thrown in all directions. The other half of the strike team, still making their descent went into a blind panic. Some opted to continue down as the high guard paced up and down below them, its jaws snapping as it growled. The second one had begun to make its way towards them also, its axe seeming to materialise in its outstretched hand as it slowly walked through the water.

Both, Ronald and Seamus, assumed that the monster had thought they were dead and decided this was the best time to make a hasty and somewhat safe retreat. They both stood up quickly and turned to run. Seamus had just got a few yards ahead and looked to see where Ronald was only to see him reach back to pick up his rifle from the ground.

"Are you fucking mad?" Seamus screamed terrified. "Leave your god damn rifle."

"I can't," Ronald screamed back. "It's my lucky rif—"

Before he could finish that sentence, he was stopped by the sight of a reaper high mage materialising in front of him. A demonic hiss coming from beneath its metallic black, skull-shaped facemask, its eyes glowing a bright green. In a split second, it'd reached behind it and drawn its sword from its back, sliced up and replaced its sword in the sheath in its back all before Ronald had time to comprehend what was happening. Seamus stopped and looked back in horror just as Ronald turned to face him, a paper-thin, blood-red line stretched up his body, a look of bemused pain struck his face. Then in an instant, the left side of Ronald suddenly slid down the line as the right side went limp and collapsed away from the rest of his body, the reaper high mage turned its back and vanished.

Seamus turned and ran; he knew instantly Ronald was gone. There was nothing he could do for him. The screams from the strike team too were dying down now and he knew he couldn't do anything for them either. So, he ran. He had to getaway.

First Impressions Never Go Well

Seamus Carmichael had been running for, what seemed to him, hours. His lungs burned from overwork as his third stitch began its attack. His legs were like jelly and in no mood to stay under him. To make matters worse, it was virtually pitch black in the jungle and every few feet, the moist and rotting foliage grasped at his feet, as vines curved around his ankles like fingers and eventually, with a yank, they finally brought him down.

He cried out with surprise as his body connected loudly with the waterlogged ground. Stagnant, black water splashed high into the air, landing on his body and covering it in an acrid smelling goop. The impact severely winded him causing him to instinctively gasp for air nearly filling his lungs with the festering liquid. Immediately, he yanked his head from the water, coughing and spluttering, the black swamp water ejecting from his lungs as he desperately tried to expel every drop of the suffocating liquid.

Desperately, he fought for breath to feed his limp muscles, but it was hopeless; fatigue had made its home in his body and it was there to stay.

He scanned the area for a hiding place and spotted, within the gloom, a hole in a large tree, big enough to fit himself in. He quietly and quickly crawled the ten or so feet to the sanctuary and crawled inside.

In the distance, though faint, he could hear gunfire, screams, falling trees and explosions. There's no way the strike team could've made it to this position, so who were they? He tried to ascertain what nationality these men may have been? But he couldn't make out any words or at least ones he recognised. Whoever they were, at least they were putting up a fight.

These sounds were getting louder though and he knew they were coming his way. The closer they got, the more he could make out and it became obvious they were speaking English or rather American English. He listened closely to try and determine who they were and why they were here.

"Sir, why's it so dark all of a sudden and what were those things?"

He heard one, young sounding voice enquire before an older voice told him to be quiet. *It was a legitimate question,* Seamus thought, he wondered the same thing.

"Yeah, but sir—" the voice whispered only to have his superior order him to be quiet again.

They'd heard something. He was fairly sure it wasn't him they heard, so who or what was it? He'd not heard his pursuers from the monastery for a while, so it couldn't be them, could it? Surely not.

But then he heard the screams, followed by the unmistakable sound of those huge beasts roaring and the whoosh, whoosh, whoosh from their massive axes as they spun through the air past his position and splintering trees as they went by. These sounds were followed by terrified screams and the sounds of the axes severing flesh and lifeless body parts hitting the swampy ground beneath them. A few seconds later, his attention was grabbed by the sounds of loud and very heavy footsteps splashing through the swamp outside his hiding place. Quickly, he held his breath as he could hear one of those beasts sniffing the air.

But as he listened harder, he could also pick out a faint rustling through the tree canopy above him. It was as if something was following them, jumping from treetop to treetop and very quickly too. It was also getting a lot closer to his position.

He heard the thud merely feet away from his position as it landed right across from him followed by a few footsteps and a long sniffing as it smelt the air, searching out its prey. He carefully peered out the hole he was in and...nothing. There was nothing there. Yet, he could hear it breathing. Then he spotted it, its faint outline shimmered as its glowing green eyes gave away its position whilst it stood up. Its attention had obviously been taken by those other men. It crouched again just as the unmistakable sound of one of those massive axes cut down the trees around him followed by the other of those massive high guards thundered past.

He could hear screams in terror and calls for a retreat coming from the men followed by shouts of 'get down' and 'incoming'. He wondered what the other being was waiting for. It was only when he could hear the men coming his way that he knew it was an ambush. He had to warn them, but how? If he moved, he'd surely be killed, but at least they might survive or have a better chance of surviving. He could try and fight but his body was too exhausted to effectively move let alone put up some sort of attack. He could see the mud beneath its feet being pushed back as it dug the balls of its feet into the ground ready to pounce. Then in a split second and with barely a sound, it leapt into the air, mud splattering down from its feet.

"Get down!" a male voice boomed, in an accent different from those other men. "Get down now!" it boomed again.

This was followed by a loud scraping sound of metal against metal followed by a loud grunt as if someone was putting a great deal of effort into something. Then that familiar whoosh, of one of those axes coming towards him rapidly followed by a splat, then the crunch of splintering bone and the screams of extreme pain coming from the being that had leapt away from his position. Suddenly, he could see one of those massive axes flying past, a trail of thick black blood, dripping from its blades quickly followed by a section of the top part of the invisible attacker barrel-rolled and bounced along the ground in front of him. Its black, skull-shaped face mask seemingly staring lifelessly at him.

What the fuck just happened? he thought to himself as he remained stock still in shock. Whatever had done this had to be extremely powerful to wield that axe and throw it like they had. Whoever they were must surely be of similar size and therefore not human.

"You men over, there," the voice boomed again, "Yes you! Get that big guy's attention so I can get the drop on him." This voice didn't fit the image he had in his mind of his rescuer. If anything, it sounded normal.

Maybe there's more than one of them? he thought to himself. *Though why would it say I need to get the drop on him if there was more than one?*

Seamus was baffled and against his better judgement fuelled mostly by intense curiosity, he felt compelled to take a look outside of his hiding place.

Keeping as low as he could and moving as slowly and quietly as he could, Seamus ventured out, his eyes gradually adjusting to the oily blackness of the jungle in front of him. After a little while, he could just about make out the three silhouettes of what remained of the other squad. In front of them was the unmistakable shape of one of those huge beasts. The men suddenly scattered in all directions as the beast closed in on them as they turned and fired their rifles to its direction. To its right, a brief blur caught his attention and he couldn't keep his eyes off it.

Whatever it was, it left the ground leaping 40 feet into the air. He knew this had to be their rescuer, though it's similar looking armour to that of their attackers made him cautious. It looked different enough though as instead of being jet black, it seemed to be a bright blue and green that shifted in and out of each other. It's shifting pattern causing his eyes to lose track of it somehow and it was only after it effortlessly launched itself downwards off a tree towards that huge beast that he got a clear view of it. It was just in time too to witness it pulling its arm back and produce an arcing violet coloured energy wave along its whole arm that it thrust out in a large curved beam in front of it. The beam cutting through the gaping jaws of the beast taking off the top of its massive skull, leaving the bottom of its jaw and tongue flapping in the air, a fountain of blood spraying skywards as its lifeless body dropped with a loud thud onto the ground. The men cheered as their rescuer landed in front of its kill, prompting them to instinctively run towards him.

However, their celebrations were short-lived as the remaining beast's huge axe spun through the air and severed the heads of two of the three men, the last of them managing to duck at the last second and avoid death.

He barely heard the beast doubling back around him and beginning to stealthily crawl past him again. It was staying as low to the ground as it could get and trying to make as little sound as possible and for its size was surprisingly little. Seamus lay perfectly still as a giant clawed hand lightly landed on the ground just beside his head as the huge beast made its way slowly past him, its deep red eyes glowed dimly illuminating its face a little, the light bouncing off its massive teeth. He glanced around with just his eyes for some means of escape and one that might give him time to warn the others. However, something else caught his eye.

Ambushes Are a Dime a Dozen

Seamus saw something in front of him that, if he timed it right, could slow the monster down at the very least and give him time to escape too. It was that smaller being's sword. It was only a few feet away, just a quick roll, maybe two. But he didn't have enough time to ponder on this decision, he just had to do it. As quickly and quietly as he could, he rapidly rolled between its front and back legs and then forwards, hand outstretched, narrowly stopping it from falling to the ground as he tightly grasped its hilt. The beast's back leg landed just a couple of feet from him as he carefully unsheathed the sword and using all his strength, he sprung himself towards the beast, striking out sideways with the sword. Its blade cut straight through what Seamus assumed was its Achilles tendon, causing it to snap violently up its leg.

The beast screamed out in both surprise and agony as it fell to the ground. With its tendon cut, it was unable to put weight on its leg causing it to stumble. It quickly swung its massive head round behind it as it swiped backwards with its huge front claw narrowly missing Seamus by millimetres.

Adrenaline coursed through Seamus' body and with a roar, he bounded up its back, spring boarded off it and leapt into the air. He raised the sword above his head angling it downwards. As he landed back down between its huge shoulder blades, he rammed the sword down, as hard as he could, into its eye as it looked up and plunged it in up to its hilt. Its eye loudly popped followed by a loud crunch as the blade punctured the roof of its mouth and continued down its throat. The beast loudly gurgled and spluttered, its blood filling its lungs as Seamus wrenched the sword from its eye socket as he lost balance, fell forward, then instinctively curled into a forward roll and landed on the ground. The surviving member of the other team cheered at the spectacle in front of him. Their rescuer, however; reacted by charging headlong at Seamus, his arm reaching back as he began to attack.

Did he see him as a potential threat? Seamus thought as he prepared for the worst. *Well, this is it then. At least I got to take out that beast before I died!*

He closed his eyes just as their rescuer was a few feet away. "Make it quick!" he shouted, feeling resolute and dropped to his knees.

But instead of his expected death, he heard the man leaping over his head just as the supposedly dead beast reared up ready to bite down on Seamus. Their armoured rescuer flicked out his hand, a blade materialising from nowhere in his hand just as he thrust it forward and effortlessly took off the beast's head, a large fountain of thick black blood shooting into the air.

"Fuck me!" Seamus said to himself, dumbstruck. "That bastard nearly had me."

Their rescuer seemingly floated to the ground slowly clapping. He appeared to be genuinely impressed as he laughed. "Well done, my boy, not a bad effort!" he said with a friendly tone and full of praise. "But always remember to take off their head from now on! They have a tendency to get back up otherwise!"

"Er…Thanks!" Seamus replied politely if a little confused.

"My name is Arkanon," he said as his feet reached the ground. "It's been a long time since I've seen someone who was able or willing to take out a high guard… What's your name boy?"

Seamus felt a little offended being referred to as a boy, but in politeness, he decided to answer this strange being. "Seamus…Seamus Carmichael."

He couldn't help be a little awestruck by Arkanon's armour that despite the similar look to their attacker's was less demonic-looking and the bright sapphire blue colouring, seemed to make mix and coalesce with the jade green colouring almost resembling oil on water. His eyes glowed a bright and vibrant violet colour that quickly dimmed as he removed his helmet.

Arkanon's blonde hair cascaded around his shoulders as he stared at Seamus with bright aquamarine eyes.

"Now then…With the formalities out of the way…" Arkanon's tone was a little less friendly now, "Do you mind telling me what the fuck you're doing here?"

Actually...Second Impressions Aren't Much Better

Carmichael family farm, Kerry, Ireland, 15 June 1995, 06:03 am.

Seamus Carmichael hadn't seen his son in over ten years and as far as he was concerned, he wasn't ever going to again. Yet here he was, walking up the driveway to his farm out of the blue. He'd this farm just outside of Kerry, Ireland since before Jason was born and was seriously regretting not selling up when he had the chance years ago. At least, he could've avoided this awkward feeling he was getting right now.

He didn't know whether to hug him or hit him and who was his other four companions. Two of them looked like African men, one was a very attractive woman, he let his eyes linger on her for a little longer than felt comfortable and he couldn't quite make out the third man with him, who was that? He found his attention unavoidably drawn to this man as he seemed to be purposefully trying to avoid his gaze. Seamus leaned forward, shielding his eyes from the sun as he stood up and walked down the steps of his front porch.

Jason and his company had got halfway up his driveway before Seamus realised who the other guy was. The trouble is he didn't want to believe it.

"No!" he said angrily under his breath. "It can't be him! He'd never shown his face here surely. Jason can't have got himself involved with him."

He strained his eyes as the fifth of them got closer. Jason waved to greet him and ushered his friends forward towards his father. To his surprise, the young attractive woman rushed towards him smiling and hugged him. She started saying something to him, but he wasn't listening; he was too busy seething something the young lady hadn't actually noticed. Jason was lagging trying to usher that fourth man up the drive, virtually pushing the reluctant guy up to his father.

"You!" Seamus boomed. "You've got a lot of nerve coming here!"

Jason looked confused as Arkanon attempted to hide behind one of the African gentlemen, did his dad know Arkanon somehow?

"Arkanon! You son of a bitch! I know it's you!" Seamus barked angrily.

Apparently, he did know Arkanon.

Seamus began to hobble quickly in Arkanon's direction. His cane clicking heavily on the gravel and gathering pace. Jason was just thinking to himself that for a guy well into his 70s, his father could sure move as Arkanon slowly edged backwards, protesting his innocence and desperately in vain to talk the ageing Seamus around, his hands outstretched and waving frantically. But Seamus was having none of it as he began to curse at Arkanon angrily in Gaelic to which Arkanon responded also in Gaelic. Jason began to wonder what it could've been that Arkanon could've done.

"Evening, chaps," Seamus, unnervingly, sounded genuinely friendly all of a sudden as he reached the two shamans. "It is very nice to meet you and all, but if you would be so kind as to excuse me?"

The two shamans nodded and smiled as they stepped aside, bowing as they did so and allowed Seamus to pass through the middle of them.

"Thank you, gentlemen," Seamus said, again he was unnervingly pleasant as he passed by.

Arkanon took this sudden friendliness to be a sign that Seamus was, at last, coming round and foolishly stopped walking backwards and outstretched his arms for a possible friendly hug. Jason, however, knew better and could see this strange change in character, for what it was, a ruse. This, to Jason, meant two, possibly three things were at play here:

1) His father was absolutely furious, seething in fact. It meant he was that special kind of mad that only came from decades of pent-up rage if he was suddenly friendly.

2) That being the case, Arkanon must have done something truly unforgettable because it was absolutely unforgivable, which he'd never imagined could be the case between his father and this man that, in all fairness, he'd only known less than 72 hours.

3) His reaction to the shaman meant that he'd likely finally got over his racism at last.

How the hell did Arkanon know his father? How long had they known each other even? Though he assumed Arkanon couldn't have known his father that well if he was falling for his friendly routine. But as soon as Seamus had passed the shamans and resumed his angry assault in Gaelic, Jason saw the sudden realisation and memory recall flood across Arkanon's face. Apparently, he knew him enough to at least remember that his father did this when incensed, so he knew him pretty well.

However, either Arkanon had forgotten what always came next, or; more likely assumed that the ageing Seamus was too old and frail-looking to do what came next.

How wrong he was?

The instant Arkanon let his guard down looking to the floor and shaking his head, he'd made a critical error assuming the cane Seamus was using was to aid his weary legs. Nothing could be further from the truth and Jason knew it. Sadly, Arkanon didn't and Jason wasn't going to be given any time to warn him about it either as the surprisingly fit and spry for his age Seamus leapt into the air drawing the cane back that had now gone from walking aid to effective bludgeon in a nanosecond. As his body checked a surprised and bemused Arkanon from the air, he brought the cane down and wrapped it around his head as he knocked him to the ground. Seamus instantly straddled the now very shocked Arkanon on the ground and proceeded to first strike the shaft of the cane repeatedly back and forth across the sides of Arkanon's head and with an impressive amount of force too. Then after around 30 or so blows, he changed to slamming the end of the cane over and over again into the front of Arkanon's face.

All this happened in a matter of seconds and it was only after Jason recognised the anguished and rage-fuelled screams coming from his father as he continued his assault that Jason could free himself from his shock.

"Dad!" Jason pleaded. "Dad! stop!…That's enough!…Dad! You're gonna kill him for fuck's sake!"

Alarmingly, all Seamus did in response to his son's plead was laugh, a murderous and maniacal grin extended across his face.

Tyler, also shaking off the shock, began pleading with him too! Both of them were getting increasingly concerned about Arkanon's wellbeing. Though judging by the jelly-like condition of his head, by this point, the prognosis didn't look good. His shamanic companions, on the other hand, didn't seem quite so concerned as they were. They appeared to be decidedly unphased by what could potentially be the murder of what they'd thought was a dear friend. They were so nonchalant about this whole ordeal unfolding before them that they were laughing and joking in their own language. It even appeared to Jason that they were actually joking about what was happening as they pointed and gestured with their hands about something before erupting into loud, roaring laughter.

Jason was horrified by this behaviour. He knew their cultures were different, but he was sure that helping a friend by stopping their murder would be kind of universal. He rushed towards his father, he had to stop him.

"Dad, stop!" Jason shouted. "I think you killed him."

"Mr Carmichael?" Tyler said softly. "He ain't breathing, hunny!"

"Not...breathing...Ha!" Seamus said dismissively as he continued his sentence between swings, "He's...not...dead...He...can't...die!"

At last, he stopped and rose to his feet. A satisfied smile like that of a job well done built gradually across his face.

"Sweetie," Tyler continued, "You basically turned his head into paste! I don't think he's ever gonna get up from that."

Jason walked cautiously over to his father, who was staring down at Arkanon's corpse. He took out a cigar and lit it just as Jason placed his hand on his shoulder to guide him away.

"You gonna explain things or am I?" Seamus waited a moment for a response before continuing when he failed to receive one. "He'll be fine, just you watch...His head will patch itself together in no time, eh, you fuckin' drama queen."

Jason and Tyler looked at each other like Seamus had finally lost the plot, which hadn't gone unnoticed by Seamus. He gave Arkanon's body a kick.

"Get up, you lazy arsehole," he said frustrated, "before these two fuckers put me in the loony bin! Just show 'em what I mean."

To their amazement, Arkanon thrust his arm in the air and gave Seamus a thumbs up.

"See!" he said, now feeling the full effects of exhaustion, now his adrenaline had worn off.

"You done then?" Arkanon said, feeling a little embarrassed. Seamus nodded. "Good...Thank fuck for that! Can we get pissed? Oh! I take it we're even now?"

"Come on then. I've got a nice malt somewhere in the house...Oh! And no, we're not even yet. Not by a long shot. But that was a good start."

Arkanon sighed and held his hand out for Seamus to help him up on his feet. Seamus obliged to a rousing round of applause by the two shamans.

"You men drink whiskey?" Seamus asked them as he made his way back to his house. The two gentlemen nodded eagerly as they followed him and Arkanon. The four of them talking like old friends as if nothing had happened.

Tyler and Jason looked at each other, utterly bemused until Jason couldn't resist the compulsion to say what they both were thinking.

"What the fuck just happened?"

Eavesdroppers Are Always Disappointed

Jason Carmichael stood with his ear pressed against the porch door of his father's house listening intently. On the other side, he could hear the hushed tones of his father and Arkanon deep in a very heated discussion. Behind him through the narrow hallway to the kitchen were the loud voices of Tyler and Arkanon's two shaman friends in the midst of playing a drinking game. The smell of Irish whiskey filtered in the air and he couldn't help but wonder how alcohol seemed to be a universal language on account of the Shaman not speaking any English, yet they could follow the rules of a drinking game perfectly well. He just wished they didn't have to be loud as they were making it extremely difficult to hear what was being said on the other side of the door.

"You know she…" he could hear his father snap in a hushed hiss before it was drowned out by yet another cheer.

"I tried…You know I tried but…" Arkanon replied, clearly upset and in an equally as hushed tone.

This was followed by angry murmurs from both parties that were gradually getting more and more heated. All he could glean from the obvious argument that followed were lots of swearing in Gaelic from his father and quite apologetic tones from Arkanon interspersed with instances of something not being his fault and his not knowing about something or other that he couldn't quite make out and ended by, "Fuck you! You shapeshifting undead son of a bitch!" coming angrily from his father followed by, "I need a fucking drink…You want one?"

Jason barely had time to take his head away from the door and stand, supposedly, nonchalantly against the wall before his father ripped the door open and stomped past.

"And if you're gonna listen at the door, boy," he growled at Jason, "at least do it quietly…That conversation wasn't for you! Now, where's that friggin' whiskey? I need a stiff one."

Jason couldn't believe he'd been caught. He was just about to apologise when Arkanon placed his hand on his shoulder and stopped him.

"I need to talk to you if you don't mind?" he said calmly.

Jason nodded and stepped out into the porch. The low setting sun caught his eyes and for a moment he remembered how beautiful his father's farm looked. It'd been so long since he'd been there and he'd not really had a chance to get used to being there again since they'd arrived. Arkanon sat down in one of the deckchairs and beckoned for him to sit beside him.

"I gotta ask," Jason said abruptly. "But how the hell do you and my dad know each other? And why's he so pissed at you?"

Arkanon smiled. He knew this question was going to come up.

"I and your father go back a long way," Arkanon began with a nostalgic air. "We were...we are...best friends! We just had a disagreement about the time you were born, as it happens!"

Jason looked shocked and a little apprehensive as to what Arkanon was going to say next. Arkanon saw this in him and laughed.

"Don't worry, I'm not about to announce I'm actually your father..." Jason let out a deep and long sigh of relief as Arkanon looked his square in the eye with a straight face. "That's for your father to tell you, not me!"

Jason went white as a sheet. Arkanon kept his gaze on Jason's eyes and all of a sudden, Jason thought he might actually be serious. Suddenly, Arkanon roared into laughter.

"The look on your face is a picture," he said between bouts of laughter. "Hey, Seamus... You were right! He really will believe anything."

Seamus Carmichael stepped out into the porch with three shot glasses and three cigars and in an equal amount of laughter as Arkanon. Jason was failing to see the joke, which wasn't lost on the other two men who found this fact even funnier.

"He doesn't look happy, does he, Ark buddy?" Seamus said as he began to calm his laughter.

"I gotta say," Arkanon replied, "no, he doesn't!"

Both men looked at Jason, who was feeling a little ganged up on by this point.

"Don't take it to heart, son," Seamus looked at Jason and winked, "We knew you were listening and decided to teach you a lesson!"

"Ha ha!" Jason was clearly unimpressed. "Well, you got me! So, are either of you gonna tell me what the hell is going here? How do you two know each other?"

Seamus and Arkanon looked at each other as if mentally assessing whether or not to clue him in or not before quite organically, Seamus started things off.

"I've known Ark since my World War II days," he said with a reminiscent smile. "We've been through so many operations together with the U.S. and U.K. forces. But Ark and I were like a kinda permanent fixture."

"I wouldn't go anywhere, on any mission without your father," Arkanon chimed in. "He's the only person I've met since a long time ago that's ever killed a high guard, I needed him to train others to do the same."

Jason was stunned.

"So, my dad killed what…What's a high guard?" Jason didn't know whether to be stunned, proud or both. But then he also had no idea what the hell they were talking about.

"Remember that big fucker?" Arkanon said matter-of-factly. "The one with the massive teeth that nearly made two of you?"

Jason nodded not completely taking in what Arkanon just asked.

"Wait…" then it dawned on him, "you're saying that my dad?"

"Yep!" Arkanon replied.

"He actually took out one of those massive…things?" Jason continued in disbelief.

"Not just one either!" Seamus butted in with a smile and nod towards Arkanon.

"Woah!…" Jason couldn't believe what he was hearing.

Seamus poured a whiskey into a glass and passed it to Jason, who immediately downed it in one go without batting an eyelid before shaking the glass for another. Seamus obliged with a chuckle, then poured one for himself and one for Arkanon.

"Sláinte mhaith," Seamus said with a smile and held out his glass.

"Sláinte mhaith," replied Jason and Arkanon as they connected glasses with a 'chink' before each of them downed their shots.

"So, when did you last see each other?"

"Well, it really was not long after you were born," Arkanon said lowering his head. He knew what was coming next.

"So, why'd you t—" Jason suddenly found that question shot down from an angry snap from his father.

"That's not for your ears, boy!" This obviously was a very touchy subject for his father. "Best you don't bring this up!"

Jason looked at the stern look in his father's eye, but his curiosity got the best of him and he was just about to insist on an explanation when his father butted in,

"Especially seeing as we're getting on so well," Jason could tell that this was something neither his father nor Arkanon wanted to revisit with him and concluded it best to ask some other time.

The three men sat in silence for a few minutes, the sounds of laughter coming from the kitchen and the sounds of passing planes overhead, the only sounds to break the silence.

Seamus passed out the cigars and lit each one at their mouths before asking, "So, what's brought you here? What he is going on?"

It took a while for Arkanon and Jason to explain what had happened to them and how they'd discovered that the U.S., too brass, had been compromised. Seamus slumped in his seat. In some way, he'd always knew this would happen. The U.S. and U.K. military had become too greedy and secretive when it came to the reapers and their artefacts. He really could see that is coming.

"Well, you guys can stay here for as long as is necessary," Seamus said insistently.

"Thanks, Dad."

"So, what now? I suppose you're gonna have to find out what exactly they know."

Arkanon nodded in agreement.

"But who is there inside the U.S. forces we can trust?" Arkanon didn't mind admitting he was at a loss here. "If the reapers have gotten that far in, who knows how much higher up they've got or how much they know."

"You mean Hoth?" Seamus sounded genuinely worried. This made Jason equally as concerned.

"You don't think they'll try and let him loose, do you?" Jason looked to Arkanon for reassurance. He wasn't going to get it.

"From what I've been able to ascertain, there's been an expeditionary force looking for something in Antarctica and I can only draw one conclusion as to why they're there."

"Shit!" Jason sighed as his father poured him another drink. He downed it quickly. "So, where does that leave us?"

"Well, I'm guessing it's only a matter of time before they find Hoth. So, it's pointless trying to prevent that!" Jason couldn't believe what he was hearing from Arkanon.

"I'm sorry," Jason snapped angrily, "but aren't you some all-powerful godlike entity? Can't you just stop them from releasing him?"

"Sadly, no…" this was clearly something of an embarrassment for Arkanon, "His release had been foretold millennia ago…I've got no power over it! I'm unable to prevent it from occurring!"

Jason was stunned. How was this even possible? How was he unable to prevent that yet able to do practically everything else he could think of?

"What I do know and what we can stop…" Arkanon continued, with a more hopeful tone to his voice. "When Hoth is released, he will need to make a sacrifice, partly to gain strength and also to open his first key—"

"His first key?" Jason wasn't sure if he wanted to hear the answer to this question.

"Hoth's whole reason for being released," Seamus continued for Arkanon, "is to open three spiritual locks in order to open a gateway for his boss to come through…"

"Sounds like something out of a bad horror movie or Stephen King novel," Jason joked, trying to lighten the mood. Only to be treated by stern looks from his father and Arkanon.

"Except it isn't." Seamus snapped. "This is reality and the sacrifice he has to make to open these gates…Well, it involves a lot of souls being taken at the same time!"

"How many souls?" Jason was really worried now.

"Hundreds…maybe thousands," Arkanon said with a sigh. "We just don't know where he'll make the first sacrifice or even how. But I think that the U.S. intelligence or military probably does."

"So, you need to find a way in?" Seamus added, "Can anyone in there be trusted? Is there anyone at all you might be able to lean on?"

The three of them fell silent as they thought. The silence was broken by a slightly drunk and very chipper Tyler staggering through the open door.

"I'm sorry guys," she began as she drunkenly fell onto Jason's lap with a giggle, "I couldn't help overhearing but…I know just the man…General Casey McCann…Hey, that rhymes!"

"Ah…McCann!" Arkanon and Seamus said in unison. As if they'd forgotten a long-lost friend. Jason once again was lost as he was the only one who didn't know who they were on about.

"Who's Casey McCann?" he said inquisitively.

Seamus sat back in his chair and smiled.

"He's another old friend of ours, son and possibly our best chance at getting in. He might be a bit…shall we say…standoffish? But don't hold that against him…He's a good sort!"

"He's probably one of the best strategists I know," Arkanon chimed in, "and fiercely loyal. A great leader and his men will follow him no matter what. We really could do with someone like him on the side? It'd really help even things up… Seeing as it looks as though we've got the entire U.S. armed forces against us right now."

"So, how do we approach this then?" Jason felt they were getting somewhere at last. "What do we need to do to convince him?"

Arkanon just slyly smiled. He'd just thought of the perfect plan.

Part 5: Unavoidable and Unwanted Reintroductions

Welcoming Foreign Dignitaries

Antarctica, U.S. and U.K. joint scientific research base, 12 July 1999.

Dr Eldwin Pierce was nervous as he waited on the helicopter pad for the Antarctic base that he was scientific director of. This was one of the biggest scientific research stations, outside of the main research stations on the coast and also had the prestige of being the furthest outpost inland. It was also one of the most secrets too. As a result, it also had a large military presence there too. On the outside, the outpost just consisted of a couple of temporary metallic containers that were converted into living spaces and a lab. But the actual base was nearly two miles below the ice sheet and a least a mile below ground.

Be hated being outside, it was not only freezing cold but due to their location was beset by regular white-out blizzards, which made visibility a constant nightmare and ensured that along with the regular thermal and below freezing protective gear, you were also forced to wear facial protection too.

This was a particularly miserable affair when you were an overweight individual such as Pierce as he was prone to sweating and in these conditions, sweat freezes. This made the already hour-long wait Pierce had had torturous and he was desperate to get back below ground.

The person he was here to greet, however, was well worth the torture he was putting himself through in his view. Today, he was going to meet his hero of the scientific field, Dr Hans Schmidt, who was making a surprise visit to his very station. The reason for this unannounced and very perilous visit was the discovery that Pierce's team had made only 36 hours prior.

Ever since the end of World War II, the U.S. and U.K. military had become obsessed with finding certain ancient relics. More specifically, something they called reaper relics. These were immensely valuable to both governments and many of them had been found mainly in the form of some kind of armour and

Pierce had even found a few specimens over his career, but what he had found under the Antarctic ice trumped anything he'd discovered before.

As the chopper made its difficult landing, Pierce slowly edged towards it to greet his hero. Dr Schmidt exited the vehicle, his head held low as he greeted Dr Pierce with a friendly smile. Pierce couldn't help be struck by how young Hans looked, especially for a guy supposedly in his 80s. He was still extremely blonde, his face still had chiselled features with his skin still quite tight looking and cleanly shaven. The only other indication of his apparent age was the thick lens he had in his glasses. So, he still showed a tiny bit of age, but if Pierce didn't know any better, he'd assume that Schmidt was only in his mid to late fifties at best.

The two men waited until they were out of the weather and safely inside one of the containers before unzipping their arctic coats and they were able to at last talk.

"May I just say, Dr Schmidt," Pierce began in a slight Brooklyn accent, "it is an honour to meet you. I've been an admirer of your work for many years and—"

Hans cut the man short. He wasn't a fan of pleasantries nor fawning fan service. He was all business and eager to see if what the message that brought him had said was indeed true. "Tell me exactly what it is that you have found here, Dr Pierce?" Hans' tone was cold and official.

He looked Dr Pierce up and down as he spoke with a slight sneer. Pierce's balding short-cropped black hair reflected the light from the container's roof as they approached a small panel on the wall.

"Of course, Dr Schmidt…If you'll excuse me for one second," Pierce said nervously as he placed his hand on the panel and placed his eye against another slightly higher up. Two fine purple-coloured beams scanned both his eye and his palm before the floor shook below them almost knocking Hans over and then it slowly began to descend.

"Forty-eight hours ago, a team taking horizontal core samples of some of the deepest layers of ice," Pierce began, trying to sound as professional as possible, "they hit something around 30 feet into that ice sheet, which mangled the drill yet also left an almost crystalline substance on the end. After taking some laser drilling equipment to the area and cutting around it, we found something…well… something extraordinary!"

Pierce smiled excitedly. Hans just stared at him unemotional and signalled for the man to continue.

"Well, I think it's something you need to witness for yourself, Dr Schmidt," Pierce continued with the same degree of excitement. "My words truly won't do it justice. But I believe we've found the finest example of complete and most well-preserved reaper specimens yet found."

This seemed to pique Dr Schmidt's interest, though Pierce couldn't be totally sure. The elevator lights gently reflected their rhythmic bars upwards along with his glasses, obscuring his eyes a little. But Pierce was certain he could detect a slight eyebrow raise from Schmidt at that point.

"Very good, Dr Pierce," Hans said again with the same cold professionalism. "How long until I am able to see the specimen for myself?"

"Oh, I think we can arrange for you to inspect it right away!"

Pierce smiled eagerly awaiting some sort of acknowledgement or positive feedback from Hans. To his disappointment, he received neither. All he got was a nod.

The two men remained silent the remainder of the three-minute journey down the elevator until they reached the bottom with a loud thud. The large metal doors opened to a busy looking ice domed tunnel that appeared to stretch on for miles. Bright floodlights on stands illuminated the tunnel every few feet or so and faintly melted the ice around them.

"If you'd like to follow me, Dr Schmidt?" Pierce asked.

"Thank you, Dr Pierce, lead the way."

The two men walked hurriedly down the tunnel and still in an awkward feeling silence. Pierce gestured for Hans to turn left down a corridor branching off and after a five-minute walk, they entered into a huge room that had been carved out the ice full of scientific equipment with scientists running around nervously and all under the watchful eye of heavily armed military men dressed in black camo gear and black berets. On the far wall was what Hans had come here for and his journey certainly wasn't for nought.

Encased still in a fairly thick layer of ice was an enormous looking being. It was wearing very intricate and golden looking armour, that was unmistakably reaper in origin but unlike anything, he'd seen before. It was at least ten feet in height and very broad and muscular looking, but what intrigued Hans the most was its lack of helmet and its apparent head still intact.

"My God!" Hans blurted out uncontrollably.

"Quite a sight, isn't he?" Pierce's glee was undeniable. He was extremely proud of his discovery. "We're not certain of its age yet. But from core samples, we're thinking it's around 10,000 to 20,000 years old. Yet, he's remarkably preserved, wouldn't you agree?"

"I would indeed, Dr Pierce," Hans replied with an awed whisper. He was utterly mesmerised by the sight in front of him.

"We're still trying to determine what or who he is?" Pierce said as he looked carefully at his notes on a clipboard and not noticing Hans gingerly edging closer to the being in front of him.

But Hans knew who this was. He somehow instinctively knew and it both excited him and filled him with absolute terror. Suddenly, everything around him barring the being in the ice vanished and left only blackness. Followed by a warm reddish hue appearing from the being's head within the ice.

"Welcome, Hans," a calm, deep and almost unnatural voice greeted him with a hiss. "You know who I am, don't you?"

"Yes, my lord!" Hans' tone was filled with fear as he knelt.

A thin, barely visible black line edged its way towards him and reared up like a cobra in front of him.

"Good! Then know that what transpires will not affect you! You are protected. We have much work to do."

"Thank you, sire," Hans whispered. "I look forward to your arrival, Lord Hoth!"

With that, Hans found himself back inside the ice chamber and kneeling on the floor with a decidedly confused Dr Pierce staring at him.

"Lord who?" Pierce said with a curious trepidation.

"It is none of your concern," Hans snapped as he stood up and turned heading for the door.

"What do you mean it's none of my conc—"

Pierce never got to finish that sentence as from a shadow that was cast onto his chest by a passing scientist, a clawed and golden armoured hand shot out grasping that same scientist's head, pulling it into the shadow on his chest. That shadow now gone fused the two of them together. The scientist's arms flailing in panic as he found himself miraculously fused inside Pierce's chest and equally panicked Pierce desperately tried to remove the head from where his heart should be. Moments later, both men fell to the floor dead just as multiple hands leapt shadows all over, ripping and tearing scientists and military guards alike. The later desperately attempting to fire at any shadow that looked remotely menacing and taking out a few guards themselves accidentally.

Still, the claws continued to rip and tear their way through the remainder of people in that room and as Hans calmly made his way down the corridor towards the lift, confused guards and scientists alike ran towards the source of the commotion only to turn tail and run when they did.

As Hans reached the large room containing the lift out of the facility, Hoth's murderous and supernatural assault had reached this room as unaware scientific personnel were suddenly flung upwards into the ice-covered ceiling by an invisible force as the lights suddenly went out.

Hans calmly waited for the lift to arrive as screams in terror and desperate orders along with periodic gunfire echoed around the room. He stepped into the lift on its arrival, nonchalantly whistling as the lift ascended to the surface. Still continuing his little ditty as he exited the container on reaching the surface and signalled for his pilot to prepare to take off. As the helicopter took off, Hans looked down at the outpost and witnessed the entire facility being violently pulled by unseen shadowy force beneath the ice.

From this moment, everything to do with his reaper research changed. Everything on earth was about to change because Hoth had just been released.

Elections and Their Electorate Never See Eye to Eye

David Rockefeller's summer mansion, Vermont, U.S.A, 19 July 2001.

"How long before Hoth is at full strength, Hans?" David Rockefeller asked between the initial draws on his pipe. "And more importantly, how badly did that greedy, prick Bush fuck things up for us? Can the plan still be implemented, unchanged and on schedule despite his stupidity and with him still in office?"

Hans Schmidt thought very deeply for a few moments. Regardless of his prolonged silence or lack of words, his silence itself spoke volumes.

"Jesus Christ, Hans!" genuine fear-filled Rockefeller's voice. "It really is that bad, isn't it?"

Still, Hans remained silent. This deeply unnerved Rockefeller. For nearly 50 years now, Hans Schmidt had been the driving force and sole visionary 'man with a plan', who had come up with and skilfully negotiated any of their dealings with the reapers. Everything from their technological leaps that they'd appropriated from the reapers to the military help that they provided, everything that gave them the edge they all enjoyed had been down to Hans' negotiations. All their technological help had been in exchange for lives, human lives. Rockefeller had never asked what those lives were being used for nor did he want to know. He just used his extensive power and influence over the U.S.'s government, politicians and their intelligence services to organise the cover story for where these people were going.

It'd been Hans' idea to use alien abductions as the cause. It was both compelling enough to misdirect the overly curious and outlandish enough to generate ridicule and disbelief. It was genius. But all that changed now that Hoth was free. Even Hans seemed concerned over this new approach to their dealings with the reapers. If Hans was concerned, then Rockefeller deemed that reason enough for great concern.

Hans stood up out of his chair and walked to the window. The faint sound of a helicopter drawing near broke up the serenity of the birdsong. He stared outside and sighed deeply. Hans knew why Hoth had chosen to contact President Bush. Not only was Bush cowardly, as well as incredibly greedy, he was also not the brightest of fellows, which made him a perfect candidate for what Hoth had in mind.

"He has what he needs?" Hans said quietly. "Bush's negations went exactly as Hoth wanted them to. As for whether or not he's at full strength…well…" Hans took a cigar from his breast pocket and sniffed it, "you know David, I've always loved these cigars, it'll be a shame to see them go!"

He let out an unsettling chuckle as he lit it and drew back slowly, allowing the smoke to roll in his mouth before breathing it back. Rockefeller's mouth was agape as Hans turned to face him. Had he just heard him right? Surely, he didn't mean what he thought he meant. Hans just smiled before continuing.

"No…No, Hoth isn't that full power. But then it matters how powerful he is, he's still far more powerful than anything on the planet."

"So, what does he want?" Rockefeller's fear was telling. He both wanted to know and didn't in equal measure. "What has Bush agreed to?"

"A sacrifice!" Hans replied in an uncompassionate matter of fact way. "That's all…Just a sacrifice…One large enough to rip open a doorway."

Rockefeller was stunned. "How big? When? Where?"

Hans just smiled back and shook his head.

"It's no longer your concern, Mr Rockefeller. Your part in this is done and your guarantee of immunity from harm is set in place. Just sit back and enjoy the ride."

Hans walked to the door and opened it leaving a stunned David Rockefeller to slump back in his chair, a look of terror and despair creeping over his face.

"Well, if you'll excuse me, Mr Rockefeller. I have other business to attend to."

He closed the door slowly behind him and set out to the waiting helicopter on the lawn.

Deposits and Negotiations

United Nations building, New York, 9 September 2001, 02:37 pm

Jason Carmichael ran down the corridor on the fifth floor of the U.N. HQ at full pelt, narrowly avoiding bowling over the people occupying the densely packed corridor. Interpreters, military personnel, reporters, no one was exempt as he barrelled towards his goal.

"General McCann," he bellowed with urgency, "General McCann, I really must speak with you!"

McCann was a tall man, around six feet and two inches with a heavyset and muscular build. His deep bronze tan accentuated his short-cropped and greying hair with his face holding the weight of a myriad of difficult decisions.

He turned to face the rapidly approaching figure of Jason and leant over to one of his attachés beside him and whispered in a thick Florida accent, "Not this fucking limey bastard, nut job again! What the hell are we gonna do about him?"

Jason stopped just short of his nose, his eyes catching McCann's angry look emanating from his dark brown eyes causing the same anger to well up on Jason.

"Is there something wrong with your brain, General? As well as your phone line, apparently?" Jason waited for an answer, one that wasn't forthcoming. All he got, by way of a reply, was a series of huffs as McCann's temper was starting to boil.

"I've been calling your office for two days now," Jason angrily continued, "without a single reply!"

He rapidly calmed himself before continuing in a whisper, "He has requested to see you. I would advise that you do so."

"Who the hell do you think you are, Colonel?" McCann quietly asked through clenched teeth. "First of all, you will address me as General Sir! Or have you forgotten the chain of command? You will show me the proper respect! Secondly, you are a Colonel in the British army and not part of the U.S. armed forces, so therefore just a visitor! Or more specifically, a tourist and therefore have no right to demand anything from me, nor issue me any kind of orders, do I make myself clear?"

McCann took a deep breath to calm himself before dragging Jason to one side and whispered, "As for our mutual friend, President Bush has already made our position on his matters abundantly clear."

Jason opened his mouth to argue his point but was cut immediately short.

"This all-conquering evil does not exist and will never show itself. He lied to you, Colonel! He's been lying to us all for decades trying to procure the alien tech we have for himself or likely someone else. Do you even know who Arkanon is, I mean really? For all, we and you know, he's some headcase escaped from some asylum somewhere?"

McCann stared into Jason's soul. His eyes first and abrupt, then calmly in a hushed tone he said, "Come on, Colonel." He rubbed Jason's shoulders firmly, passively shaking him to hammer home his point. "You don't really believe that bullshit about him being alive for centuries, do you?"

Jason looked at him dumbstruck. He couldn't believe what he was hearing. There was fully documented evidence of Arkanon showing up in WW1, WW2; Vietnam, virtually every conflict that the allied forces were involved in throughout the entire twentieth century. The files were there, though heavily redacted and Jason knew for a fact that McCann had been privy to the unredacted files. So, why was he lying? Then it all too heavily dawned on him. They were erasing any knowledge of Arkanon, distancing themselves from him. This new administration saw him as a threat, but why?

"OK then!" he snapped back quietly, looking around for would-be eavesdroppers. "If you won't listen to him or meet him, then it's up to me. Whether you like it or not, Hoth is very real and at this very moment in time lose out there somewhere. And like it or not, in the next couple of months, maybe before he's going to make a sacrifice to his boss…Something that makes a fitting tribute to his boss. Something like a few thousand souls perhaps and you have a chance to prevent that from happening."

Jason waited for some kind of reaction from McCann. A gasp of horror perhaps or at least a look of mild concern. To his horror, he got none of those.

"Will that be all, Colonel?" McCann asked dismissively. "I'm really quite busy. I need to see the joint chiefs of staff over matters of national security and—"

"Are you not listening to a word I'm saying?" Jason loudly butted in horrified. His words echoing down the now very hushed hallway. "Are you deliberately ignoring what I'm telling you?"

Jason suddenly realised that all eyes were now on them. He smiled sheepishly, before leaning over to McCann's ear and whispered, "Do you not comprehend what I'm saying? Hoth is going to commit a homicidal act of such magnitude that will forever be imprinted on this world. Or do you just not care? Are you seriously just gonna sit back and let this happen?"

This seemed to get the reaction from McCann that Jason wanted. Well, almost. McCann looked concerned, but Jason could tell that it wasn't from anything he'd said. No. Something else was going on here.

"Procedures are in place to cover all eventualities," McCann said with a hushed trepidation. "You need not concern yourself with the Hoth problem. It has and is being dealt with!"

"What? What the fuck are you talking about, what procedures? How is it bein…" It then suddenly and horrifyingly made sense to Jason, total terrifying sense, "Oh my god!" Jason couldn't contain his anger as he tried to stay as quiet as he could. "You're allowing it to happen, aren't you? The procedures aren't a preventive measure…They're a cover-up, aren't they? You've already assigned it a cover story…Which means you know when it's gonna happen? And where, don't you?"

"I'm sorry, Colonel, that information is classified," McCann replied nervously, knowing he'd let too much slip already.

"Oh fuck! You made a deal." Jason suddenly became frantic. "That's why you're distancing yourselves from Arkanon, you made a fucking deal. Don't you realise what you've done? Who made the deal? I know it wasn't you."

Jason stared at McCann, straight into his eyes and searched his face for an answer. It was an answer he really didn't want to hear.

"It was Bush, wasn't it? He made the deal." McCann said nothing, but his silence just confirmed Jason's worst fears. "Do you not know what you're doing making a deal with him? It's like making a deal with the devil…Actually, it's worse!"

"Yes, OK!" McCann blurted out as he tried to shut Jason up with a confirmation. "But this way, we guarantee the survival of our nation and…"

Jason scoffed with disdain. He couldn't believe what he was hearing. He was beginning to think the world had gone mad. "Hoth doesn't want slaves," Jason snapped, he was furious, "he doesn't want allies. All he wants is to cause death and souls…Our souls! Do you not get that? He needs them to feed himself and open a gateway for his boss!"

"No, this deal ensures we remain free," McCann sounded as much like he was convincing himself more than Jason. "We remain on top of the rest of the world and have the lowest loss of life. The President has brokered a deal ensuring our protection from—"

"Who helped him with the negotiations?" Jason knew the answer already.

"I'm sorry," McCann was taken off guard.

"Who helped with the negotiations? Who was on his team?"

"Erm… He was instructed to meet with Hoth alone, that's all I know. He settled the agreement himself."

Jason shook his head in disbelief. Then grabbing McCann by the lapels through him through a door into a side office. The three men occupying that office were quickly and threateningly asked to leave.

"So, let me get this straight," Jason began thoroughly incensed. "You allowed someone with an IQ lower than a chipmunk and a deep-seated greed for power, verging on the glutinous into a meeting with an all-powerful entity and master of manipulation and let's not forget pure fucking evil to negotiate the terms of, let's face it, humanity's surrender?"

McCann's attachés looked at each other stunned before both Jason and McCann politely told them to 'fuck off out of the room'.

"We didn't have a choice!" McCann continued when they'd left.

"You had no choice?" Jason was dumbfounded. "What do you mean you had no choice? You had a choice…Don't fucking meet him!"

Jason paced the room like an angry headmaster reprimanding a pupil of less than average IQ. He began muttering to himself angrily and under his breath.

"You're wrong," McCann snapped back. He was on the defensive now. "With this deal, a handful will die in order to save millions, possibly billions. It was the only choice. The only alternative."

"What? The only alternative?" Jason couldn't grasp McCann's logic and for good reason. "You seriously think that you've saved millions, maybe billions of lives?"

McCann nodded.

"Let me open your eyes, General. This isn't some foreign dictator, some despot you can bargain with. This is a demon. One far more powerful than anything your idiotic brain can comprehend?" Jason's voice rasped with anger. "Bargaining with him isn't like making a deal with the devil, you know? The devil's nothing on him! Why do you think the devil is referred to as the prince of darkness? Because Hoth doesn't answer to the prince, he takes his orders from the devil's boss! The true ruler of hell!"

McCann looked at Jason like this was fresh news to him. In truth, this was the first time anyone had told him this information. No one had either the knowledge or the courage to fully explain exactly what they were dealing with before. His brief had been from the Secretary of Defence and the President, who had both insisted that Hoth was to be treated like any other hostile force. That their top priority was their break up of ties to Arkanon! The lack of any due diligence on the part of the Bush administration had him more than a little concerned.

"So, what're you saying, Colonel Carmichael?" McCann began, trying to hide the worry in his voice. "Whatever deal the president has made is, in effect, utterly worthless?"

Jason nodded in agreement.

"All you're gonna succeed in doing is delaying the inevitable. Probably sending hundreds, if not thousands to die and giving Hoth a massive boost in power! Possibly even worse."

McCann shook his head in disbelief, muttering 'shit' and 'fuck' over and over under his breath as he slumped down hard into a nearby chair.

"But that's not the best part," Jason let out an angry almost evil chuckle, looked McCann deep in the eye and said sternly, "this is the first of three sacrifices, all of them needing a massive loss of life to give Hoth the power he needs to open the gate fully and bring his boss, 'Legion', through. The final sacrifice will make the other two looks like a muppet show Christmas special by comparison. Bush has likely agreed to all allowing all three to take place. It was the one thing that Hoth needed, the permission of a human soul and he got it in spades with your fucking president, didn't he, eh?"

McCann remained silent looking at the floor, staring into space. The full weight of how much he'd been outright lied to by his government, by his president and to his face was fully pressing down on his shoulders. Jason could see it too and it was now or never to persuade him over to their side.

Jason knew how much Arkanon wanted McCann on their side. Both Arkanon and his father had said how effective and respected a leader McCann was. Not only that but he was an exceptional strategist and he had men in the special forces who were fiercely loyal to him, as a result, and would follow him no matter what. To say this was something that they desperately needed was an understatement. But first, he needed to know if he had the location and/or knew when it was to take place.

Jason took a deep breath and placed his hand on McCann's shoulder and said in a softly coercive tone, "General, you know you can't let this happen." He crouched down in front of the now despondent McCann. "Those fucking white house wankers have you played for a fool! Used you and thoroughly took the piss! They're laughing at you right now, you know that? They think you're some kinda thick fuck, who'll blindly follow them no matter what."

He waited for a few moments to allow his words to echo through McCann's mind before continuing, "Fuck me, General!" he said with disgust. "You've allowed yourself to be blagged by a jug-eared, chimp-like dwarf with the IQ of a burnt sausage roll! Surely, you're not gonna let 'em get away with that."

Jason smiled slyly, making sure McCann hadn't seen it. *That should've done the trick?* he thought to himself.

"I can't believe I let those assholes trick me into this," McCann sounded ashamed, "into this madness! There's no way that little monkey fucker should've been able to do that without me seeing past it. What the fuck was I thinking?"

By this point, he was fuming. Perfect.

"Don't beat yourself up, mate!" Jason faked genuine concern and condolence. "Why not let Arkanon see you? At least hear him out, eh?"

Jason walked to the door and knocked as he continued, "He really is the best chance we've got right now and he honestly speaks very highly of you!"

The door to the office opened and in walked one of McCann's attachés. Another very heavyset fellow around six feet tall with very short cropped, flame-red hair and piercing green eyes. McCann hadn't noticed him come in as he made his decision.

"OK!" McCann said with an angry determination. "Let's go see him!"

It was then he noticed the other man in the room.

"Ah…McMillan," he tried to hide his anger not too unsuccessfully, "I'm glad you're here. Can you get me a vehicle ready there's somewhere I need to be?"

He turned to Jason.

"Where we going and how long you think it'll take?"

Jason just smiled.

"There's no need, General—" he began.

McCann quickly interrupted. A sudden realisation washed across his face.

"He's already here, isn't he?"

Jason laughed.

"He's been here a while, sir!" Jason said, unusually respectful.

"So, where is h…" McCann was immediately stopped midsentence by the sight of his attaché, McMillan's face suddenly blurring.

To his amazement, the young attaché's face suddenly melted and reshaped itself. Until eventually it repositioned and folded into that of Arkanon.

"Hello, Casey," Arkanon said with a grin. "It's been a long time my friend."

Jason left McCann and Arkanon alone for a few moments to discuss what information Arkanon needed and how much Casey could help.

Ideally, they needed McCann to fully commit and supply them with everything they required, but the reality of things was making sure to prevent such happy reunions and it was becoming clear that what began as a discussion; was rapidly developing into a full-blown argument.

"You do realise what's at stake here, don't you?" Arkanon shouted frustratedly before McCann nervously pleaded with him to quieten down.

"My family could be at risk, goddamnit!" McCann snapped back quietly. "It's too risky for me to just up and leave all of a sudden…They'd know something was up Surely you can see that?"

Arkanon had to admit, this was something he'd overlooked in his plan to get him onside and McCann could tell.

"Same old Arkanon," he said condescendingly, "jumping in with both feet, without thinking of the consequences as usual, eh?"

Arkanon gave him a deathly stare, which didn't deter McCann one bit as he leant around Arkanon and stared directly at Jason.

"You know? This is a trait you'll see quite a bit from your new friend here!" he looked back at Arkanon and shook his head in disbelief. "I'm assuming you've no plan as to how to stop Hoth barring a show of force."

Arkanon stepped back and grinned. He was right. None of them had the first clue about what they were going to do to stop Hoth. But then again, how could they when they had no idea when or where Hoth was going to strike?

"We've been told of six locations," McCann began, "two of which are most likely, one not so likely and three definitely out the question in my view."

"I'm listening," Arkanon said as he sat on the table beside McCann, who swivelled his chair to face him.

"Well...the best candidate," McCann continued, "is the world trade centre in New York. It was hit not so long back by some Islamic guys...Al Qaeda, I think they go by. Run by an ex-asset of ours...Highly trained wet worker!"

"Al Qaeda?" Arkanon snorted. "Doesn't that mean—"

"Yeah, database in Farsi," McCann butted in, trying to move him along. "Don't get hung up on semantics, it is what it is. But this is the easiest for our intelligence guys to cover up!"

"Makes sense!" Jason said worryingly in agreement with McCann. "What're the other two likely targets?"

"The next is likely the pentagon," McCann sucked through his teeth, "but that's less likely and I think it'll probably be linked in with their cover. The pentagon has been having, shall we say...financial issues with regards to providing information on how money is being spent."

"So, they're more likely to explode their bookkeepers to hide their syphoning off cash," Arkanon pointed out.

"Exactly," McCann said in a matter-of-fact way before continuing. "It's easier to hide it as part of a terror attack than the actual focus of the attack if you follow me."

"So, what's the third?" Jason wasn't sure he wanted to know but still asked anyway.

"Well, that would be the white house," McCann rubbed his chin. "But now I say that out loud that it really does sound crazy."

"So, the world trade centre is our safest bet then?" Arkanon stood up and sighed as he spoke. He hated asking this.

"Yeah, I'd say so!" McCann said solemnly. "There's not much time to get a decent plan together though, guys?"

McCann looked genuinely worried again and this, in turn, worried Jason and Arkanon.

"How long we got?" Jason snapped.

"Hours maybe?" McCann jumped from his seat. "Listen, I know just the guys to help you out. They're good men and loyal too! Just make sure to take care of 'em, OK?"

Arkanon nodded. He didn't want to tell him he couldn't promise anything, but McCann could tell by his look that that's what he meant. He smiled nervously before taking out his mobile phone and walking to the opposite end of the room to make a call.

"Well, I guess we'd better come up with a plan then, eh?" Jason said patting Arkanon on the back. "And make sure it's one where we come out alive, eh?"

All Things, Eventually,
Must Come to Head

World Trade Centre Tower 1, WTC Plaza, 11 September 2001.

Arkanon, Jason and Tyler ascended the stairs of WTC tower 1 with the seven-man team McCann had put together to assist them. They'd opted to take the stairs to avoid bumping into any of the employees working that morning. They didn't want to explain why the ten of them were not only clad in full armour but also why there were nine heavily armed soldiers with various forms of silenced weapons inside the building. This idea had proven to be a good one as they hadn't bumped into a soul so far on their long journey up to their destination, that being the 92nd floor.

On reaching this floor, however, they were greeted with an awful sight. Blood dripped from the ceiling and walls with body parts strewn everywhere. Despite there being bright blue sky outside, for some reason, this entire floor was covered in eerie, supernatural darkness.

"My God!" Tyler exclaimed, covering her mouth. "What the hell happened here?"

"Hoth happened!" Arkanon replied with an increased determination. "Come on, we need to move and fast, he's almost ready!"

"Ready for what?" Tyler's voice was full of concern.

"He's still not at full strength yet, but this sacrifice, if it goes ahead, will bring him up to full power," Arkanon replied. His gaze never moving from the corridors in front of them.

He gestured for them to move forward. As they slowly made their way down the blood-soaked corridor, both Tyler and Jason took a team each and checked the rooms on either side that broke off from their main route whispering 'clear' as they continued.

They carefully stepped over body parts, their feet making a barely audible squelching sound as their feet touched the floor. The corridor too seemed to get increasingly darker as they ventured forth and soon Arkanon's companions were forced to use their night vision in their helmets.

"What the fuck is going on?" Jason's voice was full of concern. "Why is it so god damn dark in here?"

"It's Hoth's presence," Arkanon couldn't hide the slight edge of fear in his tone, "he can suck the light out of his surroundings. Be on your guard…The shadows are his greatest ally!"

Both Tyler and Jason couldn't be sure what he meant by that. A fact that wasn't lost on the rest of the squad either. A couple of them began to mutter under their breaths, clearly extremely rattled by their situation. But found themselves quickly and angrily hushed by an unnervingly, equally as rattled Arkanon.

"Remember, people," Arkanon barked in a hushed tone. "Just like other reapers, Hoth can instil fear inside you just by his presence alone but in a far more concentrated form."

Unsurprisingly this didn't inspire confidence in them.

"Just be wary of your fear. Try to ignore it and push past it if possible," The irony and utter contradiction of what he'd just said seemed lost on Arkanon as the rest of them looked at each other somewhat bemused.

From nowhere, a loud cry of horror came from beside them. As one of the soldiers was suddenly sucked into the darkness followed by a loud crunching and squelching sound that drowned out the man's frantic, panic-stricken screams. Without thinking, the two men closest to that man suddenly let loose with their silenced guns in the vicinity of the attack. Their rounds impacting nothing but the wall behind. Rushing towards them, Arkanon slammed his hands against the top of their guns forcing them down and instantly ceasing their fire. Against his better judgment and in a desperate attempt to ease their fear, he clicked his fingers producing a dim ball of white light that hung in the air and dispersed all of the shadows in their immediate vicinity.

"Calm yourselves!" he said with a hushed and angry hiss. "Though I fear he's well aware of our presence now. We must press on!"

He gave them a moment or two to gather themselves before gesturing for them to re-engage night vision and with a click of his fingers, once again plunged them back into the danger of the darkness.

They slowly and carefully continued and had only made it a few feet when from a room to the left side of them one of the soldiers closest to its doorway heard a faint female voice call out, "Please…Help me!" her hushed voice was full of intense fear. "I know you're there, I can hear you…Please don't leave me here."

Just as the soldier was about to react and open the door, Arkanon leapt towards him and thrust his hand on the man's chest stopping the surprised man dead, shaking his head. "It's a trap," he whispered.

A faint and demonic sounding laugh began to permeate from seemingly nowhere all around them. This was followed by the anguished cries of, "No! No! Please, no," as the loud sounds of someone being ripped limb from limb quickly drowned out those cries.

This event was obviously too much for two of the soldiers to handle as they began to weep, terrified by what they were witnessing. They then suddenly broke away from the rest of the group, taking a break for the door to the stairs at the end of the corridor. Arkanon barely had a chance to call out to them to stop and come back before tendrils of pure darkness shot out from either side of the two men dragging their panic-stricken and screaming bodies into the nothingness from whence they came.

The rest of the squad, including Arkanon, stood stock still, rooted to the spot with fear. Until moments later, after he'd composed himself, Arkanon slapped each in turn on the sides of their head to break them out of their fear.

"Remember your training," he barked with a hushed tone. "I know it's difficult, but try to keep your heads. Else that'll be your fate!"

Tentatively, they continued until they reached at-junction at the end of the corridor to their left, the dim sunlight coming through the windows of another group of offices to their right, the entranceway to a large central room. An eerie red glow danced around the shadows that filtered through the doorway. Those same shadows seemed alive somehow and looked as though they were hungrily lunging outwards towards them.

"Welcome, old friend!" the unmistakable sound of Hoth's voice boomed from all around them. "You certainly took your time getting here. What took you so long?"

The doors before them were flung open and gingerly they entered the room. The soldiers aiming down their sights, checking every corner of the huge central room as they entered. Without warning, there was a deafening roar followed by a heavy thud! thud! thud! of footsteps and the crumbling of masonry and doorways splintering from something heading towards them.

Instantly, Arkanon knew what this was and stretching his arms out in front of everyone growled, "Fallback! Everyone…fucking fall back!"

From a doorway at the other side of the room, the doors bulged and cracked inwards. Followed by a brief moment of an unnatural, deathly silence. This was all too immediately shattered by the doors exploding as the unmistakable and roaring head of a high guard burst through. Wood splinters were sent in all directions, its gaping maw filled with gigantic foot-long teeth dripped with drool as it's roar echoed all around them. Before Arkanon had time to react, he was suddenly yanked to the side into an adjoining wall just as the high guard broke into a sprinting charge on all fours and sending the rest of the squad into a blind panic as they ran in all directions.

Only Jason and Tyler managed to regain enough of their composure to follow the path that Arkanon had been dragged on. Jason busted through the hole Arkanon had made, the sense of irony not lost on him either. He was quickly followed by Tyler, who dashed instinctively forward towards the crumpled and unconscious form of Arkanon on the other side of the room.

"You OK, hunny?" she asked full of concern. "Are you hur—"

She was unable to finish her question as a tendril of darkness wrapped itself around her throat and lifted her high into the air, her head barely glancing the high ceiling above.

"No!" Jason shouted terrified. "No! Please…let her go! Please…"

He rushed towards her, grabbing her ankles, trying desperately to pull her down.

"Arkanon!" he barked in angry desperation, "Wake the fuck up and help me!"

Arkanon roused himself just in time to see the shadowy form of Hoth appearing in the doorway behind Jason. His glowing and flaming red eyes, illuminating the room. Through the hole beside him, he could just make out the massive hulking mass of the high guard fending off an attack by three or four brave soldiers. Immediately, however, his attention was suddenly wrenched back to Jason as a shadowy hand wrapped itself around Jason's body and flung him across the room.

"Oh no!" Arkanon whispered to himself. "Not again!"

As Jason shook his head trying to regain his composure from the heavy impact he'd just received on landing on the other side of the room, he was shocked not just by Tyler's rapidly fading and struggling body floating in mid-air or the slowly solidifying form of Hoth at one side of the room, but mostly by the standing stock still and terrifying form of Arkanon on the other side of the room. Immediately he ran towards Arkanon.

"Arkanon! Snap out of it! For fuck's sake, snap out of it!"

Be Careful What You Wish for Lest It Bites You in the Ass

Unknown location, aeons ago.

Before our time began and before life and death here were even considered, before everything we have ever known about our universe; order and chaos coexisted as one entity.

Everything held a perfectly tuned balance that never fluctuated away from anywhere but exact. The void that this had become was the space lying between the fragile strands of other realities that, like giant strands of the thread, weaved themselves together like a huge interdimensional fishing net. Each of them was filled with either the leftover energy of order or chaos that remained after the creation of the void, which segregated them from each other. They were trapped inside their 'string-like' prison cells, like animals in a zoo or a prisoner in solitary confinement, never able to venture outside their shells lest the fragile balance of the void be broken.

Some of these strands were only the width of the tiniest particle but the length of 20 universes. Others looked the width of hundreds of universes and just a few feet long. All of them crisscrossed back and forth over and under each other. They stretched out as far as the eye could see and floated everywhere, all of them buzzing with energy, each one resonating with a near-silent hum, but all of them created their own dim pulsing light in the infinite blackness.

Within this very volatile and delicate environment stood Arkanon. The glow from the strands surrounding him radiated against his face. Light particles from the ones above fell like tiny raindrops, faintly glowing ever brighter as they trickled over his face and down his body from above before slowly fading away into the nothingness of the void that was beneath his feet.

At last, he thought to himself, *light!* It seemed like an eternity since any sort of light entered his eyes. To have this as the first thing his eyes were to see and after so long in the dark was a very welcome reward. It was beautiful. Every colour imaginable made a loose dimly lit patchwork above and around him. They looked so thin, so delicate like the slightest stray breath could break them as they wisped like strands of silk blowing in the wind across his face. It was incredible.

"This is beautiful!" he said astonished. "Where am I? What is this place? It's incredible... What have you done with me?" He waited a little while, soaking in the light particles as he waited. A calmness had begun to fill his body. He felt so at peace, so comfortable. If he was to remain anywhere and never go back home, which he thought must surely to be his fate, then he had to stay here.

"Is this to be my new home? And I know I've asked already, but who are you? I must know? No living being can have this much power to be able to bring me to this place or come to think of it, I would even say that this is way beyond the power of anything I know of."

The voice chuckled. Its quiet laughter was not of a sinister kind. Rather, it was soft, gentle and he had to admit, a little playful. It didn't seem to resemble a male or female voice either, it was just calming, nice even.

"THERE IS SOMETHING YOU MUST DO HERE, ARKANON... SOMETHING ONLY YOU ARE DESTINED TO DO... BUT FOR NOW, ALL YOU NEED DO IS WAIT. IN TIME, YOU WILL DO WHAT IS NEEDED TO BE DONE," the voice said in a slightly more coercive tone.

It very nearly hid its stealthy coercion beneath the same playfulness as before. But Arkanon saw through this, rather childish in his opinion, ruse easily. Although this entity was powerful, it still couldn't completely hide its little white lie. The tell tale signs that something wasn't being fully explained to him still stood out.

"There is something I must do? And it's my destiny to do it? But for now, I must wait?" He couldn't believe it.

Great! he thought, *more waiting.* At least the view he had was amazing if he was going to be here for any significant length of time.

Soon he began to think wildly, the curiosity was killing him, making his impatience even worse.

What the hell could it be that he was supposed to do? Was this a test? Did he have to work out what to do himself or would he be told? Why was he meant to do it anyway? Did Feron have to go through this, when he found the stone if he

193

even touched it that is? He would've had to do this as well, surely. It's no wonder he was smiling like he was when he showed me the stone... *That sly old dog*, Arkanon thought to himself... He knew! He knew what was going to happen, didn't he? No wonder he kept quiet! Sneaky old bastard! He didn't wanna ruin the surprise, did he?

He began wishing the old man was with him though right now. Partly, so he could kill him! But also, so he could share this experience with his old friend. Though mostly, so he could guide him through this and suggest what he should do. It would have been so much easier and it might not have taken as long to get to where he was now. Everything that had occurred up to this point was completely alien to him and was taking every ounce of his sanity to keep his mind focused.

Suddenly he remembered Atlantis and the soldiers that he'd left behind pretty much to die at the hands of the invading reaper army in order to get to King Feron and this very situation. How could he have forgotten about them? How could he have been so selfish? He still had no idea what had happened to them and no way of finding out either. He dropped quickly to his knees, a renewed sense of grief enveloping him as he raised his head and cried out in despair. The shockwave from his cries battered the tiny strings around him knocking them into one another and severed those that were closest to his face.

"AND SO IT IS DONE, YOUR CHOICE IS MADE... YOU HAVEN'T GOT MUCH TIME, YOU MUST PREPARE YOURSELF, ARKANON!, THIS WILL BE SHORT BUT REGRETTABLY, VERY PAINFUL IF YOU DO NOT ALLOW ADEQUATE TIME TO READY YOURSELF... IF YOU CURL UP INTO A BALL AND GET AS LOW AS YOU CAN... THAT SHOULD TAKE A LITTLE OF THE EDGE OFF THE PAIN."

Choice? What choice had he made? He didn't recall ever being told that he had to make a choice. He hadn't been told that there was something he had to choose. More to the point, he had no idea what he'd done in the first place to make that choice.

What the hell was going on and what was he preparing himself for? And why was it going to hurt? What had he done?

He was beginning to panic a little now. Something suddenly felt very wrong. Even so, he thought it was a good idea to do as he was told. Unfortunately, he didn't get the chance to do much else as a searing, burning hot explosion as bright as the sun erupted in front of his eyes before it enveloped him.

The strings, once delicate and pretty, had started to take on a more sinister air as they started colliding with each other more regularly. The opposing energies released from within them from the multitude of collisions reacted, for want of a better word, rather badly.

As the first of the shockwaves from these explosions slammed into his body hurling him backwards, he tried to fathom how something so small and delicate looking could create such a violent spectacle.? Also, he didn't know how. But somehow, he was still standing. This was, despite the fact that he was still taking the full force of that, initial violent blast. The pressure was now crushing his body and by rights should've killed him. At the very least, he should be suffocating because he was completely unable to breathe. The blast had gripped his chest tightly preventing his lungs from taking in air.

Following that first shockwave came a sound that can only be described as like the cries of a billion babies in incredible pain all crying at once. The deafening sound shattered past his ears and began reverberating around his head making it feel like it was about to explode. The pain felt excruciating. He grabbed his head tightly in his hands in an attempt to ease the pain and dropped to his knees screaming in agony. The heat that was radiating from the ever-brightening light from the widening explosion then began scorching his eyeballs, it was so intense and it was only growing ever more in intensity. Soon even shutting his eyes no longer blocked out the light or protected his eyes from the heat and it began to cut deep into his eyes. The searing heat boiling them in their sockets.

Arkanon frantically tried to decide which to comfort first, his near to exploding head or his bubbling and sizzling eyes. He wasn't being allowed much time to decide, however, as the second shockwave hitting with a force at least 1000x faster and harder than the first made the decision for him. He managed to catch a glimpse of something, though, just before his eyes violently exploded in their sockets that puzzled him and seemed, especially due to his current situation, completely impossible.

In front of him, there appeared to be someone else. He was sure there was? But the voice had told him that there was only him on this plain of existence. And yet, there, right in front of him, was the silhouette of another person and it looked as though they were experiencing the same violent end as he was doing.

How was this possible? Who was that? Could it have been just a reflection of his own silhouette, bounced back at him? He didn't have the chance to ponder on it too long, however, as another wave of burning hot radiation enveloped his body and he screamed violently in pain. Red hot blood began flowing like a raging river down his face from where his eyes once were.

His body was being held rigid by the secondary force of the blast, it held itself in one position and he was unable to change it. He longed to be able to cover up what was left of his eyes just to give them some sort of respite from the still ongoing explosions and huge flames that were being generated. Yet, even though there was just residue left where his eyes once were, he could still see. Not only that, but he could see as clear as day.

Yet again, milliseconds broke up the shockwaves and additional, far larger, explosions, so he didn't get a moment to work out how he was still able to see. For his body was now beginning to very gently burn away to ash as he was slowly and agonisingly being roasted alive. Soon his screams began to die out but only because his vocal cords had disintegrated along with his entire throat and lower jaw.

Although he was silent, it still hadn't stopped it hurting any less. The incredible heat was claiming his body, piece by piece and as his screams now fell totally silent, so did the blast. What remained of his body was almost completely gone. Almost nothing more than ash. Yet he still, in some strange way, somehow still existed.

But this was impossible, surely? he thought, though the simple fact that he'd had this thought in the first place was a convincing argument that apparently, it wasn't impossible. It seemed that although he had, virtually, no physical form, his consciousness still remained. His spiritual form still lingered on this plain. The only thing that confirmed his existence to himself was the continuing pain that he still felt.

"YOU MUST LISTEN TO ME ARKANON... CONCENTRATE ON ME, CONCENTRATE ON LISTENING TO MY VOICE AND THE PAIN WILL EASE... IT IS IMPORTANT THAT YOU LISTEN TO WHAT I'M ABOUT TO TELL YOU!" the voice had returned.

As best as he could, he began to concentrate on the voice and nothing else. Desperately trying to pinpoint its position as he fought to hear every sound. Just as the voice had said and to his relief, his pain started to subside. He continued concentrating until it was, at long last, just about bearable.

"WHAT YOU HAVE WITNESSED, ARKANON, MY CHILD, HAS NEVER HAPPENED BEFORE THAT MOMENT AND IT NEVER WILL AGAIN... YOU HAVE WITNESSED THE AWAKENING OF THE VOID. THE BEGINNING OF EXISTENCE."

Arkanon had to admit that he had no idea what the voice just said or what it meant. It seemed like it was important though, he just had no idea how important in actuality that it was. The voice, however, continued.

"I KNOW YOU MUST HAVE QUESTIONS, BUT I CANNOT HELP YOU AT THIS TIME. YOUR MIND IS NOT READY NOR CAPABLE TO CONTAIN THE KNOWLEDGE THAT YOU WILL GAIN IN YOUR LATER DAYS... YOU ARE GOING TO ACHIEVE GREAT THINGS, ARKANON, BUT IN ORDER TO DO SO, YOU WILL HAVE TO MAKE SOME, INCREDIBLY, DIFFICULT CHOICES AND SACRIFICES... I CHOSE YOU BECAUSE I KNOW WHAT YOU WILL BECOME. I MYSELF CAN NEVER WALK ALONG THE PLAIN THAT YOU INHABIT, BUT YOU CAN... YOU ARE TO BE THE MESSENGER, TEACHER, ENFORCER AND CHAMPION. MY INSTRUMENT ON YOUR PLAIN."

Arkanon was now fading fast and he could feel his life rapidly slipping away. *Looks like you were a little too late,* he thought to himself as the light that was his life started to flicker dimly away.

Shame though, it sounded kinda fun. In his mind, he smiled how he would smile if he still had a mouth with which to smile that is. But it was still, indeed, a contented smile.

The light from the blast now flickered out of view and before him was left giant clouds of gas, trillions of light-years long and belching out newly developing stars, molten metals and rocks. The beginnings of solar systems spiralled in front of him. Time began to accelerate before his eyes. He tried to make out as much as he could out of the blurring images that were flashing past his view. He saw a fledgeling solar system and the demons that inhabited the planets long before life had begun to exist on or near them. It was an incredible sight yet terrifyingly destructive at the same time. It was beautiful to behold that was until he saw it.

It was gigantic. All claws, scales, teeth and dark crimson eyes. Their glow dimly lit up the developing space surrounding them as its serpentine coils wrapped around and interwove itself between the fledgeling planets. This immense beast that he saw was the first. It was the ultimate evil. The true father of all demon kind. Though he didn't know how he knew there and then that this was the demon named Legion. Not just that, but he would be the one responsible for creating an even greater evil in the form of Hoth.

Strangely, as he floated past this monstrosity and the passage of time raced on, he was sure, though he couldn't be certain, that those glowing, deep crimson eyes followed him. Not just that, but they seemed to look right at him and then right through him. But soon he was starting to speed up and that great demon vanished as it was forcefully imprisoned within the unyielding vacuum of a supermassive black hole and then hurtled away into deep space. Years then flew by in nanoseconds, centuries in seconds, millennia in minutes.

Soon Arkanon began to see familiar-looking sights despite them being there thousands of years before he was born. They still bared some slight resemblance to the places he knew in his time. Some of them in far better condition than what he remembered from his childhood. But then over time, they soon began to fall into their eventual and inevitable ruin and decay and took on the appearance he was familiar with. Not only that, but his body was also slowly and so agonisingly slowly started to regenerate. Piece by piece, his body was returning. Not only was it returning, but his body was also feeling different somehow, changed and for the better. He just wasn't entirely sure of exactly in what way that it was better. But he was sure that he was going to find out sooner rather than later.

In no time at all, the blurry mists of time were fading and he found himself high above the ground but a few miles outside the city walls. From his high vantage point in the night sky, he could see Atlantis. Vibrant oranges, bright reds and deep yellows glowed from the myriad of burning buildings. The colours intensified further as they bounced off the bright white marble of the tall towers and thick ramparts before they mixed with the dark blue of the night sky. As he began to float downwards and got closer and closer to the ground, the faint sound of screams and intense battles drifted through the air. At least he wasn't too late, he thought as he gently landed on the grasslands below.

He slumped to floor, his legs still a little week after his ordeal. From where he was sitting, he could tell he wasn't too far from the city gates, they were still quite huge from where he was sat, maybe five or ten minutes easy run.

Explosions were filling the air with noise. The bright white walls of the city were illuminated by the raging infernos behind them. Those reaper bastards were gonna burn the whole city to the ground and he had to stop them before they did! A renewed energy and determination filled his body as he slowly got himself to his feet, but he quickly dropped back to his knees as a searing pain cut through his head. Time around him stopped still once more.

"ARKANON!" it was that voice again. But why was it hurting him now? It didn't before. "ARKANON! THERE ARE A FEW THINGS THAT HAVE CHANGED SINCE YOU VISITED THE VOID. MY VOICE TO A HUMAN IS FATAL, BUT TO YOU, IT IS MERELY PAINFUL... IT IS AN UNAVOIDABLE SIDE EFFECT OF YOUR HUMAN PART."

"Really?" Arkanon said sarcastically. He knew it was painful, after all, he could feel that. But then it struck him, what the voice had just said.

"What do you mean my human part? I am still human, aren't I?" In reality, he didn't want to know the answer to this question, but he awaited the response regardless.

"WHEN YOU ENTERED MY REALM, I HAD NO CHOICE BUT TO KILL YOU," said the voice casually. Arkanon was stunned. He honestly didn't know what to say to that.

"So, I'm dead then?"

"NO... NOT NOW... I GAVE YOU BACK YOUR LIFE." Arkanon was confused and not entirely grateful either. It had felt the need to kill him after all and then so very generously bring him back to life.

"You gave me back my life?" he said angrily. He couldn't believe what he was hearing. He wasn't exactly gonna say thank you if that's what it wanted. Whatever that voice was, it had decided to kill him in the first place, so he wasn't sure he should trust it.

"What do you mean you had to kill me? Why kill me to start with?"

"IN ORDER FOR YOU TO COMPLETE YOUR DESTINY, YOU HAD TO DIE, IF NOT, YOU COULD NOT BE MERGED WITH THE VOID AND YOU COULD NOT HAVE WHAT YOU NEEDED TO FULFIL IT... THESE ARE GOING TO BE TESTING TIMES FOR YOU, MY CHILD. YOU WILL EXPERIENCE TRIALS IN LIFE THAT NO NORMAL MAN WOULD USUALLY FACE... THE SKILLS THAT YOU HAVE LEARNED AND TAUGHT YOUR TRIBE ARE TO BE INVALUABLE AND WILL ONLY

GET MORE POWERFUL WITH TIME… IN ORDER TO DEFEAT HOTH, THOSE POWERS MUST BE CHANNELLED AND NURTURED THROUGH THEIR ORIGINAL MASTER. NO MORTAL MAN CAN GAIN SUCH KNOWLEDGE IN ONE LIFETIME. MANKIND IS HAMPERED BY THE LIMITS OF HIS LIFESPAN, SO HE CAN NEVER EQUAL HOTH IN ANY SORT OF MEANINGFUL WAY AND WILL SURELY BE CRUSHED. BUT IF THE MASTER CAN LIVE BEYOND THE LIFESPAN OF MAN, IF HE CAN KEEP ON INCREASING HIS KNOWLEDGE FOR ETERNITY, THEN HE WILL SURELY BE A MATCH FOR HOTH ONE DAY."

"What?…So, what do you mean I will never die?…You mean I can never be killed and never grow old? Or just that I'll never grow old, but I still better avoid anything that might kill me? Like falling from a great height, poisons, sharp objects or vigorous sex with a young wench in my late 90s, for example." He had to admit, this immortality idea was beginning to intrigue him.

"YOU ARE VIRTUALLY INVINCIBLE, ARKANON. YOU ARE NO LONGER HUMAN; YOU ARE SOMETHING MORE AND WITH TIME YOU WILL EVEN TRANSCEND FURTHER THAN THAT."

Invincible, eh? He had to admit, maybe dying wasn't such a bad payoff after all. But one question still burned on his mind.

"Will I be able to kill Hoth?" That question had been burning on his tongue. The anger in his tone so very pronounced. "Do I now have the power to wipe that evil bastard off the face of the planet?" There was a long pause, not a good sign.

"YOU ARE INDEED POWERFUL, ARKANON."

He could see a 'but' coming here and he knew he wasn't going to like what came after it.

"BUT AT THIS TIME, YOU ARE STILL RELATIVELY WEAK… YOU WILL NEED TIME TO… HOW CAN I PUT IT?"

Arkanon didn't care how this voice in his head was going to put it. He'd already said enough. There was no way he was going to get his revenge and deep down, he knew it. But so as not to offend his mystery companion, he allowed him to continue.

"YOU WILL NEED TIME TO MASTER YOUR NEW-FOUND ABILITIES, IMMORTALITY ISN'T YOUR ONLY STRENGTH. SOON YOU WILL EQUAL HOTH IN ALL THAT YOU CAN DO, BUT UNTIL THAT TIME, YOU MUST BE PATIENT… I HAVE OTHER PLANS FOR HOTH."

Have to be patient? Arkanon thought. *I've been patient long enough and anyway, what did it mean 'it had other plans for Hoth'. What other plans? What could it be up to?*

"NO, MY CHILD, ALL I ASK IS THAT YOU WAIT… DO NOT BE SO HASTY, THE RIGHT TIME FOR YOUR REVENGE WILL COME, BUT AT THIS PRESENT MOMENT, I AM GOING TO GIVE YOU A CHOICE… CALL IT A LEARNING EXPERIENCE."

Now, this was more like it, Arkanon thought.

"THE OUTCOME OF THIS NIGHT IS THE SAME. WHICHEVER PATH YOU CHOOSE TO TAKE, HOTH WILL BE IMPRISONED FOR MILLENNIA TO COME UNTIL THE TIME OF HIS RELEASE… BUT THE MANNER OF HIS IMPRISONMENT AND THE CONSEQUENCES SURROUNDING IT ARE VASTLY DIFFERENT. IT ALL DEPENDS ON WHAT TRANSPIRES."

The consequences wouldn't be that bad, would they? Arkanon thought as his mind wandered and pondered. The voice in his head continued, but he wasn't listening. All he wanted to do was get him whatever the consequences were. He'd deal with them as and when, but right now, he had a chance and he was damn sure he was going to take it.

"SO?" said the voice, waiting for a response to a question it'd just asked that clearly, Arkanon had just missed.

"So?" said Arkanon, smiling and shrugging his shoulders. He was obviously fishing for something to give him any sort of a clue as to what the question he just asked was and the voice knew it. However, mischievously, it didn't let on.

"SO, DO YOU UNDERSTAND THE NATURE OF WHAT YOU ARE BEING ASKED AND THE RAMIFICATIONS OF THE DECISION THAT YOU MAKE?"

It was being deliberately vague so as to catch him out. It knew Arkanon wasn't taking a blind bit of notice about what he'd just said and Arkanon knew he'd been caught out. He knew that if he could see the face behind the voice, he'd see a smug grin on its face. He thought for a minute about what it might've said. *Probably it was something along the lines of 'if you don't do this then somethin' else would happen instead or somethin',* he thought. But in the end, he couldn't be sure, so he just nodded in agreement instead.

"GOOD!" the voice seemed pleased. "THEN IF YOU WISH TO FACE HOTH NOW, HE IS IN THE THRONE ROOM LOOKING FOR THE DOORWAY THAT YOU OPENED EARLIER. HE WILL NEVER FIND IT THOUGH. AS THE POWER THAT WAS SEALED INSIDE THAT STONE HAS BEEN DELIVERED TO IT'S RIGHTFUL OWNER. YOU! WHEN YOU FACE HIM, HE WILL BE INCENSED AND WILL ATTACK WITH INCREDIBLE FEROCITY. IT WILL TRULY BE A BATTLE YOU WILL NOT WIN, BUT I WILL GIVE YOU WHAT YOU NEED TO IMPRISON HIM IN THIS STATE. THE OTHER—"

Arkanon didn't give him time to finish, "I do not care what the other option is, I must take this chance to stop him." The determination in his voice was clear and true.

"REGARDLESS OF THE CONSEQUENCES INVOLVED WITH MAKING THIS decision?"

"Yes! No matter what, I must try."

"THEN SO BE IT… THE DECISION IS MADE."

With that, time restarted. Arkanon looked at the burning city in front of him. In there, somewhere was Hoth, the source of all the pain and hurt in his heart. The reason his city, his home was lying virtually in ruins. The battle inside still raged and he could hear the cries of battle, still hear the sounds of pain and despair. Now, though, he knew he had a chance, however small it was, of perhaps turning the tide of this battle and ending this war. He was going to save his home and his friends. As the voice had already said, 'No matter what happens tonight, Hoth will be imprisoned for millennia to come and in his eyes', there was no way he could lose...

Part 6: Cliffhangers, by Their Nature, Always Leave You Hanging

'For we wrestle not against flesh and blood, but against principalities, against powers, against the rulers of the darkness of this world, against spiritual wickedness in high places.'

Ephesians, chapter 6, verse 12.

Dire Consequences

Outside Atlantis as the battle rages on.

Arkanon lay on his belly on top of one of the hills that lay to the west of Atlantis. From this vantage point, he had a clear view of the vast plain outside the city walls. A huge network of canals crisscrossed the flat plateau from north to south and from east to west. Between them lay farmhouses and suburbs, all were now either in flame or in ruin or both. Reaper troopers chased unarmed townsfolk, like cats chasing mice, everywhere, gleefully massacring them when they finally had them cornered. There were thousands of reapers all over the place, the whole army it seemed had turned out and in droves. Most were inside the city walls, Arkanon was sure of that. The ones remaining outside were lower-level soldiers. The more powerful troops were keeping what was left of the palace guard and the Atlantian army battalions busy inside the main city.

To the east, across the plain, he could see the dark forest in the distance and behind that somewhere was his village. But something caught his attention in the night sky just below the tree line that troubled him. Torchlight. Not just one, however, but thousands. All at once, he knew what it was. Hoth's plan was beginning to become a reality, the Asumertrians were advancing. They had come with a full invasion force to mop up the remnants of the Atlantian army for an easy victory. To make matters worse, in the north was the ocean and on the horizon, he could just make out the silhouettes of Asumertrian ships in the moonlight. He didn't have much time, but more to the point, he had no idea how to defeat the Asumertrians, as well as Hoth's armies. It was starting to become very apparent that Atlantis could, after all his efforts, be lost. Even so, he had to try, he just needed an idea of how or, indeed, where to start. First things first, he had to get into the city.

He got up onto his feet and surveyed the area once more. He knew that his window of opportunity was very small indeed. The Asumertrian land forces would be arriving within the hour. The naval fleet shortly after. He weighed his options carefully. Going for the front gates for any normal man would be suicide and even though he was apparently no longer a normal man, it was still going to be extremely time-consuming at the very least.

There was no way he could scale the walls of the city either. They were way too smooth. Purposefully built that way so as to stop anyone climbing them in the first place. Any of the other gates on the western, eastern and southern walls would more than likely be swarming with Hoth's hordes also. He decided it was time to face facts. He was, for want of a better word, screwed! Suddenly, that tell-tale pain seared through his head and time stopped once again.

"GIVING UP ALREADY?" it was that voice again. Only this time it was a lot more smug with its tone. "YOU SEEM TO HAVE DEVELOPED A TINY FLAW IN YOUR PLAN, HAVEN'T YOU?"

He hated to admit it, but it was right. From what he could see, the task ahead of him was virtually impossible. But there was no way he was going to let the voice know that he was stuck.

"It's just a minor setback," he said, gritting his teeth. He was trying so hard to hold back his frustration but to no avail and the voice could tell. "I'll come up with something, don't you worry."

"OH, I'M NOT WORRIED," the voice said, its smugness seemingly growing in intensity, "I HAVE NO DOUBT THAT YOU'LL COME UP WITH SOMETHING... CAN I JUST MAKE ONE TINY, LITTLE OBSERVATION?"

Arkanon seethed but still tried to hold his anger back, he couldn't believe he was being taunted for a start, let alone being taunted by a voice in his head.

"It's OK! I've nearly got somethin' thought up, just need to finalise a few things, that's all before I make a push." This was an outright lie of course and unfortunately, Arkanon wasn't a very good liar.

"YOU CAN'T GET IN, CAN YOU?" the voice chuckled to itself, it knew it was right and so did Arkanon. "YOU CANNOT SEE ANY WAY AT ALL TO GET IN WITHOUT A LONG DRAWN OUT BATTLE, THAT WILL WASTE A HUGE AMOUNT OF TIME."

"It's just a minor setback...nothing more. Now if you don't mind, I'm trying to think."

"I COULD TELL YOU HOW YOU COULD GET IN WITHOUT YOU ALERTING ANYONE IF YOU WANT ME TO THAT IS? IT'LL TAKE YOU STRAIGHT TO HOTH AND IT WON'T TAKE YOU ANY TIME AT ALL."

Arkanon laughed. *What a load of rubbish,* he thought. *There's no way of getting in without, as it so eloquently put it, a long drawn-out battle, that'd waste too much time.* It was, as far as he could see, impossible for anyone to come up with any way of getting in quickly and without alerting the enemy.

"YOU THINK IT'S IMPOSSIBLE, DON'T YOU?" Arkanon nodded silently. The only sound coming from his teeth grinding together as the voice tickled his temper. "I ADMIT THIS IS AN IMPOSSIBLE TASK FOR ANY NORMAL MAN."

At last, a result, thought Arkanon. It finally saw his point.

"BUT YOU SEEM TO FORGET, MY CHILD, YOU ARE NOT A NORMAL MAN."

Suddenly, Arkanon started to pay attention, he'd forgotten about that. He was thinking like anyone would in this situation, well, as anyone normal would do anyway. But he wasn't normal anymore, was he? But even so, he was still unsure as to what to do. He'd never been in this situation before, so he had no idea how to think in these situations or what he was capable of doing for that matter.

"I THOUGHT THAT MIGHT GET YOUR ATTENTION… YOU'D BE AMAZED AT HOW SIMPLE THE SOLUTION TO ANY PROBLEM, LET ALONE THIS ONE, CAN BE TO SOMEONE SUCH AS YOURSELF."

"I'm listening. What do I need to do?"

"THINK OF WHERE YOU WANT TO BE… THEN JUST CONCENTRATE ON THAT PLACE AND YOU'LL FIND YOURSELF THERE."

Surely not, he thought, *it can't really be that simple, can it?* Even though he had his doubts, he didn't have any better ideas and right now, anything was worth a try.

"What else does that work with?" he asked, he was intrigued more than ever now by what else might be possible for him to do. "Does this only work with wanting to travel from A to B or does this work with anything else that I might need?"

"YOU'D BE SURPRISED WHAT YOU CAN ACHIEVE THESE DAYS WITH JUST THE POWER OF A SINGLE THOUGHT, MY FRIEND." And with that time resumed. This was a whole new concept for Arkanon but one that, admittedly, was making him all the more curious about what he could achieve. Right now, though, he had more pressing matters. Closing his eyes, he imagined the throne room inside the palace and began to concentrate hard. He concentrated harder and harder still, he didn't want to open his eyes until he was absolutely sure he was where he wanted to be. He carefully listened for the slightest indication that he was no longer outside, the faintest breeze or the sounds of townsfolk screaming, but he still heard them even after a full minute of intense concentration. To his surprise though, what felt like a foot slammed into his chest with the force of a train knocking him off his feet and flying backwards at great speed.

When he had hit the floor and after getting his breath back, opened his eyes, he realised what had happened. He didn't get much time to reflect upon his mistake, however, as Hoth wrenched him up off the floor by his throat and flung him high into the air. He looked furious, the flames, that were his eyes, burned a deep crimson red. Something had really got him mad and Arkanon thought he probably wasn't keen on discussing his problem with him. Hoth slammed his hands together and sent an intense wave of energy hurtling towards Arkanon. The wave engulfed him in mid-air before his smoking and still very singed form tumbled groundward landing with a loud thud. Arkanon lay motionless. Hoth laughed with an evil smugness and calmly sauntered over to Arkanon's burnt body.

"Didn't anyone ever tell you?" he said with a menacing tone. "If you're going to sneak up on someone, at least keep your eyes open," he cackled knowingly as he approached the, supposed, corpse of Arkanon, "and now because of your rather foolhardy mistake, you are now dead." He stopped for a moment as if to pause for thought before continuing. "Actually," he said, a thoughtful tone was clear in his voice as if something had just dawned on him as if from nowhere, "how did you sneak in? I think I would've heard you, wouldn't I?" Now he was intrigued. "I mean I know I was preoccupied…but still… I would've heard you," again he paused as he tried to rack his brain looking for an answer to a question that only he had heard in his head. "Unless?" He kicked Arkanon's body, rolling it over.

"Boo!" said Arkanon jokingly,

"Ah, of course," Arkanon didn't know what troubled him more; the fact that Hoth said that in such a way as to imply he was pleased to see him or that he was now sitting cross-legged beside him. "I was wondering when you'd arrive…It would seem that I'm too late to acquire what I am looking for…because, so it would seem, you already have it."

Arkanon lay staring at Hoth from the floor, the flames danced around playfully around his eye sockets like a puppy wags its tail when it is playing a game. Hoth cocked his head to one side, an expectant look on his face as if he was waiting for a response to a question that he never asked.

"Erm…sorry!" Arkanon said, unsure of what the correct response was to give.

"Hmmm…you're sorry?" Arkanon shrugged his shoulders in response as he gathered himself to his feet, Hoth glared at him intently. The playful nature in his eyes was subsiding to something altogether more sinister. "You're sorry?…well that's nice!" Effortlessly, Hoth floated to his feet. "You're sorry? Hmmm," The calmness in his tone was deeply worrying.

Arkanon, desperately from the corners of his eyes checked for any kind of escape route that might grant him some time to develop a fighting strategy. Hoth's gaze didn't move from Arkanon's frame.

"For twenty thousand years I've waited for this day, you know? I knew it was going to come, but I still tried to fight against it." Arkanon was at a loss what to say. In the end, he decided, it was probably best to shut up and let the demon speak. "For twenty thousand years, I devised anyway I could to avoid my destiny…Sorry! I meant to say our destiny."

Arkanon had to admit, he never saw this coming. What did he mean, 'our destiny'? The only thing he could think of that he could possibly mean was this battle now. But something in the back of his mind was telling him that wasn't it. Hoth noticed the perplexed look on Arkanon's face and let out a smug chuckle.

"You have no idea what I'm on about, do you?" Arkanon had a feeling his vacant look gave that away. "Oh, dear! Oh, dear! Oh, dear!…See, I told you, didn't I? I told you, you were going to make things interesting." Hoth was loving this and Arkanon could tell. "Ah, well! No matter. You'll find out in due course…Shall we get on with this then?"

Get on with what? Arkanon thought. *What was he on about now?* Hoth took up a stance and then he knew. *Ah! That's what he meant.* He carefully readied himself. Fists clenched, stance solid, weight centred, he was ready for any blow Hoth could deal.

"Ready, Arkanon?"

"I'm ready!" he said with determination. With that, Hoth vanished.

Arkanon had to admit, this wasn't what he had expected. He thought Hoth might throw a punch at least, not turn tail and run, as he apparently had done just now. *That was surprisingly easy,* he thought as he turned his back to leave. He didn't get far.

Quietly, like a whistle on the wind, an evil chuckle floated past his ears. Quickly, he turned on the spot. *All right then! Maybe he hasn't run off,* he thought. He stood motionless trying to listen out for the slightest noise that would indicate where Hoth was coming from. It didn't help. From nowhere, Hoth manifested in front of him, ramming his fist into the side of his jaw, knocking him, spiralling skyward. Before he had a chance to return to the ground, Hoth was already plunging his fists into his stomach and sternum, knocking him higher still. Hoth followed him up and in the brief nanosecond that Arkanon had to react, he blocked the next punch, landing one of his own in the process and knocking Hoth towards the ground.

Hoth grinned with a maniacal pleasure. He could tell this was the first time he'd been hit by anyone in a long time. Worse still, he seemed to like it. Arkanon had to act fast and when his feet hit the ground, he quickly spun on his heel and launched out a kick, but Hoth saw this coming and vanished out of the way only to appear at the side of his kick. He grabbed his leg and effortlessly spun him around, throwing him behind him. Again, he vanished, appearing right behind Arkanon where he had just been thrown, grabbing him, once more, by his head this time and throwing him skyward, quickly following him with several ferocious kicks to the head and body before letting him crash to the ground.

Gently, Hoth floated down towards Arkanon's battered shell. His eyes burning bright red as he neared his prey. Slowly Arkanon gathered himself to his feet only to be met by a headbutt from above smashing him into the floor. The force of the impact was so severe that it left a deep crater in the ground where Arkanon lay crumpled and broken.

"Had enough?" Hoth said. There was no compassion in his voice, only a feeling of disdain. "I know that you cannot die whelp, but I do know you can feel pain…If I were you, I would stay down. Only suffering comes from challenging me."

Hoth's entire demeanour had now changed. Gone was the playfulness that Arkanon had witnessed earlier. It was now replaced with utter contempt and anger. He meant business now and Arkanon knew that all too well. Yet still, either out of sheer defiance or most likely, sheer stupidity, he slowly gathered himself up once again.

"Hmmm! A glutton for punishment, eh?" Hoth's demonic nature was becoming more prevalent with every second, the cruelty in his voice, striking fear in Arkanon's bones. But still, he stood, battered and bruised as Hoth silently floated to within an inch of Arkanon's face. "Your move!…You can do anything you want, anything you like!"

His lack of fear of Arkanon's still, as yet, unknown abilities was disturbing. For all he knew was that he could cast a spell that could destroy him in a single breath. But somehow, he knew, Hoth knew he couldn't. He waited a little while, staring Arkanon in the eyes. Both of their gazes never left the other's eyes as they both tried, mentally, to weigh each other up. But Hoth was growing impatient.

"Can't think of anything, eh?" he said, trying to taunt Arkanon enough to make a brash move. But he just stood there, motionless, not even blinking, just staring into Hoth's burning eyes. This puzzled him, surely, he should do something, yet he did nothing. Hoth's patience grew thinner and thinner until without warning and quick as a flash, he launched Arkanon into the air with an uppercut. He landed ten feet away with a loud boom as he hit the floor.

"You're no fun anymore…Why won't you attack me?" Hoth couldn't contain his anger anymore. "Damn it! Attack me!…why won't you attack me?"

Arkanon lay in his newly formed crater and giggled at first but that soon turned into a psychotic chuckle, then quickly turned into a maniacal laugh, Hoth was furious. Why was he laughing at him? Why was he laughing? If Arkanon was honest with himself, at that moment, he had no idea why. But it looked like it was pissing him off and that, in Arkanon's eyes, was good enough reason to him.

Hoth charged towards him scraping his long talons on his fingers along the floor, building himself up to throwing Arkanon's seemingly defenceless body skyward once more. He didn't expect Arkanon to launch himself to his feet just as he reached him and deliver a rocket-propelled uppercut of his own. The punch knocked Hoth skyward taking him totally by surprise and Arkanon followed him up. Before Hoth had a chance to comprehend what had just occurred, a flurry of punches, kicks and elbows battered his body, swiftly followed by a devastating throw groundward and for the first time, Hoth crashed into the floor making a crater of his own. Arkanon decided to take his chance and hurtled, knee first, towards his advisory. From out of nowhere, a burst of red flame erupted from the crater where Hoth once was. The shockwave from the blast knocked Arkanon back into the air, doubling him over before smashing him into the ceiling high above. Hoth slowly floated himself to his feet from his crater, an impressed chuckle escaped from his breath.

"Fair attempt," he said with a telling tone. "It looks as though you might have just become a match for me after all…given time."

Arkanon still lay crumpled in the ceiling high above, his body, barely visible in the deep crater he was in. Hoth leisurely floated towards him, a confident grin filled his face with razor-sharp teeth. Arkanon lay motionless again, his mind preoccupied with other things. *Surely, he couldn't fall for it twice?* he thought, *Even he wouldn't be that naïve.* Patiently, he waited for Hoth to come closer and for a little while at least he did. He was a mere 20 feet away when he stopped. He tutted wagging his finger as he let him know he wasn't going to fall for the same trick twice. *Time for a different strategy,* he thought, just what that was going to be, he didn't know.

"What now? You seem to be at a disadvantage here." Arkanon knew Hoth was right. He was at a disadvantage, he was stuck in a hole in the ceiling, kind of a bad position to be in. "Well, looks like this is it, my new friend, I'll be seeing you around. At least you tried your best."

Hoth drew back his hands to his side and began to generate an ever-increasing in size ball of shimmering red light. *Why can't I do that?* Arkanon thought, *Why haven't I got something like that?* He began to dwell on this problem more intensely as the ball in Hoth's hands grew bigger. He knew this was really going to hurt. He knew that he'd probably be out of action for a while, but at least he wouldn't be dead. All he could think about was why he didn't have something like that? He'd have a chance then.

Suddenly, something began to change, his body was getting hotter and hotter and hotter. Waves of energy began to pulse through his arms. The pulsing started to shake the walls of the crater around him sending debris crashing to the floor. Hoth looked on dumbstruck. This was even enough to break his concentration and the flaming ball whisked away into nothingness around his hands. With a victorious roar, Arkanon extended his body outwards sending clouds of dust and shards of marble in all directions, masking his position in a thick dusty fog.

When the fog cleared, to Hoth's surprise, Arkanon had vanished from sight. Frantically he searched the ceiling from his position below but to no avail. Where was he? he thought to himself, slightly panicked by what had just occurred. As far as he knew, he shouldn't be able to do that yet and the fact that he did, worried him greatly. It seemed that Arkanon was a fast learner and a little too quick for his liking.

Arkanon watched him from his new vantage point behind the throne. *I could get used to this newfound power,* he thought, a newfound confidence filled his thoughts. He knew all he had to do was concentrate enough and he could practically do anything, but combining whatever that energy wave that he did was and teleporting together had taken a lot out of him. His new position, thankfully, gave him time to rest and recuperate, for a little while at least, whilst he formulated a plan. What that was, however, was beyond him at the moment. He watched Hoth, from his hiding place, gently float to the ground, searching with his eyes every nook and cranny in the vicinity of where Arkanon at last was. Thank God he hadn't figured he could teleport as well straight after his explosive escape. He breathed a very quiet sigh of relief. Hoth's ears pricked up instantaneously. *Surely he hadn't heard that?* he thought. Panic was starting to set in. *I'm nearly 50 feet away from him and I hardly made a sound...even a bat couldn't hear that.* His eyes never left Hoth's demonic form as he scoured the surrounding area near to where he was hiding. But his attention soon moved elsewhere. Cautiously, he began to relax. He just needed a couple more minutes and then he, hopefully, would've come up with something. Unfortunately, that was not to be.

Without warning, Hoth destroyed the huge throne Arkanon was hiding behind exposing his venerable form from behind his barrier. Arkanon had to think fast. Curiously, for no apparent reason other than it was there, he spied a giant window behind Hoth and without even thinking hurled himself at Hoth, picking him up in a rugby tackle and crashing them both through the glass. Hoth laughed as they both fell hundreds of feet down towards the courtyard below. Both of them twisted and turned each other in the air, both trying to make sure the other was on the bottom when they landed. Each of them exchanged blow after blow as they tried to get the upper hand. Hoth was the unlucky one, who was on the bottom and as they hit the ground, the ground shook violently. Some reaper troopers nearby rushed forward to investigate what all the commotion was about only to be greeted by a deep, giant crater in the ground after the dust had settled.

Arkanon launched himself skyward, high out of the crater, bolts of searing hot lightening ejected from his hands as he blasted at the downed Hoth. Hoth realised he was right, Arkanon was learning fast, too fast! With an angry roar, he retaliated, firing searing hot death of his own at his skyward target, missing by mere inches as Arkanon landed safely on the ground a few feet away. Hoth had decided he'd had enough; it was time to bring out the big guns. These fireballs were just party tricks, it was time to show this young upstart the true meaning of power.

He stood up facing Arkanon in the great courtyard of the Atlantian palace. A menacing grin filled his face filling Arkanon's heart full of dread. His body arching forward as if trying to make himself look bigger and meaner than he already was. *What is he up to?* Arkanon thought worriedly. *Should I attack or should I wait?* Hoth just motionless stood in the same position, his gaze, yet again, firmly fixed on Arkanon's eyes. He was a frightening sight, made even more so by the lightning crashing down only metres away. There was a storm brewing and it was unnaturally close to where they were. Even so, Hoth didn't move, didn't flinch. Even as a bolt of lightning slammed inches away from his face, he still stood firm. *What was is doing?* This really was causing him great concern. But at the same time, Arkanon could also see the point of why he could be doing this. It could just be a scare tactic, nothing more than that. How wrong could he be?

The reaper troops retreating or should that have been running for their lives, should've given it away. But still, Arkanon watched him, still watched Hoth waiting for his next move. It didn't take long.

With an evil laugh, he shimmered out of view. *Had he turned invisible again?* Arkanon thought as he frantically struggled to hear the faintest sound through the rumbling thunder and clashing lightning. Soon it became apparent that the rumbles weren't thunder and what he thought was crashing of lightning, wasn't that either as the whole ground beneath his feet began to shake.

"Shall I show you real power, boy?" Hoth's voice boomed. The anger in it caused it to reverberate around the city walls, but he was nowhere to be seen. "This is real power!"

Suddenly, huge boulders began to fall from the sky. It took a moment for Arkanon to realise that Hoth was pulling meteors from the heavens and not just small ones, but huge town-sized ones and most of them directed against him. Not only that, but he was generating huge earthquakes ripping the ground apart beneath his feet. It was then that he realised, why the voice in his head wanted him to battle Hoth so badly and why, at this time, it didn't think he was ready yet.

This demon had awesome power, far greater than he could've possibly imagined. With a click of his fingers, Hoth could quite easily destroy the world. The importance of why it was foolhardy to battle him now suddenly dawned on him. Worse still, at this point, he had no idea how to stop him. The world was literally being torn from beneath his feet and once again, Arkanon felt powerless to do anything, pain seared through his head once more, oh, sweet welcoming pain. He knew what this meant and time stopped once more.

"Got yourself into a bit of a pickle here, haven't you?" It was that voice, the one that gave him his powers. He'd never thought he'd be so glad to hear it. "Hmmm! Wonder how you're gonna get outta this one, eh?"

"OK! I'll admit you were right." The sheer horror of what was happening, what he had caused was driving him to despair. If he hadn't been so foolhardy, so sure in himself, then none of this would be happening. "How do I stop him?...He's going to destroy everything...What do I do?"

"Look in the distance...Look out to sea and tell me what you see." To be honest, it didn't seem like much help, but the voice was always right before, so he did as he was told.

In the distance, he could see nothing, only blackness. It took a moment or two before he realised that it wasn't quite right. Where was the moon, over the horizon? More to the point, where was the horizon and why was the Asumertrian fleet floating in mid-air. Then he realised, the horizon wasn't there because in its place was a tidal wave, hundreds of miles long and at least a mile high. But what had caused such a wave, did Hoth do it?

"That wave is your solution...But your solution comes at a terrible price." At this point, Arkanon didn't care, he just wanted this whole thing to stop, for the world to survive, no matter the cost.

"Tell me what to do?" he whispered. His soul ached as he tried to estimate what that cost might be, but the more he thought, the more his soul was crushed under the weight of all the suffering he'd caused.

"Before the wave hits, Hoth will appear once more...he's predictable like that, he likes to gloat before the big finish...That is your time to strike."

What did it mean my time to strike? In what way? Arkanon thought.

"Just think very cold thoughts, think freeze...Channel all your energy into that one thought...Remember, freeze!"

With that, time again restarted and not a minute too soon, the wave was gaining speed with every second and it was gaining ground even quicker. The ocean, suddenly withdrew far out to sea tens of miles exposing the ocean bottom, leaving fish stranded on dry land for what seemed like an instant. Then with a loud boom, it hit. Hundreds of thousands of people, Atlantian, Asumertrian and reaper alike ran for whatever safety they could find. None of it was any use. They were all doomed. Nothing could save them.

Arkanon, unconsciously, began to make himself float. He didn't realise until he was high in the air looking down as the mile-high wall of water consumed the land. As predicted, Hoth manifested, foolishly, to survey his work and laughed proudly, as he looked up at Arkanon. Water now covered the land where Atlantis used to be, beneath him. It sickened him to see his home destroyed in this way. But Hoth, he was proud and the sight sickened him.

Whilst Hoth's back was turned, Arkanon took his chance. With all his might he blasted Hoth in the back with enough force as he could muster, sending him crashing deep into the monstrous wave as it began its retreat. Then with every last ounce of energy that he had, he did as the voice asked. *Freeze!* All his concentration went into that idea. *Freeze! damn you, freeze!*

The air around him became colder and colder and as he opened his eyes, he could see where his proud kingdom once stood and where his friends and countrymen had lived their lives. Now there was only ice. A mile-thick chunk of ice. He groaned in agony as his head felt like it was going to split once more.

"YOU HAVE DONE YOUR FIRST TASK, MY CHILD... HOTH IS NOW SEALED... HE WILL NOT RETURN FOR QUITE SOME TIME TO COME... BY THAT TIME, YOU WILL BE READY FOR HIM, I HOPE YOU HAVE LEARNT YOUR LESSON?"

Oh, he'd learnt his lesson all right. Because of his arrogance and his ego, everything that he ever loved or held dear was now gone. This was the cost of his foolhardy attitude and it was a huge price to pay. The shock of what transpired was beginning to prove too great for his rapidly developing mind. But one thing was for certain, he would never forget what he had done tonight. Nor, indeed, what it cost him. But right now, he just needed to rest and with that, he plummeted towards the ice below…

Well...It Could be Worse I Suppose?

World Trade Centre Tower 1, WTC Plaza, New York, 11 September 2001.

Arkanon suddenly found his attention being violently ripped from the comfort of his memories back to a sickening reality. Before him stood Hoth, his eyes burning bright crimson red, the flames burning furiously within his eye sockets, the flames licking high above his brow line.

Behind him, he could just make out the hulking form of the high guard from earlier followed by screaming and tearing flesh before a fountain of bloodshot past.

In front of Hoth was Tyler hovering in mid-air about four feet from the floor. Her head was completely covered by shadow, her hands clawing at where her face should be as if the shadow over her face was preventing her from breathing. Her legs flailed wildly beneath her, panic well and truly set in.

Beside her, desperately trying to grasp hold of her leg to hopefully pull her free somehow was Jason, who was looking directly at Arkanon at rapid intervals, screaming something that he couldn't quite make out just yet.

Arkanon shook his head trying to shake off the ringing in his ears and almost wished that he hadn't as the full brunt of the absolute chaos hit his senses at once.

"Fucking hell, Arkanon, help me! He's killing her, for Christ's sake!" Jason screamed in desperation. "Snap the fuck outta whatever has got you and help me!"

"No! Not again," Arkanon whispered to himself, he felt petrified, "I...I...can't let him do it again."

He looked up at Hoth and what he was doing. He reminded himself of what Hoth had done! He'd taken everything from him. Everything he loved held dear and cherished. His father! His tribe! His best friends, his brothers in arms! His nation of Atlantis. But most of all, his humanity and a chance of normal life and death. And now he was going to take even more from him by killing Tyler and then Jason.

Quickly that intense fear he felt turned into an uncontrollable rage. "I won't let you do this to me again!" Arkanon screamed at the top of his lungs. His screams were so powerful, they sent a shockwave out from him at the epicentre. It splintered and shattered wooden doors and plasterboard walls as it travelled outwards, forcing first Jason to cover his ears to soften the blow as the shockwave hit him and launched him along its path.

Tyler, however, was unceremoniously dropped as the wave struck Hoth and broke his concentration enough for him to drop her. The wave seemingly strengthened as it travelled further outwards, so by the time it reached the high guard it literally ripped it to pieces before obliterating it. Sadly, those men still fighting the beast suffered the same fate but mercifully a lot quicker.

As Hoth raised himself back onto his feet, he laughed loudly and did appear genuinely pleased by what just happened. Jason remained on the floor still trying to recover as he watched Hoth walking calmly towards Arkanon.

"Very good!" Again he appeared genuinely impressed. "Shall we?"

He bowed and beckoning invited Arkanon forward to fight. Arkanon didn't even think about it as he charged forward. His unstoppable rage making him so fast that he was just a very faint bluish blur to Jason's eyes. But he was certain that Arkanon was throwing hits at Hoth because he looked as though he was effortlessly evading every single strike. This was followed by Hoth appearing crouched on the floor below a rapidly ascending Arkanon as he slammed his fist into the floor.

"That's enough distractions," Hoth sounded furious. "I have a task I must complete, after all."

Turning his fist like a key in the floor, a deep green jet of energy blasted upwards surrounding him. This was followed by a loud and almost distant rumble. Jason suddenly realised what that was. An explosion. An explosion in what sounded like the basement of the building they were in.

Arkanon had stopped his ascent and flipped himself over to hang in the air above Hoth. Then what can only be described as his scream in reverse began to buffet everyone in the room with increasingly stronger waves growing with ferocious intensity. These sound waves began to get so powerful that they became intensifying gravity waves.

They were so strong that Jason could feel them slowly and agonisingly begin to crush him, blood started trickling down his nose. The pressure in his head bursting the capillaries in his brain. He began to hold his head and scream in intense pain. But these were drowned out by the now low hum of a rapidly growing gravitational vortex.

In one of the brief moments, he could open his eyes, he could see Tyler now woken up by the pain, writhing in agony and mouthing for it to stop. As best as he could, he crawled over to her and cradled her beneath his body in an attempt to protect her from Arkanon's attack.

Hoth was surrounded by the energy wave and slowly starting to burst through the floor causing Arkanon to become further incensed as he realised his attack was having no effect on Hoth. This caused him to strengthen his attack even more without thinking.

Without warning, Hoth vanished taking everyone by surprise. Only to appear above and behind Arkanon in the air and then smashing his fist into the back of Arkanon's head. This snapped him out of his rage-induced blindness just in time to witness a plane having been wrenched out of the air and driven into the side of WTC1, bursting through the wall of the floor they were on. Terrified Jason and Tyler looked on in horror first at the plane then at Arkanon. Their faces full of helplessness as burning white-hot flame engulfed the area they were laid.

Arkanon turned to face Hoth just in time to see a wry smile creep over his face before he too was engulfed first by the jet fuel fireball and then by the basement explosion's energy roaring through the floor and propelling Hoth ever skyward through the remaining upper floors.

Then those flames came for Arkanon but inexplicably extinguished as quickly as they came. He sat on the floor of WTC1 motionless staring at the column of continuous deep green energetic light that shot through the building. Surrounding him were the souls of those who died on the plain being sucked into a vortex-like spiral into that green shaft.

Suddenly, an explosion coming from the opposite tower snapped him out of his catatonic state replacing it with overwhelming despair.

He'd failed and Hoth had opened the first seal. There wasn't too much time for him to dwell on this too long, however, as some unnatural and immensely powerful force picked him up and flung him through the window behind him.

On his way down, though it was faint, he was sure he could hear what can only be described as both one voice and several at once laughing as he plummeted to the New York pavement below.

"What the fuck just did that to me? How did I not see that hit coming, I should've felt a presence at least?" Arkanon said to himself, genuinely puzzled. "More to the point, who the fuck wa—"

His question abruptly stopped by a loud squelch followed by blackness…

To be continued in:

Chapter 1: Under the Shadow of Legion's Wing